ALSO BY V. S. NAIPAUL

NONFICTION

The Overcrowded Barracoon
The Loss of El Dorado
An Area of Darkness
The Middle Passage

FICTION

In a Free State
A Flag on the Island
The Mimic Men
Mr. Stone and the Knights Companion
A House for Mr. Biswas
Miguel Street
The Suffrage of Elvira
The Mystic Masseur

GUERRILLAS

"When everybody wants to fight
there's nothing to fight for.
Everybody wants to fight his own little war,
everybody is a guerrilla."

—JAMES AHMED

GUERRILLAS

V.S. Naipaul

ALFRED A. KNOPF New York 1975

THIS IS A BORZOI BOOK
PUBLISHED BY ALFRED A. KNOPF, INC.

Copyright © 1975 by V. S. Naipaul
All rights reserved under International and Pan-
American Copyright Conventions.
Published in the United States by Alfred A. Knopf,
Inc., New York.
Distributed by Random House, Inc., New York.
Originally published in Great Britain by
Andre Deutsch Ltd., London.

Library of Congress Cataloging in Publication Data
Naipaul, Vidiadhar Surajprasad. Guerrillas.
I. Title.
PZ4.N155Gu3   [PR9272.9.N32]   823   75-8236
ISBN 0-394-49898-4
Manufactured in the United States of America

First American Edition

Published November 21, 1975

Second Printing, December 1975

GUERRILLAS

P.A.N.

AFTER LUNCH Jane and Roche left their house on the Ridge to drive to Thrushcross Grange. They drove down to the hot city at the foot of the hills, and then across the city to the sea road, through thoroughfares daubed with slogans: *Basic Black, Don't Vote, Birth Control Is a Plot Against the Negro Race.*

The sea smelled of swamp; it barely rippled, had glitter rather than color; and the heat seemed trapped below the pink haze of bauxite dust from the bauxite loading station. After the market, where refrigerated trailers were unloading; after the rubbish dump burning in the remnant of mangrove swamp, with black carrion corbeaux squatting hunched on fence posts or hopping about on the ground; after the built-up hillsides; after the new housing estates, rows of unpainted boxes of concrete and corrugated iron already returning to the shantytowns that had been knocked down for this development; after the naked children playing in the red dust of the straight new avenues, the clothes hanging like rags from back yard lines; after this, the land cleared a little. And it was possible to see over what the city had spread: on one side, the swamp, drying out to a great plain; on the other side, a chain of hills, rising directly from the plain.

The openness didn't last for long. Villages had become suburbs. Sometimes the side wall of a concrete house was painted over with an advertisement. In the fields that had survived there were billboards. And soon there was a factory area. It was here that the signs for Thrushcross Grange began: the name, the distance in miles, a clenched fist emblematically rendered, the slogan *For the Land and the Revolution,* and in a strip at the bottom the name of the firm that had put the sign up. The signs were all new. The local bottlers of Coca-Cola had put one up; so had Amal (the American bauxite company), a number of airlines, and many stores in the city.

Jane said, "Jimmy's frightened a lot of people."

Roche, slightly clownish with the cheap dark glasses he wore when driving, said, "Jimmy would like to hear you say that."

"Thrushcross," Jane said.

"Trush-cross. That's how you pronounce it. It's from *Wurthering Heights.* Like 'furthering.' "

"I thought it sounded very English."

"I don't think it means anything. I don't think Jimmy sees himself as Heathcliff or anything like that. He took a writing course, and it was one of the books he had to read. I think he just likes the name."

The hills smoked, as they did now every day from early morning: thin lines of white smoke that became the color of dust and blended with the haze. Above the settlements lower down, which showed ocher, drought had browned the hills; and through this ᵒwn the bush fires had cut irregular dark red patches. The asphalt road was wet-black, distorted in the distance by heat waves. The grass verges had been blackened by fire, and in some places still burned. Sometimes, above the noise of the car, Jane and Roche could hear the crackle of flames which, in the bright light, they couldn't see.

Traffic was heavy in this area of factories. But the land still showed its recent pastoral history. Here and there, among the big sheds and the modern buildings in unrendered concrete, the tall wire fences and the landscaped grounds, were still fields, remnants of the big estates, together with remnants of the estate villages: vegetable plots, old wooden houses on stilts, huts, bare front yards with zinnia clumps, ixora bushes, and hibiscus hedges. Grass now grew in the fields beside the highway; billboards offered building plots or factory sites. Sometimes there was a single rusting car in a sunken field, as though, having run off the road, it had simply been abandoned; sometimes there were heaps of junked vehicles.

Jane said, "I used to think that England was in a state of decay."

Roche said, "Decayed from what?"

They left the factories behind. Traffic thinned; and when they turned off the highway they were at last in what seemed like country. But the bush had a cut-down appearance and looked derelict in the drought. Paved areas of concrete and asphalt could be seen; and sometimes there were rows of red brick pillars, hung with dried-out vines, that suggested antique excavations: the pillars might have supported the floor of a Roman bath. It was what remained of an industrial park, one of the failed projects of the earliest days of independence. Tax holidays had been offered to foreign investors; many had come for the holidays and had then moved on elsewhere.

Roche said, "I hope there's something to see. But I doubt it."

"You told him I was coming?"

"He was very much on the defensive when I told him. But I thought he was pleased. He made the usual excuses. The drought. But that's Jimmy. Always hard done by." Roche paused. "He's not the only one."

Jane said nothing.

Roche said, "He said that some of the boys had left. Run back to the city, I imagine. And I don't think they like to feel that people are coming to spy on them."

"You mean all they want is the publicity."

Roche smiled. "It will do them no harm at all to be taken by surprise. It's the only way, to corner them into doing what they say they want to do."

The roads of the former industrial park were narrow and overgrown at the edges, and parts of the rough, graveled surface were eaten away. The land, part of the great plain, was flat; but now the areas of low bush were fewer, and they lay between sections of secondary forest. There were still many roads; but one turning was like another, and it would have been easy for a stranger to get lost. Since they had left the highway there had been no signs for

Thrushcross Grange. But then, abruptly in the wasteland, there was a new sign in yellow and red and black, with the emblematic clenched fist at the top.

THRUSHCROSS GRANGE
PEOPLE'S COMMUNE
FOR THE LAND AND THE REVOLUTION
Entry without prior permission strictly forbidden at all times
By Order of the High Command, JAMES AHMED (Haji)

In a strip at the bottom, in letters cut out white on red, was the name of the local firm, Sablich's, that had put the sign up.

Roche said, "We had to tone down Jimmy's copy." Roche worked for Sablich's.

Jane said, "Haji?"

"As I understand it, a haji is a Muslim who's made the pilgrimage to Mecca. Jimmy uses it to mean 'mister' or 'esquire.' When he remembers, that is."

Not long after the board was a side road. They turned into that. A little way down there was a sentry box painted in diagonal stripes of black and red. It was empty; and the metal rail, also striped black and red, weighted at one end and intended as a barrier, was vertical. They drove on. The road was as narrow as the road they had turned off from, irregularly edged, the asphalt surface eaten into by crab grass and weeds from the wild verge. They drove through secondary bush and forest; there was as yet no sign of cultivation.

Jane said, "They have a lot of land."

"That's it," Roche said. "Jimmy's absurd in nearly every way. But he somehow gets things done. Sablich's were thinking of buying it all up. Investment, I suppose. Then Jimmy stepped in, and they disgorged this bit. A twenty-five-year lease. A gift. Just like that."

Roche laughed, and Jane saw his molars: widely spaced, black at the roots, the gum high: like a glimpse of the skull.

The road curved, and they saw a big cleared area, walled on three sides by forest, the forest walls seemingly knit together by the thin white trunks and white branches of softwood trees. The cleared land had been ridged and furrowed from end to end. The furrows were full of shiny green weeds; and the ridges, one or two of which showed haphazard, failed planting, were light brown and looked as dry as bone. Far from the road, against a forest wall, there was a low open shed, thatched with whole branches of carat palm. Near this, and half into the forest, was a red tractor: it looked as abandoned there as those rusting automobiles in the tall grass below the embankment of the highway. The field looked abandoned as well. But presently Jane saw three men, then a fourth, working at the far end, camouflaged against the forest.

Roche said, "That's laid on for us. Or laid on for you. It's their official rest period now. No one works in the fields at this time of the afternoon."

After the cleared area there was forest again, threaded with the thin white branches of softwood trees and pillared with forest palms, their straight trunks bristling with black needles, hung with dead spiky fronds, and with clusters of yellow nuts breaking out of gray-green husks the shape of boats. Then the forest opened out again into clearings on both sides of the road. On one side the forest had been cut down to stumps and low bush. On the other side of the road the land was bare and clean, stripped of trees and palms and bush, the earth in places scraped down to pale red clay. At some distance from the road, on this side, on a smooth brown slope, there was a long hut with concrete-block walls and a pitched roof of corrugated iron. It stood alone in the emptiness. The roof was dazzling and hot to look at; it barely projected over the wall and cast no shadow.

The car stopped and there was silence. Even when the car doors slammed no one came out of the hut. There was no wind; the forest wall, dead green, was still; the asphalt road was soft below the gravel. Jane and Roche crossed the dry ditch by the bridge of three logs lashed together. The stripped land baked. Jane wanted shade; and the only shade lay within the dark, almost black, doorway of the long hut.

She walked ahead of Roche, as though, as always, she knew the way. He had paused to look about him. When he saw Jane walking up the slight slope to the hut door he felt, as he had feared, that her presence there was wrong and looked like an intrusion. The flowered blouse, through which her brassiere could be seen, the tight trousers that modeled stomach, groin, and cleft in a single, sudden curve: that could pass in the city, and in the shopping plaza of the Ridge would be hardly noticeable, but here it seemed provocative, overcasual enough to be dressy: London, foreign, wrong. And again it occurred to Roche that she was very white, with a color that wasn't at all like the color of local white people. She was white enough to be unreadable; even her age might not be guessed. He walked quickly toward her, protectively. A fawn-colored pariah dog, ribby and sharp-faced, came round from the back of the hut and stood and watched, without expectation.

At first it seemed cool in the hut; and, after the glare outside, it seemed dark. They saw, as they entered, stepping up directly from clay to concrete floor, a steel filing cabinet in an unswept corner, an old kitchen chair, and a dusty table with what looked like a junked typewriter, a junked duplicator, and some metal trays. Then, as their eyes became accustomed to the interior light, they saw two rows of metal beds all the way down the concrete floor of the hut. Not all the beds were made up; some had mattresses alone, thin, with striped ticking. Clothes hung on nails above the beds that were in use: colored shirts of shiny synthetic material, jerseys, the jeans that looked so aggressive on, so shoddy off.

Four or five of the beds were occupied. The boys or young men who lay on them looked at Jane and Roche and then looked up at the corrugated iron or at the opposite wall. Their shiny black faces were blank; they did nothing to acknowledge the presence of strangers in the hut.

Roche said, "Mannie."

The boy spoken to said without moving, "Mr. Ahmed bathing."

Roche laughed. "Bathing? Jimmy's been working with you?"
Mannie didn't reply.

Jane could feel the grit on the concrete floor through the soles
of her shoes; it set her teeth on edge.

Roche said to Jane, and it was as if he were speaking to the
boys, "They built everything themselves." He took off his dark
glasses and looked less of a clown; he looked more withdrawn than
his voice or manner suggested. He sucked at the end of one temple
of the glasses. "Mannie, you were the mason, weren't you?"

Mannie sat up and let his feet hang over the bed. He was
small and slender. Beside his bed, on a gunny sack on the floor,
there were about a dozen green tomatoes.

The hut that had at first felt cool now felt less so; Jane was
aware that the corrugated iron was radiating heat. And the hut
was more open than she had thought, was really full of light.
Oblong windows, fitted with frosted-glass louvers in aluminum
frames, were spaced out at the top of the wall that faced the road.
Everything was exposed, lit up, and open for inspection: the boys,
their faces, their clothes, the narrow beds, the floor below the beds.

On the wall next to the filing cabinet what had looked like a
large chart could now be read as a timetable. Jane was considering
it—ablutions, tea, field duties, barrack duties, field duties, breakfast, rest, barrack duties, dinner, discussion—when she heard Roche
say "Jimmy," and she looked and saw a man in the doorway at the
far end of the hut.

The man was at first in silhouette against the white light
outside. When he came into the hut he could be seen to be naked
from the waist up, with a towel over one shoulder. As he came
down the wide aisle between the metal beds, moving with short,
light steps, he gave an increasing impression of physical neatness.
The neatness was suggested by the slenderness of his waist, the
width of his shoulders, by the closed expression of his face, by his
full, closely shaved cheeks, by his trimmed mustache, and by his
trousers, which were of a smooth, fawn-colored material, and tight,
so that he seemed smooth and tight from waist to shoes. The shoes
themselves were thin-soled, pointed, and shining below a powder-
ing of red dust.

Jane had been expecting someone more physically awkward and more Negroid, someone at least as black as the boys. She saw someone who, close up, looked distinctly Chinese. The heavy mustache masked the shape of his top lip and stressed the jut rather than the fullness of his lower lip. His eyes were small, black, and blank; that, and the mustache, which suggested a mouth clamped shut, made him seem buttoned up, tense, unreadable.

To Roche he said, "Massa." He nodded to Jane without seeming to see her. Not hurrying, indifferent to the silence, he took the green towel from his shoulder and put it on the back of the kitchen chair, and took a gray-blue-green tunic from a nail on the wall. The drab color killed the contrast between his face and his paler chest and made him less disturbing. Dressed at last, he pulled at the table drawer and said, "Yes, massa. As you see, we're still holding out."

Jane said, "I see you have a duplicating machine."

"Secondhand from Sablich's," Jimmy said. "More like last hand."

Roche said, "It would be a help if you learned to use it."

"Yes, massa." He took out some duplicated sheets from the drawer and gave them to Jane. "This will fill you in on background."

The top sheet was dog-eared and felt dusty. Jane read: *Communiqué No. 1. CLASSIFIED.*

Roche said, "That's the fairy story. I see the tractor's still out of action, Jimmy. Didn't Donaldson come?"

"Hmm. Is that what they told you at Sablich's?"

"Didn't he come?"

"Yes, massa. Donaldson came."

Roche let the subject drop. He said, "All right. Let's go and see what you've been doing about the septic tank."

The two men went out into the sunlight. Jane stayed behind. She felt the eyes of the boys on her now, and she looked at the duplicated sheets in her hand.

All revolutions begin with the land. Men are born on the earth, every man has his one spot, it is his birthright, and men must claim their portion of the earth in brotherhood and harmony.

In this spirit we came an intrepid band to virgin forest, it is the life style and philosophy of Thrushcross Grange.

That was how the communiqué began. But Jane, reading on, found that it soon became what Roche had said: a fairy story, a school composition, ungrammatical and confused, about life in the forest, about the anxieties, dangers, and needs of isolated men, about the absence of water, electricity, and transportation. And then it was full of complaints, about people and firms who had made promises they hadn't then kept, about gift equipment that had turned out to be defective.

Jane, looking up from the duplicated sheets, caught the eyes of one of the boys. On the wall above his bed she saw a poster: a pen drawing of Jimmy Ahmed that made him all hair, eyes and mustache, and more Negroid than he was, with roughly lettered words below: *I'm Nobody's Slave or Stallion, I'm a Warrior and Torch Bearer—Haji James Ahmed.*

The oblong windows showed a colorless sky. But Jane had a sense now of more than heat; she had a sense of desolation. Later, on the Ridge, in London, this visit to Thrushcross Grange might be a story. But now, in that hut, with the junked office equipment on the table, the posters and black pinups from newspapers on the walls, with the boys on the metal beds, with the light and the emptiness outside and the encircling forest, she felt she had entered another, complete world.

She heard a hiss. It was one of the street noises she had grown to recognize on the island. It was how a man called to someone far away: this hiss could penetrate the sound of traffic on a busy road. The hiss came from a boy on one of the beds. She knew it was meant for her, but she paid no attention and tried to go on reading.

"Sister."

She didn't look up.

"White lady."

She looked up. She took a step toward the beds. Then, made bold by this movement, she walked between the beds, looking for the boy who had spoken.

Only Mannie was sitting up; all the other boys were lying

down. One boy seemed to stare through her as she passed his bed. But then she heard him say softly, as though he was speaking to himself, "So you know your name." And the boy on the next bed said more loudly, and in an abrupt tone, not looking at her, his shining face resting on one side on his thin pillow, his close-set bloodshot eyes fixed on the back doorway: "Give me a dollar."

His face was oddly narrow, and twisted on one side, as though he had been damaged at birth. The eye on the twisted side was half-closed; the bumps on his forehead and his cheekbones were prominent and shining. His hair was done in little pigtails: a Medusa's head.

She took out a purse from her shoulder bag and offered a red dollar note, folded in four. Raising his arm, but not changing his position on the bed, still not looking at her, he took the note, let his hand fall on the bed, and said, "Thank you, white lady." And then there was nothing more to do or say. She walked back past the beds, feeling the silence behind her, and went out into the sunlight, stepping from the concrete floor of the hut onto red, hot clay.

She considered the forest palms, their straight trunks hazy with black needles, their living, rotting hearts bandaged, it seemed, with tattered sacking. The land was shaved and bare and bright all the way down to the road and up to the forest wall. But the land at the back of the long hut already seemed derelict and half abandoned. She saw empty chicken-coops, roughly knocked together with old boards and with sagging walls of soft wire netting, like the chicken-coops in the open yards of the redevelopment project in the city, so that already, in the midst of bush, the effect was of urban slum. She saw piles of old scantlings and corrugated-iron sheets, rolls of old wire, drums: back yard junk. She saw a pit of some sort: dried-up mounds of clay, a heap of concrete blocks. At the edge of the clearing there was a corrugated-iron latrine on a high concrete base. It was silver in the hard light, and the door was open. A thatched roof had been fixed to the back wall of the concrete hut, at the far end. It began halfway up the wall and sloped down almost to the ground. In the black shade of the thatch, on a wash stand made of trimmed branches, there were unwashed enamel bowls and plates and basins; the ground below was dark and scummy. Desolation: she had the urge now to get away.

When she saw Roche and Jimmy Ahmed coming to where she was, she could tell, from the melancholy and irritation in Roche's face, that he had been quarreling with Jimmy. But Jimmy was as expressionless as before, his mouth as seemingly clamped shut below his mustache.

Roche said, "You're going to have an epidemic on your hands one of these days."

Jimmy said, "Yes, massa."

Roche smiled at Jane. His irritation was like her own; but his smile depressed her. That smile of his, which had once seemed so full of melancholy and irony, issuing out of the largest vision of the world, now seemed to hold only a fixed, meaningless irony. And less than that: it held sarcasm, frustration, pettishness.

They walked to the car to drive to the field. Jane sat with Roche; Jimmy sat in the back. Too soon for Jane, who would have preferred to consider the visit over, they got out, to the renewed shock of heat and glare, and crossed from the road to the path at the edge of the leveled field, beside the wall of forest. They walked one behind the other: Roche, Jane, Jimmy. Roche was still irritable. Jimmy's impassivity had turned to something like calm. To Jane he was even considerate: she was immediately aware of that.

He said, in his light voice, "How did you get on with the boys?"

"We didn't say very much."

Roche said without turning round, "They don't have too much to talk about."

Jimmy gave his grunt. "Hmm."

The sun was full on them and full on the forest wall, less green, drier, and more pierced than it appeared from a distance. There was no play of air. The path was hard and bumpy and they kicked up dust as they walked. Jane was sweating; dust stuck to her skin.

Roche said, "Did they ask you for money?"

"One of them asked me for a dollar."

Jimmy said, "That was Bryant."

"A boy with pigtails. Very black."

"Bryant," Jimmy said.

Roche said, "Did you give him a dollar?"

"No."

Jimmy said, "Hmm."

They walked between the forest and the dry field, past the furrows where shiny green weeds grew out of the caked earth; past the abandoned red tractor marked *Sablich's*; past the crumbling thatched shed where long-stalked tomato seedlings yellowed in shallow boxes of dried earth; past human excrement laid in two places on the path itself. They went silent after stepping over the excrement.

Then Jane said, thinking of shade, and thinking at the same time of something that Jimmy and his boys might find easier to do, "Are you planting any fruit trees?"

Jimmy said, "That's long-term. In this phase of the project we need cash and we are concentrating on cash crops."

They came to the end of the field, where four boys in jeans and rubber boots stood in weed-choked furrows and straddled four dry ridges. As if in parody of nineteenth-century plantation prints, which local people had begun to collect, the boys, with sullen downcast eyes, as though performing an unpleasant duty, were planting tomato seedlings which, as fast as they were set in their dusty little holes, quailed and drooped.

Jimmy said to Jane, as though speaking of a purely local vegetable, "Tomatoes. You can pay eighty cents a pound in the market. Marketing, massa—that's going to be a problem."

Roche said, "We'll cross that particular bridge when we come to it."

They left the boys behind and walked to where clumps of bamboo grew at the edge of the forest and arched over the field. It was cool in the shade of the bamboo, and the ground was soft and padded with dead bamboo leaves. The bamboo stalks, of all the colors from bright green to chrome yellow to straw, swayed under their own weight and rubbed creaking against one another. One clump had ignited; but green shoots were already sprouting from its blackened, ashy heart.

In that part of the field shaded by the bamboo, weeds had

grown almost to bush. Through this they walked to what Jimmy said was the vegetable garden; the vegetables grown there were intended only for Thrushcross Grange. The vegetable garden was knee-deep in weeds, with no sign of furrow or ridge. Neither Jimmy nor Roche appeared surprised. Jimmy, suddenly energetic, pulled back weeds, looking for what had been planted, and showing what had grown: deformed, pale eggplants, stunted okras. He was excited; he was like a man discovering the simplicity of nature, its unchanging laws, the processes that worked for him as they did for others.

JIMMY DIDN'T live at Thrushcross Grange. His house was a little distance away, separated by a block of forest from the commune hut. There was a path through the forest, but there was also a way through the side roads of the former industrial park, and they went in the car.

The invitation was unexpected; Roche had always found Jimmy secretive about his house. But Jane was not surprised. She had already begun to feel that Jimmy's initial coldness had only been a form of anxiety; that he had considered the visit important and had prepared for it, had prepared his entrance, his set blank face; and that gradually he had unwound, had become more and more a man anxious to make an impression, to display himself. There had come a moment in the vegetable garden when, as Jimmy had bent down to separate weeds from vegetable plants, Jane had thought: He is a candidate. And her irritability, which until then had been the irritability of heat and disgust, had altered, had become the irritability of the woman who knew she was being courted. She had become more at ease.

Even before they had got as far as the striped sentry box, Roche, shut in behind this dark glasses, had recognized her new mood. It was something he had remembered from their early days in London: that irritability, mixed with an abrupt coyness, which was her special style. The sea anemone, he thought, waving its strands at the bottom of the ocean. Rooted and secure, and indifferent to what it attracted. The dragon lady, infinitely casual, infinitely unconsciously calculating, so indifferent to the body, so apparently willing to abuse it, and yet so careful of the body, so careful of complexion and teeth and hair.

The house stood by itself at the end of a narrow road that stopped some distance away from the forest wall. During the days of the industrial park it had been the house of an American factory manager. The enterprise had, within its period of grace, withdrawn its capital and its machinery; the factory buildings, shells of corrugated iron or timber, had been auctioned off as building materials and dismantled; and all that remained now of the factory was the dead-end road, the flatness on either side of the road, and the house at the end of the road.

Pink and white oleanders had grown tall around the house, and bougainvillaea had run wild: sudden bright color in the brownness. The house, which stood on low concrete pillars and had ocher-washed concrete walls, looked simple in plan; but the corrugated-iron roof was complicated: an attempt at what was known locally as the California style.

As they arrived, a small blue van came out of the yard: *CHEN BROS The Quality Grocery*. Roche pulled aside to let the van pass, and then drove in, past the white glare of the front porch, to the shelter and cool of the car port at the side of the house. On the concrete steps at the far end were cardboard boxes, full of parcels and packages.

Jane said, "They deliver here?"

"And they deliver free," Roche said, taking off his dark glasses. "It's the next best thing to living off the land."

"My Chinese brothers," Jimmy said. As they walked back into the sunlight, to the front of the house, he addressed Jane directly: "Do you know about the Chinese?"

She was coy, interested, amused.

"I was born in the back room of a Chinese grocery. But that must be pretty obvious."

Jane said, "I don't know anything about Chinese groceries."

"I suppose that's why I've always felt hungry. My Chinese brothers understand the situation."

The garden looked at once scorched and overgrown. Crab

grass had grown long, with more stalk than grass, and had dried, leaving bare patches of earth. But the drought that had killed the land and set the hills on fire had drawn out the tenderest blooms from the unpruned bougainvillaea and the almost stripped hibiscus shrubs. It was the season of new leaves; where these had appeared they were still of the freshest green.

Sunlight struck full on the terrazzo porch, and the living room caught the glare. A square of English carpet, electric blue with splashes of black and yellow, almost covered the floor. The furniture was also English and had a similar innocent stylishness; it was of a kind seen in the windows of furniture shops on the main streets of English market towns. A three-piece suite, square and chunky, with fat cushions, was covered in a tiger-striped synthetic material, thick and furry. On the fitted bookshelves a number of books in the same magenta binding stood solidly together: The Hundred Best Books of the World; there were also some paperbacks and a neat stack of records. A blue-tinted glass vase held three sprays of bougainvillaea. It was a room without disorder; it had obviously been prepared for this visit.

Jane felt that some comment was expected of her. She said, "But it's like being in England."

Jimmy said, "All the stuff here comes from England. You know what they say. You may not be able to make a living in England, but England teaches you how to live."

On two of the fitted shelves, below the books and the records, there were unmounted photographs in cheap stand-up frames: Jimmy in London, with various people. Jane recognized some celebrities: an actor, a politician, a television producer. They were people outside Jane's circle, and in London she had been indifferent to their names. But they seemed glamorous here; and the perception came to her that in this setting, which was his own, Jimmy was a diminished man.

She said, "Your English mementos."

He picked up the automatic irony in her voice, and his eyes went restless. Then his mouth was clamped shut below his mustache.

She saw another photograph in a frame. The photograph had

been mutilated, irregularly cut down the middle, to exclude someone. What remained showed two children of mixed race, with plump faces and thick features, hair kinkier than Jimmy's, and skins that were not pale. A mutilated photograph, a reminder of the person cut out: it was odd that a man so fond of photographs didn't have portraits of the children alone.

A triangle of white light was advancing from the porch into the sitting room, over the curling edge of the electric-blue carpet, which lay untacked on the terrazzo floor. Glare picked out fine dust on the smoked glass top of the oval center table. On this table Jane saw, as though laid out for inspection, airmail letters with English stamps.

She said, "You must miss England?"

She saw him hesitate: it was as though she had asked him a trap question.

Roche said, with that weary tone that had once set her looking for deeper meanings in his words, "England is in the eye of the storm. It's part of their great luck."

Turning half-coy from Jimmy, her complexion so fresh, so well cared for, she said, irritation coming quickly to her eyes, "Is it lucky to be half dead?"

It was what he had taught her, what she had picked up from him and incorporated, as words, as a passing attitude, into the chaos of words and attitudes she possessed: words that she might shed at any time, as easily as she had picked them up, and forget she had ever spoken them, she who had once been married to a young politician and had without effort incarnated an ordinary correctness, and who might easily return to such a role. She was without memory: Roche had decided that some time ago. She was without consistency or even coherence. She knew only what she was and what she had been born to; to this knowledge she was tethered; it was her stability, enabling her to adventure in security. Adventuring, she was indifferent, perhaps blind, to the contradiction between what she said and what she was so secure of being; and this indifference or blindness, this absence of the sense of the absurd, was part of her unassailability.

Jimmy said at last: "I miss my children."

He offered soft drinks. He was a Muslim, he said, and drank no alcohol. After he had served them he sat down in one of the furry chairs. With two small, deft movements he hitched up his trousers, holding each crease between a thumb and forefinger. He rested his bare arms flat on the arms of the chair, and began very gently to rub his palms over the thick synthetic fur. Jane noted the rubbing gesture and stroked the fur on her own chair. It was smooth and felt almost oiled; her palms tickled and her teeth were set on edge. He was so neat, with his tight, creased trousers; his gestures were so small and precise. His full lower lip was moist and very pink in the middle, it seemed to Jane it had been worn down to this color by the constant little licks he gave with the tip of his tongue. He shaved very close; the stiff hair was embedded deep in his coarse skin, and his cheeks and chin were bumpy from the razor, with a whitish bloom on the bumps.

The soft drink he had offered was disagreeable. It had the tainted-water taste of the pale fluid at the top of an unshaken bottle of orange juice; and the frosted tumblers, more or less full, running with wet on the outside, remained on their wooden coasters on the glass-topped table.

Roche had withdrawn from the conversation. His brow had puckered; his irritation showed. Jane was calm.

Jimmy said, "England isn't real."

"What do you mean, it isn't real?" Roche said. "Do you know what you mean?"

Jane said, "I know what he means."

Jimmy gave a little lick to his lips. His hands went still, fingers spread on the arms of his chair, and he held his back flat against the back of his chair. "The problems aren't going to be solved there. You know what happens in England. Everybody goes to the demo and the meeting and then they leave you and go home to tea."

Roche said, "Do they still go home to tea in England?"

Jimmy looked at Jane. She was interested, smiling, coy, very pink. He said, "I got away in time. I was lucky. Over there the black man can become"—he fumbled for the word—"like a play-boy. They make you like a playboy in England."

It was the wrong word. Jane, fumbling after him, worked out what he meant: plaything.

She said, "Playboy. That was the impression the papers gave."

So, in London, she had heard of him. He said: "Hmm."

Roche said, "I didn't see Stephens. What's happened to him?"

"I suppose he's run out on us, massa."

Jane said, "I want to hear more about England."

Roche said, "I'm asking him about Stephens."

Jane smiled and crossed her legs.

"These people want overnight results, massa. Stephens was the wild one. You thought you were sending me a worker. You didn't know you were sending me a little boy who wanted to kill me dead. He thought he should be here." He waved his hand about the room. "Everybody wants to be a leader."

Roche said, "So Stephens has left?"

"I don't know, massa."

Jane said, "It must be a hard life, here."

"I don't know about a hard life," Jimmy said. "To me it's life. It's work. I'm a worker. I was born in the back room of a Chinese grocery. I'm a *hakwai* Chinee. You know what a *hakwai* is? It's the Chinese for nigger. They have a word for it too. And that's what they thought I was going to be when I got back here. 'Oh, he's a big shot in England and so on, but over here he's just going to be a *hakwai*. Let him start up his movement. Let him take on the niggers. Let him see how far he'll get. This isn't England.' They thought they were trapping me. Now they see they've trapped themselves. Eh, massa? They've got to support me, massa. Sablich's and everybody else. They've got to make me bigger. Because, if I fail—hmm. I'm the only man that stands between them and revolution, and they know it now, massa. That's why I'm the only man they're afraid of. They know that all I want in my hand is a megaphone, and the whole pack of cards will come tumbling down. I'm not like the others. I'm not a street-corner politician. I don't make any speeches. Nobody's going to throw me in jail because I'm subversive. I'm not subversive. I'm the friend of every capitalist in the country. Everybody is my friend. I'm not going out on the streets to change the government. Nobody is going to shoot me down. I am here, and I stay here. If they want to kill me they have to come here. I carry no gun." He raised his bare arms off the chair and held them up, showing the palms. The short sleeves of the drab-colored tunic rode down his pale, firm biceps and revealed the springs of hair in his armpits. "I have no gun. I'm no guerrilla."

He stopped abruptly and lowered his arms. The words had carried him away; he had spoken too quickly and hadn't ordered his thoughts. He hadn't said the right things; he had mixed too many things together. His eyes went hooded; his lower lip jutted. His hands lay flat on the arms of the chair, fingers stiffly together.

Jane said, "Was your wife English?"

Jimmy stood up. His eyes were more hooded; his lower lip had begun to curl. On his smooth forehead creases appeared, and the skin below his eyes darkened. He said, "Yes, yes."

Roche saw that it was time to go.

.

"EVERY TIME I meet Jimmy," Roche said, as they drove away, "I make it a point to lose my temper with him at least once, to bring him back to earth. He was unusually excited today. I suppose it was because of you."

"He was showing off a lot."

"There's always a little truth in everything he says. That's the odd thing."

"That ghastly shed. Those moronic-looking boys. All that shit in the field."

"Did you give that boy any money?"

"No."

"Once you allow them to blackmail you it's hard to have any authority with them."

Jane said, "Harry de Tunja was saying that Jimmy was sinister. I found those boys infinitely more worrying."

"Just playing bad, as they say. But they're only dangerous if you start playing with them. That's another reason why I always try to lose my temper with Jimmy."

"Is it true about the rape and indecent assault in England? Was that why he was deported?"

"I don't have any reason to doubt it. But you have to work with what's there."

Jane said, "I wonder what little Doris made of it all."

"Doris?"

"I was thinking about the wife. I think she must have been a Doris, don't you?"

"It wasn't the Dorises who went for Jimmy in London. You have the world in front of your eyes, and yet it's funny how your mind prints out comic strips all day long. To call someone Doris isn't to have a point of view. You're not saying anything. To talk about Doris and the shit in the field doesn't add up to a point of view."

"Perhaps I don't have a point of view."

"I wish you wouldn't pretend you had. You remember how you stopped the conversation at the Grandlieus'? You thought you were being so concerned, talking about the shantytowns and the horrible little black animals crawling about in the rubbish. You thought you were talking about things no one had seen before you. You thought you were being so much more concerned than everybody else. But you were saying nothing. It was just a cheap way of showing off."

"Well, I've stopped seeing the shantytowns now."

They were on the highway. The sun was slanting into their faces. The hills smoked; but, in spite of the continuing still heat, the light on the hills had altered, had turned from the light of midday to the light of afternoon. The yellowing smoke haze above the hills held hints of the sunset to come; already, high in the sky, the end-of-day clouds had begun to form.

They came to the factory area: traffic, blackened verges, factory buildings still looking impermanent in the flat landscape of the old plantations, ornamental trees and smooth-trunked young royal palms standing on browned factory lawns like things rescued from the forest. Here and there, deep in the fields behind the factories, were automobiles in the trunks of which men were loading bundles of cut grass, fodder for the cows and other animals they still kept, the pens sometimes to be seen at the back of the huts and houses on the highway.

There was a man running steadily on the road ahead of them, indifferent to the traffic and the fumes: an elderly Negro, long-necked, lean-faced, in black running shorts and a soaked white vest. He was a well-known figure, a disordered man, who at odd times of day and night took to the roads and ran for miles. And Jane thought that that was something else she had stopped seeing: people like the runner, people like the wild men who lived in the hills, among the new developments, or down in the city, in the back yards of certain thoroughfares: derelicts, a whole parallel society.

She said, "Is the government really afraid of Jimmy?"

"The government's afraid of everybody. And Jimmy is right. They've got to build him up and pretend they are supporting him. The doer. And Jimmy has this English reputation. He can't just be got out of the way."

"What a strange idea he must have of England."

"I suppose he understood it well enough for his purpose."

Jane said, "You don't sound as though you like him."

"It isn't a matter of liking. And I don't mind Jimmy. He's like the others. He's looking for someone to lead."

"Of course, he's having everybody on, isn't he? And everybody's having him on. Everybody is pretending that something exists that doesn't exist."

Roche said: "You have to work with what's there."

"But he must know those fields are in an appalling state. Doesn't he know that? Or is he just mad like everybody else?"

Slowly in the thickening traffic, and always with the sun in their eyes, they came, through the suburbs, to the city: to the burning rubbish dump, with its mounds of fresh garbage; to the new housing estate, with its long red avenues now full of men and women and children; to the market, where refrigerated trailers stood in the unpaved forecourt; to the sea road, where there had once been talk of a waterfront cultural center, of walks and restaurants, a theater and a marina, but where now red dust from the bauxite loading station settled on everything. The road was bumpy here, irregular at the edges; on the unmade sidewalks, tufted with hardy grass, there were sections of concrete pipes on which slogans had been daubed, and old flattened heaps of gravel and other road-mending material, mingled now with bauxite dust, yellowed scraps of newspaper, and bleached cigarette packs.

Jane said, "What's a succubus?"

Fine red dust powdered Roche's dark glasses, so that he looked unsighted. He said, "It sounds like an incubus. But that must be wrong."

"That was what Harry de Tunja said, when I told him we were going to Jimmy Ahmed's. He said that Jimmy was a succubus."

"It sounds like a grub of some sort. Something you have to carry. A kind of leech."

They turned off at last into the city proper. This was the area of the merchants' warehouses, and there were many rum shops. From each rum shop came a din. This was once part of the city center. But the city no longer had a center. With the coming of the motorcar, in numbers, the hills had been opened up and developed as self-contained suburbs, with their own shopping and entertainment plazas; and the peasants who had cultivated and impoverished the hillsides had sold out and moved down to the flat land. To go up to the Ridge was to go up to a more temperate air; it was to lose the feel of the city and see it as part of a larger view of sea and mangrove and great plain. It was to see it, as it could be seen now, as part of the colors of the late afternoon, smoke haze and pink cloud rising from the edge of the sea to blend with the glory of gray and red and orange clouds.

An amber light fell on the brown vegetation of the hills. But in that vegetation, which to Jane when she had first arrived had only seemed part of the view, there was strangeness and danger: the wild disordered men, tramping along old paths, across gardens, between houses, and through what remained of woodland, like aborigines recognizing only an ancestral landscape and insisting on some ancient right of way. Wild men in rags, with long, matted hair; wild men with unseeing red eyes. And bandits. Police cars patrolled these hillside suburbs. Sometimes at night and in the early morning there was the sound of gunfire. The newspapers, the radio, and the television spoke of guerrillas.

The house was set on a large bare lawn, cut out flat from a piece of irregular hillside, with a natural wall of earth on one side. Tawny where it remained grassed, and almost bald near the earth wall, the lawn was now gold where the low sun touched it; every bit of grass and every little clod of clay cast a shadow, so that the whole surface was dramatized. The house was nearly as wide as the lawn; it was low, on one floor, and the wood-tile roof projected far over the rough-rendered concrete wall, on which a kind of ivy grew. From the open porch at the back the land sloped down to a dry gully and woodland. The city lay far below, a small part of the flatness. The rim of the sea still glimmered, but elsewhere sea and swamp were darkening to the color of the great plain.

"So bogus," Jane said. "So hidden away. The High Command. All the publicity. All that food. Of course, it's a perfect cover for the guerrillas, isn't it?"

THE SKY went smoky and the evening chill fell on the hills. The hidden city roared and hummed, with ten thousand radios playing the reggae, as they so often seemed to do. As though somewhere the same party had been going on, with the same music, month after month. The same party, the same music, at the foot of the hills, in the thoroughfares across the city, the redevelopment project, the suburbs beyond the rubbish dump. The same concentration of sound, the same steady beat of people and traffic and radio music which, dulled during the day, at night became audible. As the fire on the roadsides, invisible in daylight, could now be seen, little smoking flares beside the highways.

At Thrushcross Grange it was dark and quiet. The sky had darkened to the deepest blue and then had gone as black as the forest walls. Every footstep and every shuffle resounded in the hollow hut; every sound, bouncing off concrete and corrugated iron, was sharp, reminding the boys of the emptiness and the night outside; and they, who in the towns never spoke without raising their voices, here spoke quietly, almost in whispers. The two oil lamps threw shadows everywhere.

Once, even when the hut was less finished, when the walls were unplastered and the glass louvers hadn't been fitted, the hut had been noisier and gayer. That was when Stephens was there. But Stephens had gone, and other boys had followed him; and now more than half the beds were empty, with bare mattresses that looked alike, and with only the newspaper and magazine pin-ups glued to the wall above (the yellow glue making what was printed on the other side of the paper show through) speaking of the boys who had occupied those beds.

The boys who had left were boys who had places to go back to; somewhere in the city they had mothers or aunts or women they called aunts. Those who had stayed had nowhere to go. They were like Bryant, boys spawned by the city, casually conceived, and after the back yard drama and ritual of their birth gradually abandoned, attaching themselves as they grew up to certain groups and through the groups to certain houses that offered occasional shelter or food.

Bryant grieved for Stephens. Stephens had made Thrushcross Grange a happy place. Stephens talked a lot; Stephens read books; Stephens had ideas and a lot of common sense. Little Stephens, with the funny blob of a pimply nose: funny, until he began to talk. Stephens didn't have to stay in a place like the Grange; he had a mother and a house. But Stephens had come to the Grange because of his ideas; and that had made a lot of the boys feel better. Bryant didn't understand all the things Stephens said; he knew only that he felt happy and safe being where Stephens was. Stephens knew how to give a man courage. And now Stephens had gone away. He hadn't gone back to his mother's house in the city; Bryant had checked. No one knew where Stephens had gone.

Without Stephens, and the boys who had left one by one after Stephens, Bryant didn't like being in the Grange at night. He didn't like being with the boys who had stayed behind. They were too much like himself; with them he felt lost. He wanted to be outside, among other people. He had the dollar the woman had given him, and some other money; and the money made him restless.

Almost as soon as he had seen the woman he had decided to take the risk and ask her for money. He wasn't sure that she would give; she might even complain; but as soon as he had seen the fright in her face, when he had called to her, he knew it was going to be all right. The little victory had set him apart from the other boys in the hut. But then he had begun to feel that the victory might somehow turn sour, and he became nervous. He didn't talk; he kept to himself and behaved as though something had happened to offend him.

They ate early, rice and a meat stew. When he was finished he took his plate out to the thatched lean-to at the back of the hut, dipped the plate in the bucket and put it on the wash stand. He didn't go back inside. He walked round to the front and, avoiding the light from the doorway, went down to the road. Soon he had left the dim lights of the hut behind and was walking in the dark to the highway. He didn't like the dark and the nighttime scuttlings and squeaks of the bush, but his excitement gave him courage. It was a three-mile walk. He walked fast and was sweating when he came to the highway.

He knew it wouldn't be easy to get a taxi. Thrushcross Grange had a reputation; he remembered how, in the time of Stephens, on occasions like this, they had relished that reputation and sometimes acted up to it. The cars went by, four or five a minute, and their headlights picked him out: a young black man in jeans and a striped jersey, small and venomous in appearance, with his twisted face sweated and shiny, deliberately ugly with his pigtails, the pigtails like serpents, signals of aggression. He waved and the cars didn't stop; and there on the highway, the bush all around him, he began to feel lonely and frightened, excitement turning to a sick sensation in his stomach at the thought of the evening being lost, going sour, of having to walk back unsatisfied the way he had come.

At last a taxi stopped. It was nearly full; that was no doubt why the driver had risked stopping. He sat next to a fat woman and he could feel her shifting away from the contact of their shoulders. Fifteen or twenty minutes later the taxi turned off the highway and they came to a little town that had grown up around crossroads in the factory area. The taxi stopped near the center, at a shop with an illuminated clock, and Bryant got out.

It was just after eight. Half an hour before the evening movie shows began, half an hour before the streets grew quieter, that precious last half hour of the evening when, with the relaxed groups on the pavements, the coconut carts doing brisk business, the cafes and the rum shops, the food stands and the oyster stands below the shop eaves, even a little religious meeting going, with the neon lights, the flambeaux smoking in stone bottles, the acetylene lamps like Christmas sparklers, so many pleasures seemed possible. But Bryant was wise now; he was no longer a child. He knew that these moments were cheating. He had money, he had to spend it; it was like a wish to be rid of his money, and it went with the knowledge that it was all waste, that the day would end as it had begun.

He went into the green Chinese cafe, a barnlike old wooden building, two unshaded bulbs hanging from the ceiling, and asked for a peanut punch, banging on the counter as he did so and shouting "Ai! Ai! Ai!" for no reason, only to make a little scene, and to see the look in the eyes of the Chinese man in vest and khaki shorts behind the counter. The man hardly blinked. The peanut punch had gone rancid and bad; but Bryant didn't spit it out. Instead, he put the waxed carton on the counter, paid, and went outside.

He thought of the movies. He had seen most of the films: in these country movie houses certain films were shown over and over. When he was younger he used to go to the interracial-sex films with Negro men as stars; they were exciting to see but depressing afterward, and it was Stephens who had told him that films like that were wicked and could break up a man. He chose the Sidney Poitier double feature. He went into the shuttered little movie house with the noisy electric fans and was alone again, the evening almost over.

In the first film Poitier was a man with a gun. Bryant always enjoyed it, but he knew it was made up and he didn't allow himself to believe in it. The second film was For the Love of Ivy. It was Bryant's favorite; it made him cry but it also made him laugh a lot, and it was his favorite. Soon he had surrendered to it, seeing in the Poitier of that film a version of himself that no one—really no one, and that was the terrible part—would ever get to know: the man who had died within the body Bryant carried, shown in that film in all his truth, the man Bryant knew to be himself, without the edginess and the anger and the pretend ugliness, the laughing man, the tender joker. Watching the film, he began to grieve for what was denied him: that future in which he became what he truly was, not a man with a gun, a big profession, or big talk, but himself, and as himself was loved and readmitted to the house and to the people in the house. He began to sob; and other people were sobbing with him.

The usher scrambled about, turning off the electric fans, creating a kind of silence, opening the exit doors and pulling curtains to shut out the street lights. It was quiet outside; traffic had died down. Bryant was already afraid of the emptiness, the end of the day. He had already come to the end of his money and was as poor as he had been in the morning. The excitement of money was over. The cafes would be closed when the film finished and he went outside; the rum shops would be closed; there would only be a coconut cart, more full of husks than coconuts, a few people sleeping below the shop eaves, drunks, disordered people, and an old woman in a straw hat selling peeled oranges by the light of a flambeau. There would remain the journey back, the taxi, the walk in the night along roads that would barely glimmer between walls of forest and bush. So even before the film ended he was sad, thinking of the blight that came unfairly on a man, ruining his whole life. A whole life.

It was even worse getting a taxi back. He stood under the illuminated clock; but there were not many travelers at that late hour, the taxis were empty, and the drivers pretended they didn't see him. Eventually a long-distance taxi came with two other passengers, and Bryant got in. He waited until they were on the highway before he said, "Thrushcross Grange."

When they were out of the factory area the driver fumbled for something on the floor of the car, next to the accelerator; and Bryant, sitting at the back, heard the sound and understood the signal: the driver had a cutlass. Bryant was nervous. He said, "But like everybody is a bad-John these days"; and was surprised at the tough way the words came out. The driver didn't reply. He gave a little grunt; and he grunted again when some minutes later—Bryant saying, "Here! Here, nuh! Where you going?"—he set Bryant down and took his money. The headlights of the taxi swept on, the red taillights receded; and Bryant was left alone in the darkness.

He had got off at a junction some way beyond the road to Thrushcross Grange. It wasn't to the Grange that he was now walking. This was a shorter walk: soon the bush flattened out and he saw the house against the forest wall. A light was on, not the dim car port bulb that burned all night, but the light in the living room.

Jimmy was up, and Bryant knew that Jimmy would be writing. Jimmy wrote a lot. For this writing of Jimmy's Bryant had a great respect; and Bryant knew that when Jimmy was up so late writing it was because something had happened to make his head hot.

JIMMY WAS writing. The mood had come on him late, after the disturbance of the afternoon, which had stayed with him through dusk and sunset and the night. This was how he usually wrote, out of disturbance, out of wonder at himself, out of some sudden clear vision of an aspect of his past, or out of panic.

As he had been talking to Jane and Roche, as they had let him run on, he had began to feel unsupported by his words, and then separate from his words; and he had had a vision of darkness, of the world lost forever, and his own life ending on that bit of wasteland. After they had gone he allowed himself to sink into that darkness, keeping the memory of the afternoon close: the memory of Jane who, by her presence, manner, and talk, had suggested that darkness reserved for himself alone. Yet at the same time, in his fantasy, she washed away the darkness; he carried the picture of her standing outside the hut on the bare, bright earth, nervous, tremulous in her flared trousers.

I wonder how a man of those attainments can waste his life in a place like that with all those good-for-nothing natives for whom to speak in all candor I cannot have too high an opinion, seeing them shit everywhere just like that, just like animals, they don't even shit in the high grass but on the path, because wait for it they're afraid of snakes.

This is not the kind of thing I am accustomed to with my own class of people, but Peter doesn't turn a hair, the buzzing of the flies around the shit is like music to his ears I'm sure. He wants to beat it out on the drums that he likes being with the natives, so he says. What a laugh, the reason is that they make him feel good and with them he enjoys a position he wouldn't enjoy anywhere else, never mind all the talk about revolution and his sufferings in South Africa for the black man.

Ever since I arrived here I have been hearing about the man they call Jimmy. I had heard about him in London, he was like a celebrity there, but I never dreamt that Fate would throw us together. Out here he is a controversial figure, no one is indifferent to him, he is discussed in every quarter. For the ordinary people, the common people, he is like a savior, he understands and loves the common man, and that is why for the others, the government people and the rich white firms and people of that ilk, he is something else, they're scared of him and they queue up to give him money. And Mr. Roche of Sablich's too, he thinks he's using Jimmy for his own purposes, he is scared too.

So I scheme to see this man, knowing full well that he is not accessible to visitors like myself and resents intrusion, and when on the appointed day I make the journey to Thrushcross Grange and see this man with the naked torso, not black, but a lovely golden color, like some bronze god, I am amazed, my heart is in my mouth. He says nothing and I'm scared of this cold reserve, and yet I am amazed at the perfection of his form and the way he gets these black louts to respect him and behave with a little discipline; that's not something they know much about.

You wouldn't believe that he can be so different from them. They live in poky little shacks on the highway and up the hills, any old piece of board and pitch-oil tin would do for them, you should see those shacks and then it will occasion no surprise that I have no great regard for these natives. But Jimmy's house is something else, I can scarcely believe my eyes when I enter, wall to wall carpeting, everything of the best and everything neat and clean and nicely put away. And what a collection of books, no skimping there. He's obviously a man of considerable refinement rare for these days.

I said, "Do you mind," and went to the shelves. He said, "By all means, they're not dummies," and I took up Wuthering Heights. "Ah," he said, breaking into my thoughts, "you are looking at that great work of the Brontës. What a gifted family, it makes you believe in heredity. Would you like some tea?"

I can see that he is of a difficult disposition but he is making some effort to be civil, and yet in spite of his unwonted readiness to indulge in the tittle-tattle of the tea table I can see that he is revolving great thoughts and projects in his head. Little of this escapes him however, he is a man who knows how to keep his own counsel. He lives in his own rare world, his head is full of big things, he is carrying the burden of all the suffering people in the world, all the people who live in shacks and grow up in dirty little back rooms.

I am drawn to this man, I can't help it, my eyes light up when I look at him, and Peter is getting jealous. But this is no surprise, this is always how the revolution and the love of the black man ends. All the way home I am in a daze, I don't see anything, and I find at night that Peter's touch is repugnant to me. There wasn't much that way between us anyway, but suddenly now he is in heat, and he knows why, and I can see that Peter will soon be on the side of the others, the people who want to destroy this man.

I dream about this man but I don't know how we will meet again. I know he will never forgive a second intrusion and I have no desire to aggravate his impatience. He is an enemy to all privilege and I am middle-class born and bred and I know that in spite of his great civility and urbane charm he must hate people like me. I only have to look in his eyes to understand the meaning of hate.

He had begun without conviction, simply putting down words on the pad. But then excitement had possessed him; the words became more than words; and he felt he could go on for a long time. Now, out of that very excitement, he stopped writing and began to walk about the room. As he walked he became aware of the night and the bush; and he was undermined again. Melancholy came over him like fatigue, like rage, like a sense of doom; and when he went back to the desk he found that the writing excitement had broken and was impossible to reenter. The words on the pad were again just like words, false.

One day I was driving on the highway and suddenly in the middle of the traffic my car broke down, when who should appear in my moment of need but Jimmy driving about in his Aston Martin . . .

Words alone: again he stopped.

At the beach one day of glorious sunshine amid the sands and dunes and motorcars below the coconut trees, the splendor of the scene marred only by a gang of louts . . .

He heard footsteps in the road, and waited. Bryant came in from the front porch, red-eyed, exhausted, null. His movements were abrupt, as though, having hurried to the house, he wanted now only to draw attention to his own mood. Saying nothing, not looking at Jimmy, he sat down heavily on one of the furry chairs with his legs wide apart, rested his head on the top of the back cushion and looked up at the ceiling. There were fresh tears in the corners of his eyes.

Jimmy said, "You went to the pictures, Bryant?"

Bryant didn't reply.

"For the Love of Ivy?"

Bryant wiped the corner of one eye with a long, crooked finger.

Jimmy knew the film and he knew the effect it had on Bryant. He said, "Go and make yourself a little Ovaltine."

Bryant didn't move.

Jimmy said, "Stay and watch the milk. Don't let it boil."

He watched Bryant rise, his movements less abrupt now, and he watched him leave the room. He sat for some time looking at the door through which Bryant had gone. Then he faced the desk and turned over to a new page on the pad.

Dear Roy, In my last I sent you some clippings from the local rags which I thought would amuse you and give you some idea of our activities. No one here who is in charge seems to know how close the crisis is, how this whole world is about to blow up, and when I consider the world as it is presently constituted, when I think of the boys I work with here at Thrushcross Grange, I feel that to destroy the world is the only course of action that is now open to sane men.

The destructive urge comes on me at times like this, I want to see fire everywhere, when I stop and think that there is no hope of creative endeavor being appreciated, it is all for nothing, and on a night like this I feel I could weep for our world and for the people who find themselves unprotected in it. When I think how much I expected of my life at one time, and when I think how quickly that time of hope dies, I get sad, and more so when I think of the people who never expected anything. We are children of hell.

Perhaps after all, Roy, the world is only made for the people who possess it now, and there are some people who will never possess anything. The people who will win are the people who have won already and they're not taking chances now, like the liberals. You know better than I how they let me down when the crisis came, you would think that after making me their playboy and getting me deported from England they would leave me alone. But they do not. Even here they are coming after me, well I ask you. These liberals who come flashing their milk white thighs and think they're contributing to the cause.

Still everybody has their uses, even Mr. Peter Roche, I call him massa but he doesn't see the joke. He's the great white revolutionary and torture hero of South Africa. He's written this book which I don't think you would know about, but over here of course he is a world-shaking best-selling author, and now he is working for one of our old imperialist firms, Sablich's great slave traders in the old days, they now pretend that black is beautiful, and wait for it they employ Mr. Roche to prove it. I play along, what can you do—

He broke off. The charm did not work. Words, which at some times did so much for him, now did not restore him to himself. He was a lost man, more lost than he had been as a boy, in his father's shop, at school, in the streets of the city, when he saw only what he saw and knew nothing.

Bryant, sitting quietly in the furry chair, had been watching him. The empty Ovaltine mug stood on the glass-topped table. Bryant's eyes had cleared; expression had come back to his face and he was calmer; his pigtails looked limp.

"Bryant, did you ask the lady for money?"

"Jim?"

"Did you ask her?"

"Jimmy, you know it isn't the sort of thing I does do."

He offered comfort to others, but he needed their comfort more. He went to Bryant, the very ugly, damaged from birth, who expressed all that he saw of himself in certain moods. He embraced Bryant.

IT WAS fashionable here, in the new houses on the Ridge, to have instead of glass windows louvers of redwood which, when closed, created total darkness. It was in this darkness, the louvers closed to keep out insects, that Jane awoke in her own room every day, and recaptured for a moment something of the mystery of her arrival. The long airplane journey through the night: the noise of the engines that obliterated past and distance; the memories—more like dreams than memories of actual events—of getting off at various airports, brilliantly illuminated; excitement then going, fatigue deadening response; so that, just hours away from London, she felt she had entered another life.

The strangeness had begun at the London airport. They had all boarded the plane; then there had been a fog alert and they had all got out; then they had got in again and there for five hours they had stayed, on the ground. London was outside; but they inside were already in another world, of passengers and stewardesses, stewardesses who, on the ground part of London and not noticeable, in the airplane became English and exotic, wearing a particular uniform. Change came to the passengers as well: the restless and the assertive began to stand out, mainly men who had taken off their jackets and slackened their ties; and among the black passengers differences of clothes, manner, and speech became more pronounced.

London all afternoon; New York at some time of the night or early morning. Some Americans got on, and two men sat in the empty seats beside Jane. She was too tired to mind, too tired to do more than note the pornographic books, their titles printed small on plain white covers, that both men were always reading whenever she awakened from her doze. Nassau airport: the transit lounge closed, a dim light in a kind of corridor, a half-embarrassed Negro, a workman in spite of his jacket and tie, trying to pick up a red-haired girl. Later, in the plane, Jane had reached out for *Easy Lay*, now resting in a seat pocket; but the American beside her, to whom the book belonged, had put his plump hand on hers and taken away the book, saying, "Not for little girls. It's the hard stuff." Awake again, connected sleep no longer possible, bright light in some windows; trays, brisk stewardesses now with aprons over their uniforms, so that their character changed again. The American said to Jane, "You need intensive care."

After the landing—black men in khaki uniforms, continuing a loud conversation of their own, hurrying into the plane to spray it—after the sting of insecticide and the shock of light and heat, the Americans had taken Jane with them through concrete corridors to the immigration hall, her clothes getting sticky as she walked, her eyes registering the bad French signs. They had taken her to the head of the queue that had already formed; and they must have been important men, because they were let through without formality, and Jane had been let through with them, without handing over her disembarkation card or showing her return ticket or having her passport stamped.

In the customs hall, waiting for her luggage, Jane had begun to be more alert. She had begun to think of one of the Americans: He is a candidate. He had given his local address; she noted it was not in the city. He asked where she was staying and who was meeting her. She mentioned Roche's name, speaking it as a famous name, casually, and expecting that it would get some response, of surprise or apprehension, from the Americans, whom she now judged to be business types. But they hadn't heard of Roche or the firm he worked for.

And the surprise, disappointment almost, which showed on

their faces when, leaving the customs hall, they saw Roche, under medium height, without a jacket and slenderer than he had appeared in London, almost thin, leaning against an iron rail, indistinguishable in dress and posture from the taxi drivers and the freelance porters among whom he appeared to be lounging at the exit gate, this disappointment, this abrupt coolness of the Americans, communicated itself to Jane and almost immediately became her own response to the meeting.

It was not their custom to kiss or embrace in public.

Roche said, "You travel with big people."

"They spent all the time on the plane reading pornography. The hard stuff."

"They are the bauxite company. They own the place."

"They got me through immigration. I didn't have to show my passport or return ticket or anything."

"I hope that doesn't create problems when you're leaving."

"I need intensive care."

They drove through a flat green land, already hot, the windows of the car open. The hills to the right were breathtaking, green below a blue haze, the folds of the ridges soft in the morning light. The vegetation was new to her, all a blur of the brightest green. She thought: Later. Later I will get to know this.

The junked cars; the little houses in Mediterranean colors set beside the road at the edge of fields of tall grass. The factories, set in ordered grounds behind fences; and then the rubbish dump, the endless town, the pitched roofs of separate little shops and houses jammed together, the rusting corrugated iron, jalousies and fretwork, the greenery of back yards, the electric wires, crooked walls, broken pavements, unswept gutters, the slogans: Black Is Basic, Don't Vote; and then the ride up to the Ridge, the pavements giving way to grass verges, the houses getting bigger, still little clusters of shacks about them, but then no shacks at all, just wide roads, big gardens, big houses, and vegetation hiding the city and the plain she had just left; going up to where it still felt like early morning, with sometimes, as the road twisted higher, a view of the hazy flat land below, indistinguishable from swamp and sea.

A concrete wall, stepped down a hillside, two strips of concrete at the side of a lawn still in shadow; an ivy-covered bungalow, but more than a bungalow, a great spreading house, overlooking a green hillside splashed with red. A shuttered room, the redwood louvers creating total darkness; a black maid, coffee. And Jane began to fall asleep to confused images of her journey, of Negroes, stewardesses and the Americans, airport buildings at night and the morning drive through the green land; the noise of the plane still with her, like something obliterating the life she had left behind, exhaustion and strain becoming part of her sense of violation, of having made the wrong decision. She awakened to darkness; she was momentarily confused. Then, tilting the redwood louvers, she had been startled by the light.

That was only four months ago. And that day and night and morning of travel, that succession of images that were like dreams, remained the most vivid of her new experiences. When she had arrived everything was green and the flame of the forest was in bloom. Drought had since occurred, the worst drought, she had been told, for forty years. The hills had turned brown; many clumps of bamboo had caught fire; and the woodland on the Ridge had acquired something of the derelict quality of the city. Trees had been stripped; vegetation had generally dried and thinned; and neighboring houses could now be seen. But the city and the flat land remained as unknown as it had been on that first day; and nothing had happened to alter the conviction she had had, at the moment of arrival, that she had made a wrong decision.

It was what she had half expected. She had come to expect that her decisions would be wrong; and she had begun to feel that it was part of the wrongness of the world.

In London Roche had seemed to her an extraordinary person; and she had prided herself on her perception in picking him out. He had appeared to her as a doer; and none of the people she knew could be considered doers. They grumbled—journalists, politicians, businessmen—responding week by week to the latest newspaper crisis and television issue; they echoed one another; they could become hysterical with visions of the country's decay. But the little crises always passed, the whispered political plots and business schemes evaporated; everything that was said was stale, and people no longer believed what they said. And failure always lay with someone else; the people who spoke of crisis were themselves placid, content with their functions, existing within their functions, trapped, part of what they railed against.

She was adrift, enervated, her dissatisfactions vague, now centering on the world, now on men. One evening in her house, before dinner, this happened. She was with her lover, a left-wing journalist whose views no longer held surprise for her, whose insincerities and ambition she had grown to understand and whose articles she no longer read. His beauty was something she loved, but only as she might have loved a picture: the body that promised so much offered little. She went cold when he was on her; she turned away when he tried to kiss her; she was dry and he had trouble entering. Abruptly, she made a movement and threw him off and he stood beside the bed exposed and vulnerable. Without any attempt at taunting, she drew up her right knee and lit a cigarette. He said, "Why did you do that?" She said, "Because I wanted to." She was slapped, so hard that her jaw jarred, her cigarette fell from her hand; and then she was slapped again. Her face flamed; she began to cry; and in one swift action, rescuing her cigarette from the bed, she got up, gathered the sheet around her, and went to the bathroom. She allowed her tears to flow but was careful to make no sound. She was expecting a knock at the door: she intended not to reply. She heard his footsteps in the bedroom, heard them in the passage; but then the footsteps went down the carpeted stairs, and she heard the front door closed. She stayed in the bathroom for some time, waiting for a ring at the door, waiting to be rescued. But he didn't come back; and then she discovered to her dismay and disgust that she was moist.

It was not long after this that she met Roche. He had just published a book about his experiences in South Africa. He had been arrested, tortured, tried, imprisoned, and then, after international protests, deported, his assets in the country frozen. He had made little impression on her at their first meeting. But later she had read his book, and she had then approached him through his book. And this was soon to strike her as strange, that she should have assumed from his book and the experiences he described in it that she knew him.

Roche had appeared to her as a doer, unlike anyone she had known. He talked little; he had no system to expound; but simply by being what he was he enlarged her vision of the world. He seemed to make accessible that remote world, of real events and real action, whose existence she had half divined; and through him she felt she was being given a new idea of human possibility. It pleased her that there was nothing extraordinary about his appearance, and that some people wondered what she saw in him: this small man in his mid-forties, sad-faced, with sunken cheeks, deep lines running from his nose to the corners of his mouth, and with eyes that were slightly mocking and ironical.

They had never talked about South Africa or discussed his book; about the torture and the imprisonment she preferred not to think. He came from the more important world; and she thought he had a vision, like hers, of her own world about to be smashed, and that he acted upon this vision. He was a doer; his book and his life proved that; and she assumed that his old life was claiming him, that it was to some new and as yet unsuspected center of world disturbance that he was going, when, suddenly, not stopping to enjoy such reputation as his book had given him, he had decided to leave London, to take this unlikely and not well-paid job on the island with a firm that sounded like a firm of colonial shopkeepers.

She had already committed herself to him and to what she conceived to be his kind of life. She had already committed herself to following him out as soon as she had arranged for her house to be let. Then one day something happened that awakened doubt. Roche laughed; until then she had only seen him smile. Roche laughed, and the corners of his mouth rode up over the receding gums on his molars, which showed long, with black gaps between them. It was like a glimpse of teeth in a skull, like a glimpse of a satyr; and she felt it was like a glimpse of the inner man. She had thought him distinguished-looking, and had begun to find him beautiful. This was like a glimpse of a grotesque stranger. She allowed the irrational moment to pass; she was committed. But then, at the moment of arrival, doubt had come to her again. In these relationships some warning, some little hint, always was given, some little sign that foreshadowed the future. And now the thing foreshadowed was with her.

She knew now, after four months, what she had known on that first day: that she had come to a place at the end of the world, to a place that had exhausted its possibilities. She wondered at the simplicity that had led her, in London, to believe that the future of the world was being shaped in places like this, by people like these.

The Ridge was self-contained, shut off from the city; and at first the hysteria in which her neighbors lived had interested her. Here, where she had come as to the center of the world, the talk was of departure, of papers being fixed for Canada and the United States: secretive talk, because departure was at once like betrayal and surrender. No one was more of a Ridge man than Harry de Tunja, no one seemed more local and settled. But overnight these virtues became alarming, and offensive, after it had accidentally come out that, during his many business trips to Canada, Harry had also been securing his status as a Canadian landed immigrant.

Harry's air-conditioned den, fitted up like a bar, with a little illuminated sign on the shelves that said *Harry's Bar*, with a collection of Johnny Walker figures and other bar objects, was an established meeting place. The temperature was low enough for cardigans and pullovers; the lights were dim; psychedelic bar advertisements from various countries created the effects of shifting circles or bubbles or fountains. Here, in an atmosphere of extravagance and holiday rather than of crisis, with Harry standing behind his bar, people were used to talking about the air conditioning and the degree of coldness achieved that evening and also about the local situation.

Jane had at first waited for details of that situation to become clear, for the personalities of whom people talked, the doers and demagogues down in the city, to define themselves. But the personalities were so many, the principles on which they acted so confusing, and the issues so evanescent, that she had soon lost interest, had closed her mind to talk of new political alliances that so often seemed to come to nothing anyway, and to analyses of new political threats that could also quickly disappear. Nothing that happened here could be important. The place was no more than what it looked. And Roche didn't occupy in it the position she thought he did when—it seemed so fresh—she had given his name to the Americans in the customs hall of the airport and had awaited their astonishment.

She saw that Roche was a refugee on the island. He was an employee of his firm; he belonged to a place like the Ridge; he was half colonial. He was less on the island than he had been in London, and she still wondered at the haste with which he had thrown up his life there. She doubted whether half a dozen people on the island had read his book. Of course he had a reputation, as someone who had suffered in South Africa. Without this reputation he would not have been employed by Sablich's, and he certainly would not have been given a work permit. For this reputation there was respect, but there was also something else: a curious attitude of patronage.

It was strange that there should be patronage for Roche, and regard, almost awe, for someone like Mrs. Grandlieu. Mrs. Grandlieu was of an old planter family. She was an elderly brown-skinned woman; and at her cocktail parties and dinners she always did or said something to remind black people of the oddity of their presence in her house, where until recently Negroes were admitted only as servants.

Mrs. Grandlieu's accent was exaggeratedly local. She spoke the English her servants spoke; it was part of her privilege, and her way of distancing herself from the important black men, some with English accents, whom she asked to her house. At these gatherings Mrs. Grandlieu always managed to say "nigger" once, as if only with a comic intention, using the word as part of some old idiom of the street or the plantations which she expected her guests to recognize. She might say, of something that was a perfect fit, that it fitted "like yam fit nigger mouth"; and the black men would laugh. Once Jane heard her say, of someone who talked too much, that his mouth ran "like a sick nigger's arse."

Yet the people who considered it a privilege to be in Mrs.

Grandlieu's house, assumed an exaggerated ease there, laughed with her at her antique plantation idioms, and avoided the racial challenge that she always in some way threw down, these very people could be tense and combative with Roche. They knew his South African history; they felt safe with him. But it was as if they wished to test him further, as if each man, meeting Roche for the first time, wished to get some personal statement from him, some personal declaration of love. Such a man might begin by attributing racialist views to Roche or by appearing to hold Roche responsible for all the humiliations he, the islander, had endured in other countries. Jane had seen that happen more than once.

There was this that was also strange. The very people who avoided the subject of race with Mrs. Grandlieu probed Roche about South Africa. They wished to find out more about the humiliations of black people there; and they reacted with embarrassment, unease, or resentment when they heard what they had expected to hear. Jane had seen the cold hatred one evening when Roche had spoken of the climate, of the passion for sport, of the fine physiques of the white people. Roche had seen it too. Even when pressed—the word had got around—he never talked of that again.

Mrs. Grandlieu challenged the black men in her old and old-fashioned house; they challenged Roche. Far more was required of Roche than of Mrs. Grandlieu; and Jane saw, over the weeks, that in spite of the real respect for his past, Roche had become a kind of buffoon figure to many. He was not a professional man or businessman; he had none of the skills that were considered important. He was a doer of good works, with results that never showed, someone who went among the poor on behalf of his firm and tried to organize boys' clubs and sporting events, gave this cup here and offered a gift of cricket equipment there. He worked with Jimmy Ahmed, whom he took seriously, more seriously than the people who gave Jimmy money; he bribed slum boys to go to Thrushcross Grange.

On the Ridge and elsewhere it was the privilege of the local people, black and not black, to be cynical about the future, about the politicians and politics. Roche, because of his past, because of that book that almost no one had read (and how far away that seemed, how much belonging to another life), and because of his job, was the man to whom some more positive view of the future was attributed. He was called upon to defend himself. But he never said much. He seemed indifferent to satire, indifferent to the looks that were exchanged when someone tried to get him to talk about his activities.

So Jane saw that on the island, which in her imagination had once been the setting of action that would undo the world, Roche was a refugee. He was a man who didn't have a place to go back to; he was someone for whom room had been made. His status on the Ridge was that of an employee of a big firm, high enough to be given a house, and as such he was accepted. He could be boisterously greeted in Harry's bar; he passed as a kind of Ridge man, odd but solid. And he seemed to accept this role.

It was his passivity that disappointed and repelled Jane. In the early days of their relationship his unwillingness to explain himself, his calm, had encouraged her to think that he had some long view, some vision of the future. There were still moments now when she thought, considering not her disappointment but his life, that he might be a saint, looking down from a great height on the follies of people and being limitlessly forgiving. But there was his satyr's laugh, the glimpse of those long molars, black at the roots and widely spaced. Nothing escaped him, no look, no comment. That she had learned; and there were times when she thought that he was bottling up resentment, resentment at what had happened in South Africa, resentment at a life that had gone awry, and that one day he would speak and act. But she no longer believed him capable of passion. All that he seemed capable of was a cheap sarcasm, directed mainly at her. She had decided that there was no puzzle, that he was a man with nothing to revenge, that some part of his personality, some motor of action, had been excised.

While she had expected something of him she had never asked about his experiences in the South African jail, not wishing to get him to talk about his humiliations. But one day, when in her own mind she had given him up and put an end to their relationship, she asked him whether he felt no bitterness about what had happened to him in jail; and she had been astonished by his answer. He said, and he might have been exposing a wound or speaking of a virtue or simply stating a fact, "You must understand I have always accepted authority. It probably has to do with the kind of school I went to."

SO THIS morning Jane awakened, as she had awakened in the middle of that first day, to the darkness of the room with the redwood louvers and to the knowledge that she had made an error, that she had once again seen in a man things that were not there.

She went down the parquet passage past Roche's room, his door, like hers, left ajar for the sake of air. In the big and almost empty room at the back, a room without a function, part of the unfurnished spaciousness of the company house, she unlocked the folding doors that opened onto the raised brick porch. The metal table and the lager bottles and glasses were wet with dew; the empty cigarette pack was soaked and swollen; dew had collected like water in the seats of the metal chairs.

The sun had not yet risen; and down below, beyond the brown hills, the plain and the silent city were blurred by mist, which was white over the swamp. She walked round to the front of the house. The lawn—or lawn area—was wet; dew was the only moisture it received these days, since the drought had set in and the watering of gardens had been forbidden. The wall of earth on one side showed what had been cut away from the hill to create this level place: grass and grassroots in a thin layer of topsoil, a kind of sandstone, red clay. The lawn surface near the earth wall was rubbled with little clods of clay.

Jane thought how lucky she was to be able to decide to leave. Not many people had that freedom: to decide, and then to do. It was part of her luck; in moments like this she always consoled herself with thoughts of her luck. She was privileged: it was the big idea, the one that overrode all the scattered, unrelated ideas deposited in her soul as she had adventured in life, the debris of a dozen systems she had picked up from a dozen men. She would leave; she would make use of that return ticket the immigration officers hadn't bothered to ask for the day she had arrived.

She was lucky, she was privileged. And yet, as always in moments of crisis, and her crises were connected with these failures with men, she saw the world in crisis, and her own privilege, for all its comfort, as useless. She would return to London; that society which she had given up, and whose destruction she thought he had awaited, continued. She would be safe in London, but she would be safe in the midst of decay.

She had always seen decay about her, even while going through all that the society asked of her. Slot machines on railway stations were full of sweets, but she knew they would be empty again; they were meant to be empty, as they had been when she was a child, pieces of junk that no one yet thought of taking away. She saw great squares that were no longer residential, houses that no one was ever rich enough now to live in. She saw spaces getting smaller; she saw buildings everywhere being put to meaner uses than those they were originally intended for. The sight of a London County Council plaque on a house reminded her that the people around her were no longer great, that no house of today would deserve a plaque in the years to come. Neither houses nor personalities would be remembered. She knew that, she felt it. Yet she was attached to her own house, and looked for men who would be doers. She was alert to every change of fashion, yet saw the tinsel quality of most fashions; and in the decor of a fashionable new restaurant, in the very newness, she could see hints of the failure and shoddiness to come.

She lived in the midst of change, repetitive and sterile; it did not disguise the fact of the greater impermanence. But she was privileged: she told herself that once a day. Security was the basis of her privilege. Yet she saw, with a satiric eye, the people around her as accumulators, concerned about dead rituals and dead forms, unmindful of the approaching catastrophe. She saw the girls who were her friends as empty vessels, waiting to be filled by men, who in time appeared, their names echoing and reechoing in conversation, Roger and Mark and John, as empty as the girls. But Roger and Mark and John could have been models for the men to whom she had once given herself, and in whom she had seen extraordinary qualities. Out of this contradiction between what she did and said and what she felt, out of this knowledge of her own security and her vision of decay, of a world running down, she moved from one crisis to another.

But now she was not at home, and the sense of impermanence was stronger here. The brown hills held guerrillas; so the newspapers and the government said. The stripped hill at the back of the house, the back garden, sloped down to woodland and a gully; and in that hidden gully there was a regular traffic of people on foot, wild people, disordered and unkempt, who chattered as they passed, briskly, in groups, morning and evening, going to and coming from she knew not where.

About the Ridge, so high, so seemingly secure, there was an unknown human turbulence. These big houses, these big gardens. The houses would never be completely furnished, would never be allowed to become like family houses that had been lived in for two or three generations. They would never be like Mrs. Grandlieu's old timber house, with its worn decorative woodwork, its internal arches of fretwork arabesques that caught the dust, its mahogany-stained floor springy but polished smooth, the hard graining of the floorboards standing out from the softer wood. These new houses of the Ridge, while they lasted, would only be what they were now: concrete shells. And, for all the truck loads of topsoil, the gardens would never mature, would never be cool, with green walks. The gardens were too big; they would contract. The disorder of the city and the factory suburbs: that would spread up and up, through roads and woodland, and eventually overwhelm. This was a place that had produced no great men, and its possibilities were now exhausted.

The sky brightened; the white mist above the swamp thinned. Soon the coolness of the day would go, the fires would start all over the great plain, and from the height of the Ridge it would look as though here and there, through minute punctures, the land was leaking smoke. Far away, the airport was just visible. The airplanes, their shapes not distinct, were little gleams of white.

Mrs. Grandlieu used to say, "Sometimes I does just look at the airport and think it damn far, you know." She said it only to unsettle; but it was easy to imagine the Ridge cut off and under siege. Already, something like a state of siege existed every night. There were police roadblocks on all the main hillside roads, so that a dinner party or cocktail party or a visit to Harry's bar had an added adventure, and gave point to the hysteria of the people who lived on the Ridge, people who felt threatened by what lay below, and moved higher and higher up the hills until, like the people who had held the house before Jane and Roche, they could move no higher and had flown.

Within the house very little remained to mark the passage of these people. The ocher-washed concrete walls were virgin; no nail had been driven into them, no picture had been hung. A few scratches and black scuff marks on the baseboard in the empty back room hinted at games, a child or children; but that was all.

There were more reminders of the previous people outside. In the half-rockery half-flowerbed against the stepped concrete wall at the front they had planted roses; and on the spindly yellow stalks of those that survived little single-petaled blooms still occasionally came, opening and wilting in one day. The shrubs they had planted had remained static in the clay and had dried down. The only things that really grew at the front were young trees that had seeded themselves: a flame of the forest between the rocks of the rockery, three or four pink poui in a crack in the concrete at the edge of the gateway, a thorn bush with hundreds of little yellow flowers on spiky black branches.

At the back of the house concrete steps went a little way down the eroded hillside to where there was a retaining wall of concrete blocks. The cypresses planted beside the steps were stunted, and against the retaining wall were choked growths of Bermuda grass where, during the rains of another season, grass seed from the front lawn and the area around the back porch had washed down.

Beyond the wall the land flattened, the soil was better, and there was the remnant of a vegetable garden, with banana trees. Neither Jane nor Roche had touched the vegetable garden. This lower part of the garden, beyond the steps and the retaining wall, Jane seldom walked in; it was some weeks after she had arrived that she had discovered, at the end of the garden, at the edge of the gully, a row of Honduras pine seedlings.

The most substantial thing the previous people had left was a children's house or hut on this flatter part of the land. It showed the local carpenter's hand: it was less a miniature than a replica of many shacks in the city. It stood flat to the ground on a timber frame, with one room and a pitched roof; the walls were multicolored, with old boards from other buildings; and it had been fitted with an old paneled door. It looked whole, but it had begun to rot. There was a great gritty black ants' nest below the eaves. Jane had imagined this to be alive with ants; but she saw this morning that the nest had cracked and broken away in parts and was dry and empty.

The door was slightly ajar. Jane pushed at it. It yielded. Then there was some resistance. A length of coarse, shredded string brushed across her hand like an insect; and as she started, slapping at the affected hand, she saw that the hut was tenanted.

Within, in the darkness, striped with the light that came through the gaps in the boards, in a smell of stale smoke, dirt, old clothes and something like the smell of dead small animals, a wild man of the hills was asleep. His matted hair was done in long pigtails, reddish brown in places and with a kind of thick blue grease; his face was broad, very black and shiny where the light caught it. He was in rags; and he lay amid other rags.

He stirred at the sound of her slapping hand, and gave a grunt. She saw a cutlass beside his bundle and his old paint can, and she turned and walked very fast to the concrete steps, leaving the hut door open. She began to run up the steps, past the Bermuda grass clumps, the stunted cypresses, not looking back. How long had he been there? For how long had that hut in the garden been his home? At the top of the steps, near the hibiscus bush, she stopped and looked back. There was nothing to see.

She thought of Bryant in the hut at Thrushcross Grange, with his aggressive pigtails. He, like the man asleep in the children's hut, had issued out of the city and the plain below, which from this height could be seen all at a glance. Down there, in the garden, the scale had altered; it was like being taken, for a moment, into the intricate life contained in that view.

The sun was out; it caught her on the temples. The woodland and the children's hut cast shadows. The haze on the plain was going. Once the hills were green and had only been part of the view, a foreground spattered with the red and orange of the flame of the forest.

She thought of Bryant. She thought of Jimmy Ahmed. *Succubus.* In the house, through the half-open door of his room, she saw Roche asleep. She changed her mind and didn't awaken him. She went back down the passage to the large sitting room, with a view through the picture window of the front lawn in shadow. From the paperbacks on the nearly empty fitted shelves she took down the Academy English Dictionary. She found the page she wanted. She read: *Succubus: demon that mates with a sleeping man.*

He called from his room: "Jane."

When she went to him he said, "I've just had a terrible dream. Just after you came in from the garden. I was about to be tortured. There was a doctor in a dark suit. He said, 'We'll get the coitus out of you.' And I knew I didn't want him to use those things in his box on me. And that the coitus I had to get rid of I could get rid of just by going to the lavatory."

He had never spoken of a dream like this before, and she was disturbed. He had begun with real distress, but his distress seemed to go as he spoke, and at the end he was even smiling. She didn't know what to do; and the moment for sympathy and response passed.

She said, "We dream all kinds of strange things just before we wake up."

A car or van had stopped outside the house. It turned in the road, and then it could be heard going away banging down the hill.

She said, "The paper's come. I'll go and get it."

A radio came on in the far end of the house. It was Adela, the maid, in her room, listening to the morning program of hymns sponsored by a church of the American South that specialized in Negro souls.

Adela was young but devout. She was plump and healthy, but she went to all the faith healing meetings that itinerant Southern American preachers held in the city. It had at first amused Jane to hear of these meetings, to hear Adela's stories of crippled Negroes who had thrown away crutches and ripped off bandages and run up shouting to the platform, of bewitched boys whose bodies had been made to give up nails and other pieces of metal that had somehow, during their bewitchment, been absorbed into their flesh. But Jane had soon regretted the encouragement she had given Adela; for Adela, when she understood that Jane and Roche were not married and were living "in sin," became permanently annoyed. In her white uniform, on which she insisted, she walked through the large house like a Friday night woman preacher, filling the rooms with her annoyance, and looking for fresh signs of sin.

Jane, going out to the front gate to get the newspaper, heard Adela shriek. And she knew the cause: the lager bottles on the metal table in the back porch.

"The an-amount of rum!" Adela shouted. "Rum! Rum! Oh my God, but the an-amount of rum they does drink in this house!"

After breakfast—Adela back in her room, the radio going again: music, commercials, government announcements—Jane said to Roche, "What would you say if I told you I was going back to London?"

He was reading the police news in the newspaper: the events of the previous day and early evening: the raids, the shootouts, the slum brawls: for many people down there in the city life had reached crisis in the last twenty-four hours.

He said, "I would say I wish I was going back with you."

"But if I was going for good. If I wasn't coming back."

He didn't put the paper down. He continued to read; and then, as he unfolded the paper and turned the page, he said, in his precise way, "That would be more complicated."

He said no more. His calm robbed her of impatience or combativeness. Mood, emotion, events, led her to action. So it had always been with her; so it was going to be now. She had decided; the time for acting on that decision would come. When Roche returned for lunch they talked of other things; it was as though the crisis had passed.

4

THIS MAN fills my whole mind to the exclusion of all other trivial concerns and I don't know how I can get to see him again. He's suffered so much in England, I don't believe he will want to see someone like me. Over here they see him only as a hakwai, but a woman of my class can see what he really is, I can understand what all those other people in England saw in him. They say he was born in the back room of a Chinese grocery, a half black nobody, just a Chinaman's lucky shot on a dark night, that's a good laugh, but I can see that he is a man of good blood, only someone of my class can see that, to me he is like a prince helping these poor and indigent black people, they're so shiftless no one will help them, least of all their own.

He's the leader they're waiting for and the day will come, of that I'm convinced, when they will parade in the streets and offer him the crown, everybody will say then, "This man was born in the back room of a Chinese grocery, but as Catherine said to Heathcliff, 'Your mother was an Indian princess and your father was the Emperor of China,' we knew it all along," and that was in the middle of England mark you, in the days when they had no racial feeling before all those people from Jamaica and Pakistan came and spoiled the country for a man like him. They will see him then like a prince, with his gold color.

I drive past his solitary forbidding house many times and often *late at night I see the lamp burning in his study, he's wrapped up in his thoughts and I have no wish to intrude and aggravate his impatience because I know he's writing that book he has a contractual obligation to write. One day I summoned up the courage to telephone him, my heart was beating when he answered, I put the phone down, though I'm dying to hear that soft and cultivated voice, that dark brown voice as it has so aptly been described by many . . .*

Jimmy put aside the pad and considered Bryant, sitting on one of the furry chairs and trying to read the newspaper without making the sheets rustle.

Bryant wasn't a reader. But Stephens made a point of reading the newspapers every day, and Bryant was copying Stephens. Stephens read newspapers in his own way. He especially read the evening paper. Stephens didn't pay much attention to the foreign news or the big stories about politics; he concentrated on the police items, which were longer in the evening paper, fresher, and with those casual details, usually edited out of the same stories in the morning paper, that he looked for. Stephens could tell, from the names of districts, from the description of an incident by police and eye witnesses, from the places where motorcars were stolen and where they were later found, what his friends and enemies were up to. This was how Stephens read the evening paper, like a private circular. And this was how Bryant tried to read the paper, going through the finely printed paragraphs of little facts, half hoping that in this way he might get some news about Stephens.

Now that he had stopped writing, now that he had broken the mood and was aware only of the desolation outside, Jimmy felt enervated by his writing. He considered Bryant, the twisted face, the little pigtails, the lips working as they shaped the words, the thin legs in their old blue jeans; and Jimmy was as sad for Bryant as he was for himself.

He got up. He walked about the blue carpet. He went to the bedroom and stood near the telephone on the chest of drawers. He hesitated. Then he dialed, and waited.

Adela said, "Roche residence."

He didn't speak.

"Roche residence."

He put the telephone down. He went back to the living room and sat at the desk.

This man possesses me. He's a loner, I can see that. Over here they're jealous of him, cut him down to size, that's their motto, it's all they know, leave him in the bush to rot, and in England too they tried to destroy him, talking of rape and assault, he became too famous for them to stomach, they thought he was just a stud, that's how they wanted to keep him, send him back to rot. But he's a man not easily destroyed, he's surprised them I bet, he's a man once seen never forgotten.

And then one day scanning the paper as usual for news of his doings I see that he's going to address a big gathering of the Lions, local and foreign big shots, everybody of course wants to know what he has to say about the issues of the day. He's addressing this meeting at the Prince Albert Hotel one lunchtime and I make it my business to be there at the appointed hour.

I see his name and photo on a board in the lobby and I notice that everybody is in a state of suppressed excitement, the waiters themselves are congregating in hushed groups outside the room where he's addressing the assembly. In the end I heard one set of applause, it seemed there would be no end to the acclamations, and one of the waiters cried out "But that is man," and then he comes out with all those big shots local and foreign hanging on to his every word, they're in their suits, he's so casual in his well-creased trousers and his Mao shirt, but very respectable and polite, with a kind and relevant word for everyone, casual his clothes might be but they reveal the lines of his lithe, pantherlike body.

My heart is in my mouth, I don't know whether he will recognize me and whether it will be right for me to accost him, but then he said, "But isn't it Clarissa," and I said, "So you remember me." The big shots fall back and I'm very proud indeed to be seen in the company of this famous man who is so essentially modest. He said, "Of course I remember you, I owe you a dollar."

A little smile comes in his eyes and I'm amazed, because nothing is hidden from this man's gaze, he must have seen how frightened I was that day at the Grange and I suppose that even now when he's talking to me he can see the terror in my light-colored eyes, because when I'm with him I feel like a mesmerized rabbit, I just want to give up and when I revive he will bring water in his own cupped hands and I will drink water from his tender hands and I will not be afraid of him anymore.

He was enervated, sick with excitement. He could feel that his pants were wet. He was tormented and deliciously saddened by that dream of beauty. It had come to him years before, when he was a schoolboy; it had only been a story, but it had become like a memory of something seen. It was a Monday morning story at school, a story that had penetrated the back yards of the city over the weekend and had then been brought to the school by various boys, who told the story as it might have been told by the older women of the back yards, awed rather than shocked at what had happened, fearful of the punishment about to come to all, and half protective, half resigned.

It was the story of the rape of a white girl at the beach by a gang. The girl had bled and shrieked and fainted. One of the men had then run to a brackish creek in the coconut grove and had tried, using his cupped hands alone, to bring water to the girl.

The boy from whom Jimmy had first heard the story that Monday morning—and in the boy's voice could be detected the accents of the women of the back yard where he lived—the boy had told of this episode of the water as part of the lunacy and terror after the event. But to Jimmy it was the most moving part of the story, and it had stayed with him, in a setting that had grown as stylized as a tourist poster: the soft light and blurred shade below the coconut palms, the white sand, the sunlit breakers, the olive sea and blue sky beyond the crisscross of the curved gray coconut trunks, the bleeding girl on the front fender of the old Ford, the cupped hands offering water, the grateful eyes, remembering terror.

He could write no more. He wakened from his dream to the emptiness about him, to the interior he had so carefully prepared, for an audience that didn't exist. He was restless; he could have screamed like the girl on the Ford fender. At such a time he needed crowds, adventure, encounters, something in which he could forget himself. There was only the stillness of the bush and the abandoned industrial park.

He went and stood beside Bryant's chair, Bryant the loveless, the rejected, the lost. Almost like himself. Yet even in Bryant what beauty was concealed. He put his hand on Bryant's shoulder and his fingers touched Bryant's neck. Bryant said, "Jimmy," and let the paper fall. Such beauty, if only it could be known. His hands moved down inside Bryant's jersey, felt the nipples twitch and harden, felt the well-defined chest and then, moving lower, felt the firm molding of Bryant's stomach. Bryant began to swallow; his stomach muscles tensed and dipped. Lower, past the navel, to the hard curve, the springy hair, a man after all, the concealed complete beauty.

"Jimmy, Jimmy."

But then, almost roughly, he withdrew his hands, and went to the bedroom and the telephone.

Jane answered. "Hello."

He didn't say anything.

"Hello." She spoke the number.

"Jane? Jimmy Ahmed."

"Oh yes."

She was caught: he could tell.

He said, "What an English way you have of answering the phone. Only people in England answer the phone like that."

"You mean giving the number?"

"How are you?"

"Harassed. And hot."

Mock irritation: she was going coy, was beginning to act.

"Jane. I'm coming in to town tomorrow. I am under an obligation to meet some business executives at the Prince Albert. They are giving me lunch. Could you be there at two o'clock in the lobby? You know the Prince Albert?"

"What do you want to see me for?"

"We can talk about England. It will make a change after the business executives."

"Do you want me to come alone?"

"You can bring massa if you like. But I want to give you your dollar back."

He began to wait for her response; he wanted to laugh, to break the tension he sensed developing. He wanted to say: Bryant's a bad boy. But then, sternly, he put the telephone down.

The stern face remained when he went back to the living room. But his restlessness had been appeased. Bryant recognized the new mood; he picked the paper up and began to read again. And Jimmy felt his head grow clear; he had the clearest vision of the world.

HE TOOK a hired car to the Prince Albert and arrived some minutes after one. The uniformed doorman opened the car door. Jimmy hadn't lost his self-consciousness about the Prince Albert and preferred to arrive by car. In the old days, just before and just after the war, before the airplanes and the tourist rush, the Prince Albert had been the big hotel of the island; and to Jimmy, even after London, the very name still suggested luxury.

Once the area around the main park had been residential and fashionable. But the people who had lived there had emigrated or had moved up to the hills; and the big private houses around the park had been turned into government offices or restaurants or business offices, and later, with independence, into embassies and consulates. The Prince Albert was still, in spite of renovations and additions in concrete, and in spite of its internal iron pillars, like a grand old-fashioned estate house, an affair of timber and polished floors, with an open verandalike lobby. Once it had been barred to black people and received tourists from the cruise ships coming down from the north, sightseers only in those days, before the beaches were discovered. Now it had an air of having been passed by; the tourists went to beach hotels; the Prince Albert had become local. The uniforms of doorman and waiters were not as crisp and starched as they would once have been; the building itself had begun to go in parts, with yielding floorboards in the lobby. At lunchtime the renovated air-conditioned bar was busy with people who worked in the offices nearby, so that the atmosphere was casual where once it had been exclusive. But to Jimmy the name, Prince Albert, still had a wonderful sound, still suggested privilege and splendor.

He sat in a wicker chair in the open lobby, just outside the air-conditioned bar, and ordered an orange juice. By half past one the lunchtime drinkers had left the bar to return to their offices; the lobby was almost empty; the travel desk, with BOAC posters of London on the wall at the back, was empty; the elevator was not busy; and elevator man, doorman, and waiters were relaxed in the great heat.

The hotel faced the park. Drought had burned the grass, and scattered midday walkers, moving briskly, kicked up little puffs of dust. The view of the park, in ordinary times one of the attractions of the Prince Albert, was now the view of a dustbowl; dust had settled on the floor of the lobby. The rails of the park had been taken down during the war, part of the island's war effort; and little metal stumps showed. The rails had not been replaced, and there was no longer a true division between pavement and park. The pavement had buckled here and there from the spreading roots of great trees, and patches of the park had been worn smooth. Beyond the park was the first ridge of hills, scarred with housing settlements, with red gashes that marked the zigzag of roads, with red roofs, silver roofs, and yellow-white walls against a background of brown.

The orange juice was finished. She was late. He was half relieved. She came at about a quarter past two. She was in tight trousers, curving down the groin; she came into the lobby without fuss, the Prince Albert obviously less to her than to him.

He couldn't read her mood. Seen against the glare of the park, she was less tall than he remembered, and she had a clumsy, slightly dragging walk. Her arms were a little too short for her body, and she held them close to her sides. Her face was the puzzle: he hadn't been able to remember it, and now he thought he saw why. It seemed characterless, soft, without definition; it could become many faces. He noted the mouth, as though for the first time: it was too big, the top lip slightly puffy, as though from a blow, and the creased vertical lines suggested a healed wound. It was the kind of mouth he associated with certain children and with adults who remained childlike: weak, spoiled, with the cruelty of the weak and the spoiled.

He had been preparing a face and a mood for her. But now, as he studied her face, he found that an attitude had come to him. He stood up, walked toward her, and said, "My car is waiting."

"Where are we going."

"My house."

"It's been bad enough getting down here. I'm going to have something cold to drink."

He walked back with her to where he had been sitting, at the far end of the lobby. The position was open: the lobby in front, and on one side a wide passage like an internal veranda, beside a patio where, within a concrete border, a little forest garden had been created: lit up now by the sun which was directly overhead, a garden of thick green vines and creepers with large heart-shaped leaves that grew in the shade of the deep forest, the lower leaves browned in the drought, the black earth dry.

He sat in his chair against the wall and pressed for the waiter. She sat in the chair that was half in the veranda; her posture was easy. She put her bag down on the floor, and he noted that: the woman with time, awaiting developments.

He said, "In public places these days I always prefer to sit with my back against a wall. It's a simple precaution. Remain observable in public places. Never sit with your back to a door."

She lit a cigarette with a lighter, a blue cylinder; and he noticed, with slight disgust, how her bruised top lip came down over her teeth and then fitted tightly over them. Her eyes were beginning to grow moist; she was no longer as casual and cool as when she had arrived.

He hitched up his trousers, feeling the neatness of his own gestures and the neatness of his own clothes. He passed the thumb and middle finger of his right hand over his mustache.

He said, "That's a nice lighter."

"It's French. You throw them away when you're finished with them. Sahara gas, I suppose."

She passed it to him. But her eyes were beginning to cloud with irritation. When the waiter came she ordered a rum punch. And she smoked her cigarette, looking at the forest garden.

He stood the lighter upright on the table.

He said, "You would find this hard to believe, but when I was a boy my big ambition was to be a waiter in this hotel. They didn't allow black people."

"It's a pretty tatty place."

"We get things when we don't want them. The world is for the people who already have it. For the people who don't take chances."

The rum punch came.

"Like the duplicator you saw at Thrushcross Grange. We get things last hand and they expect us to be grateful."

She appeared to revive after sipping at the rum punch.

She said, "How did it go with the executives?"

He didn't understand. Then his mind raced, and he felt betrayed. As in a dream he saw confused swift events: a drive to his house, her reading of his writings, exposure. He didn't know what to do with his eyes. Then he remembered their conversation on the telephone.

He said, "The Lions?"

"Peter is a Lion. Was he there?"

"Massa wasn't there. These business people, they're all on your side now. But I'm not giving anybody any certificate of good conduct. I'm not giving massa a certificate. That's what Sablich's want and that's what they're not going to get."

"Nobody likes Sablich's here."

"I hate them. Do you know how the Sablich fortune was made? Sablich was an immigrant from Prussia or somewhere in Germany. He came over in 1803. He went to Trinidad. They were giving away land there. The more blacks you brought in the more land you got. Free. In 1807 the slave trade was abolished. It was like immigration controls in England: everybody rushed to beat the ban. Sablich ordered a boatload of Negroes from a Liverpool firm. Nobody knows how many. Two or three hundred, at a hundred pounds a head. They got here just in time. And then Sablich refused to pay. When the fuss died down Sablich was a very rich man. And then he left Trinidad and came over here. That was the start of that very, very respectable firm."

Jane's irritation had returned. Her eyes were moist; to Jimmy it seemed that she was either about to cry or to lose her temper.

She said, "I don't know why everybody feels obliged to tell me that story. I can't tell you how often I've heard about the origin of the Sablich fortune."

"Massa's firm."

"But not mine."

Jimmy said, "Look. I don't want us to be friends."

And she was instantly alert, on the defensive.

He noted that. He said, "In England I had too many women friends."

She understood his meaning. He studied her eyes alone.

He didn't give her time to say anything. He jerked his chin toward the park. "When we were at school we used to come to play there some afternoons. Cricket and football. The white people would watch us. And we would act up for them. When I was in England I met a girl who had been here as a girl. She passed through with her parents and they stayed at the Prince Albert. All she remembered of the place were the little black boys playing football in the park outside the hotel. We worked out the dates. And I realized she must have seen me. That I must have been one of the black boys. What do you make of that?"

"Was she one of the women with whom you were not friends?"

The woman courted, ready to be courted.

He said, and he spoke solemnly, "I was nervous about seeing you this afternoon. I don't notice hair. I don't notice clothes. What I felt about you I felt as soon as I saw your eyes. They looked as they look now. Half screaming."

She was unwilling to let the topic pass. She said, "Why were you nervous?"

"I thought my imagination might have been playing tricks."

"Was it?"

He didn't reply. He pressed for the waiter. "Bryant is waiting for us. He wants to give you back your dollar. The car will bring you back."

She would object. But he knew now that she was going to come.

THE DOORMAN stopped leaning against the iron pillar of the portico and blew on his whistle. Across the road, the driver, sitting on a park bench with other drivers in the half-shade of a big tree, stood up, short and very fat, and shook out the seat of his trousers. The big American car turned wide in the road and entered the semicircular hotel drive.

Through the haze of heat and rum punch Jane noted the size of the car. It was absurd, pathetic; she could have giggled. The doorman opened the door; Jimmy tipped him. It was pathetic and absurd. The car seat was hot; the sun burned her arms. They turned toward the city center, away from the dustiness and glare of the park and the view of the red-scarred hills, into a deader heat; the wind that came through the windows was warm. Black asphalt streets, still residential-looking; white or yellow-white buildings; shadows contracted and black. Beyond the blue-tinted windscreen, a pale sky.

The car was so wide they sat at far ends of the seat. Jimmy sat erect and formal, his left foot on his right knee, his narrow trousers riding up above his thin nylon sock, his right hand resting on his exposed lower calf. Jane sat directly behind the driver. The driver's bright blue shirt, of a shiny synthetic material, showed the black skin below and a white reticulated vest; on his neck, half hidden by his shirt collar, was a thick roll of black flesh with scattered springs of hair; a blue light, from the tinted windscreen, fell on his bare fat arms.

Jimmy said, "The Tennis Club."

She didn't turn to look. She was aware only of buildings close to the road: no openness there, no sign of courts. But the area was like that: new buildings standing in the grounds of old, open spaces everywhere filled in.

Jimmy said, "That girl I was telling you about, her father was in Intelligence. When he came here he went to the Tennis Club one day. I think it was the championships or something. Of course, no blacks allowed. He got mad when he saw the local whites behaving as though there wasn't a war on. He felt that the Vichy people in Martinique could seize the island at any time. He asked one of the players—the boy was sitting next to him, very cool and don't-care-a-damn—whether he didn't think he should be fighting for the mother country. The boy said, 'I prefer playing tennis.' "

Jane was only half listening, sitting at the far end of the seat, withdrawn, in a haze of rum punch and heat which was like a sense of the adventure she had committed herself to. Half amused at the reference to that girl, unnamed, whose father had been in Intelligence, knowing it to be something laid out to catch her attention, she yet allowed herself to wonder about the girl; she yet allowed herself to play with the images he had set floating in her mind.

She had driven through the city many times and had long ago ceased to see it. Now, in the excitement that amounted to stupor, the feeling of a dissolving world, she found herself catching at details: the top galleries of old-fashioned Spanish-style buildings overhanging pavements where ragged beggars sat vacant, beside old women selling muddy-looking cakes and colored sweets and sweepstakes pinned to boards. In this sense of being transported out of herself, transported out of a stable world into something momentarily unstable, lay the adventure. She had been half prepared for it. What she hadn't been prepared for, what gave her little twinges of alarm, was this feeling of a sudden descent into the city itself, until then unknown, unexplored. And yet, with another part of herself, she continued to be amused by the absurd motorcar and her position in it, by the glances that the car and she in it and Jimmy with her were getting. Such a misunderstanding; so absurd.

Jimmy was saying, "Now, they've all gone. Canada, England, America. Australia. They've all gone."

The tennis players. So strange, this elegy for them, in the heat. He spoke, she noted, as from a great distance. As though he had been left behind.

They came to the main square, once an area of trees and asphalted walks, now full of parked motorcars and rough wooden booths. The reggae shrieked from a dozen amplifiers, now above the roar of motorcars and trucks, now below it. Diseased pariah dogs wandered about; some lay prostrate on the crowded pavements; and she studied one, dead-eyed, with a growth like raw flesh protruding out of its mangy yellow fur. The sea, when they came to it, gave no feeling of air and lightness: the fine red powder of bauxite, sheds of corroded corrugated iron, the reek of the burning rubbish dump, everything here—hillside, forest, sea, mangrove—turned to slum.

Excitement grew on her, studying these things as though she had never seen them before, taking them in detail by detail. And now, as they began to race along the highway, past the shacks on the hillside and the long red avenues of the redevelopment project, every little house casting an identical angled shadow, as they raced, the hot air and the noise of the car, the sense of speed, were like the things she was surrendering to: the little delirium, of which she thought she remained in perfect control, knowing that it would soon be over, that the world would become solid again, and her own vision clear.

Jimmy spoke occasionally, making little comments on what they passed. His words were indistinct and she didn't concentrate on what he said. The little delirium became the adventure; this was what she wanted to stay close to and be contained within, this dizzying mood, of which, curiously, his presence formed no part: the exaltation produced by the heat, the drive that was coming to climax, and that vision of decay piled on decay, putrefaction on putrefaction.

She fixed her gaze on the driver's neck, on the black roll of almost hairless flesh within the collar of the transparent shiny blue shirt, and on the subsidiary roll above, lost in little kinky springs of hair, as black as the skin.

"Where did those come from?"

Jimmy was speaking to her directly. They were now well out of the city, in the factory area, driving beside the charred verges and the sunken fields in which lay the wrecks of motor vehicles.

She fingered the silver necklaces he was pointing to. "Morocco." She was going to say: Someone gave them to me. But she didn't say that. She said, "They cost about sixpence. They were given me by a lover."

He was still sitting erect at the end of the seat, formal and buttoned up, embarrassed by the drive and her silence, and giving little licks at his lips. As buttoned up as he had been when he had first presented himself to her at Thrushcross Grange, but now distinctly absurd.

She added, "He didn't believe in gifts of great value. He didn't want money to come between us."

He caught her tone. He said, "Something for the girl who has everything."

Yet when they turned off the highway into the abandoned industrial park, and there was only bush and foundations of buildings among bush, her excitement began to quicken into something like uncertainty. And when the car stopped in Jimmy's yard, and there was only silence in the heat, with the bush bounding every view, and she noticed the short squat driver with his powerful fleshy arms, she began to feel dismay.

Excitement was dying; she could exercise clear judgment again. The house was as she had remembered it: the horrible blue carpet with the meaningless black and yellow splashes, the books on the shelves, the photographs, including that one with the girl or woman—with the father in Intelligence?—torn out. It had happened so often to her, who had known so many men, who had found so many men to be candidates: this altering of the character of a room or a house which, at first seen and judged in a detached way, then all at once became another kind of room, full of a man's intimate attributes. And this room now repelled her; and from her new lucidity she tried, swiftly, seeking to reestablish her balance, to re-create the chain of happenings that had brought her here, that had so altered the nature of the day for her.

Jimmy said, "Your eyes look half screaming."

She turned to him almost with irritation, her eyes moist, as if with tears.

He put his hands on her shoulders, and he was astonished at her response. She fixed her mouth on his, her lips opened wide. He was taken by surprise and couldn't react immediately; and as her tobacco-tasting tongue and her lips—that healed wound—did what they thought they had to do (no secrets here, and words no longer helped, no bravado about lovers who brought gifts from Morocco), as the action of her mouth became insipid to him and then meaningless, he thought, first of all, and without surprise: But she is starved. And then: But she is like a girl, she knows nothing, she is looking for everything in the kiss, she believes she has to be violent to show that she knows.

Her blouse was wet below the arms; he had not noticed that before. Her breasts were pressed against him, so that he was hardly aware of them as breasts, only as flesh. She had given him so little time. He would have liked, as it were, to witness the moment, but now he felt he was losing it. He edged his mouth away from hers at last and, holding her tight against him, drew breath. He felt that the moment had gone and was irrecoverable.

He said, with odd formality, still holding her, "Shall we go into the next room?"

She said quickly, in a whisper that held nothing of intimacy, "Don't ask stupid questions." And immediately she disengaged herself from him.

Coolly, with that slightly dragging step he had noticed as she had walked across the lobby of the Prince Albert, and still with her shoulder bag, she went into the bedroom, ahead of Jimmy, as though she knew the way. A maroon carpet with a large bright flowered pattern, a yellow candlewick bedspread on a double bed, bedside tables with imitation-wood graining, a lamp, a dressing table, a telephone on a chest of drawers: it was like a bedroom display in the window of an English furniture shop, and it looked as artificial. The carpet lay loose on the terrazzo floor, the ocher-washed concrete walls were bare, and the light in the room was hard and even. The open windows gave a sense of stillness and heat: a hot pale-blue sky, limp bush, not even the tops of the spiky palms moving.

Very quickly, ignoring the hand he placed on her wet arm-pits, she put her bag on the dressing table, eased off her shoes, and undid and rolled down her trousers and pants together and, still with her blouse on, lay on the middle of the bed and turned her face to the wall, as though he were not in the room. Her speed alarmed him; he feared he was losing the moment again. He felt isolated by her indifference and began to fear that he might be losing her as well. He saw the white of her belly and the tan on her legs. She had very little hair on her groin; perhaps she shaved; and the cleft was like a dumb, stupid mouth.

Without undressing he lay down beside her and again he was swallowed up by her hard big kiss, her mouth opened wide. He put his hand on her groin, felt the thin hair and moved his fingers lower. She took her mouth from his, slapped his hand away, and said, with the irritation that now accompanied all her words, "Don't tease me." He sat up and undid his shoes. And already she was withdrawn; and again he felt alarm. He took off his trousers and pants. Then the telephone began to ring. He sat still. He heard it ring and ring.

Jane said, "Answer it, for God's sake."

He got up and she saw him black and barely tumescent, little springs of hair scattered down his legs; his hair was more Negroid down there. And now, only in his Mao shirt, and looking absurdly like one of the children of the shanty towns, who wore vests alone, their exposed little penises like little spigots, he walked to the chest of drawers and took up the telephone.

From somewhere in the house, in the sudden stillness after the ringing stopped, could be heard footsteps, the sound of rubber soles on concrete.

Jimmy shouted through the door, "It's all right. All right."

As soon as Jane heard the voice at the other end of the tele-phone she recognized it.

Jimmy said, "Yes, massa."

Jane turned over on her belly and shouted, whether with

laughter or rage it was hard to tell, "Put that in your next classified communiqué."

She sprawled face down on the bed, her blouse tight over her shoulders, her legs apart and graceless, her hips very wide, her pale buttocks flat and spreading, smoother than her tanned legs.

"I haven't seen him, massa," Jimmy said into the telephone. Jane tucked her arms below her chest.

"I know, massa. I know. Massa, I'll telephone you back."

He put the telephone down and came back across the scatter of clothes to the bed. Jane, still face down and with her arms below her, was as if asleep. He put his hand on her hip. She didn't respond. He lay down beside her and she didn't move. He lay on top of her, and again had only the feeling of flesh below him, again missed the sense of knowing the shape of her body. She remained still. Sudden anger swept over him. He seized her shoulders, lifted himself off her, and sought to enter her where she was smaller. She shouted: "No!" and turned over so violently that she threw him off, her elbow hitting him on the chin. He raised his hand to strike her; but then, with closed eyes, she said strange words. She said: "Love, love." He lay upon her clumsily; he was swallowed by her wide kiss; he entered her and said, "I'm not good, I'm not good, you know."

"All men say that."

And then, just like that, without convulsions, his little strained strength leaked out of him, and it was all over. And he raged inside.

He rested his head on her shoulder, on her blouse, smelling, too late now, her sweat.

She said, "Love, love."

He shrank, and unwillingly he slipped out of her. He shifted off her and lay face down on her arm.

She said, "Do you always make love in your Mao shirt?"

There wasn't even mockery in her voice. She was already quite remote. And when he opened his eyes to look at her, he saw that her right leg was drawn up, that the part of herself she had forbidden him to touch with his hand was displayed, as though she were alone. That drawn-up leg, so slender above the knee, and held slightly to one side: there was something masculine about the posture, something masculine about the hand that stroked that leg now. And she was looking at leg and hand. But how carefully she had tanned herself! With what care she had rendered that leg hairless! The skin looked abraded; but already there were the beginnings of new hairs.

She said, "What did Peter want?"

"Something about Stephens. That boy who used to be at the Grange."

She said, twitching her arm below his head, "I'm getting up."

He was close to the edge of the bed. He got up and stood beside the bed in his Mao shirt.

She got off the bed on her side, moving with quickness now, swinging both legs to the floor at the same time. And then, with one large gesture, she pulled the yellow candlewick bedspread off the bed, knocking the bedside lamp over; and, before he had time to consider her nakedness, she with her instinct to conceal herself after an act of casual sex, to reduce the man to a stranger again, she wrapped the spread about herself; and then, nimbly, in spite of the big bedspread, she moved about the room picking up everything that was hers, everything she had seemingly so casually discarded, almost as items that might be abandoned, her shoes, her bag, her trousers and her pants within the trousers; and, with everything that was hers, having cleared the room of her presence, she went into the adjoining bathroom, as though she had been there many times before, and slammed the door shut.

Half naked, Jimmy considered the room. He had lost the moment; he began to know again that emptiness he had lived with for so long; he began to feel that great pain in two places above his groin. He heard her using the lavatory, heard her flush the toilet. Later she tried to flush it again, but there was no water. He began to dress; and it was only then that he noticed, where Jane had lain on the bed below him, a great damp patch on the white sheet, a great circular patch that had soaked through the candlewick spread. So that her body seemed independent of her manner, her words, her attitudes; and yet he had lost the moment.

And when, presently, she opened the bathroom door, she was dressed, her hair rearranged; and she was cool, almost a stranger

again, someone who would have to be wooed all over again, someone who had surrendered nothing. Through the open bathroom
door Jimmy saw the yellow candlewick spread hanging over the
low tiled wall of the shower area, untidily tossed, wet. The starved
woman had had many lovers, nevertheless; she was as inexperienced
as a girl, yet she was spoiled; and, without knowing it, she had
developed the bad temper, and the manners, of a prostitute, one
of those prostitutes who after defeat and degradation celebrate a
triumph, revenging themselves on the maid of a brothel hotel,
creating work for that creature, the low punishing the lower. So
cool she looked now; so triumphant. He was full of hate for her.

He said, "The car's still here."

She said nothing.

But he walked out with her. In the car port at the side of the
house she saw the driver in the blue shirt and the boy with pigtails. She opened the door for herself, got into the car, and waited
for the driver.

She said, "I hope you get what you wanted from the executives."
Almost without looking at him.

The pain in the two places above his groin grew and grew after
she left. He longed for the feel of Bryant, for Bryant's warm firm
flesh and his relieving mouth and tongue.

6

THE LITTLE delirium had gone; it had begun to die even before she had reached Jimmy's house. Now, in the car, sitting again behind the driver, and studying the little roll of hairy flesh above the bigger roll of almost hairless flesh, hardly aware of the desolation through which she drove, aware only of the heat, she knew something like distress. Distress as a settled mood, bearable, not a pain. She had memories of sensations; but images of the house and the bedroom broke into those. Words began to go through her head, words addressed to no one in particular, yet words that she fancied herself speaking with tears, like a child: "I've looked everywhere. I've looked and looked."

The internal storm passed. The words spoke themselves more calmly, became a statement. She looked at the driver's mirror: his little red eyes were considering her, and they held her return stare. She looked out at the fields; the junked automobiles beside the road; the men far away, small and busy, stuffing grass into the trunks of cars to take home to their animals; the smoking hills, yellow in the mid-afternoon light. But she was aware of the driver's intermittent stare; and whenever she looked at the mirror she saw his red, assessing eyes. A whole sentence ran through her head, at first meaningless, and then, as she examined it, alarming. She thought: I've been playing with fire. Strange words, to have come so suddenly and so completely to her: something given, unasked for, like an intimation of the truth, breaking into the sense of safety, of distance put between her and the desolation of that house.

They began to enter the town: safety. The rubbish dump was burning: unusually thick brown smoke, oily and acrid, which made her turn up her window: mounds of rubbish like confetti, trucks and men and women and children blurred in the smoke, lightening occasionally into yellow flame, the carrion corbeaux, nervous of men, restless and squawking near the wire fence. Fire: the smoking hills, the charred verges: it explained the words. But the explanation didn't satisfy her, didn't free her. All the way through the noisy afternoon city and then up to the Ridge, the air getting cooler, the plain dropping away behind her, lower and lower, she thought: I've been playing with fire.

At the end, the driver did not get out and open the door for her. When she got out she said, "Thank you." He acknowledged that only by jerking his chin up and making a slight nasal sound. Immediately, lifting his squat, heavy body off the seat and twisting round to look back, one fat black arm embracing the shiny plastic cover of the front seat, he reversed at a great rate down the drive and through the gateway into the road, and was gone.

She was wet between the legs. The smell of the man was strong on her, tainting the perfume with which she had tried to cover it in the bathroom at that house. She fancied the smell was particularly strong on her fingers. She needed a bath. Through the redwood louvers the sun struck into the white-tiled bathroom, hot and dry. She closed the louvers and took her clothes off. But the taps didn't run. Water was short and was turned off in the afternoons.

She was tired but she didn't lie down on her bed; and when she had put on the trousers and blouse again she didn't stay in her room. She walked about the bigger rooms of the empty house, and then she sat on one of the metal chairs on the back porch, waiting first for Adela, who started her evening duties at five, and then for Roche.

When he came she said to him, "There's a man in that little house in the garden."

Her anxiety seemed to make him calmer. He said humorously,

"Perhaps it's one of Adela's friends or relations. We must be careful."

He walked down the sunlit concrete steps at the back, between the stunted cypresses. She watched him from the porch. He opened the door and then he looked up at her, the afternoon sun on his face, smiling, making gestures of puzzlement. She went down. The door swung open easily, the little house was empty. The wild man with the rags and the matted locks had taken up his tin and bundles and left. There remained only a vague warm smell of old clothes, dead animals, grease, and marijuana.

He said, "When did you see him?"

"Yesterday morning. But I was too frightened to tell you."

"It looks as though he was much more frightened of you."

At about six Adela called from the kitchen, "Water! Water!" and almost at the same time pipes and cisterns hissed all over the house. The light on the hills was golden and thin; the smoldering sky was growing dark; the evening haze covered the plain and the sea. She had a bath.

She said to Roche that evening, "Can I sleep with you tonight?"

He said, "Wouldn't it be better if I get used to sleeping alone?"

"This isn't for your sake. It's for mine."

He said no more. She took her pillows to his bed.

7

THE SITUATION is desperate, Roy, the people here have been betrayed too often, it's always a case of black faces white masks, you don't know who your enemy is, the enemy infiltrates your ranks all the time. Massa Mister Roche he's very importunate in his inquiries about one of the boys they sent here, Stephens, a little gang leader from the city, a big coup for them, they thought he was going to take over from me, as though I was going to let that boy draw me out on the streets for the police to shoot me down. No, Roy, I'm staying here in my unfortified castle, the time will come for me to move, the people will come of their own accord to their leader. But the situation is getting desperate now, in the still of the night I lose my courage, I feel it's a losing battle, they're sending other agents, I don't know how to cope . . .

He broke off. The words had circled in on the wound that was still fresh. He considered his violated room: the books, the photographs, the carpet, the upholstered chairs, everything so nicely put away. And there was the bedroom, with the stained bed, where he was still unwilling to go. The desolation! And where was Bryant? Bryant, with whom he could share the pain of the moment, in whose rejection he might annihilate his own. The night and the bush outside. The silence.

Here's a laugh, let me tell you about it. The other day one of our church big shots, a bishop or something, he held a service not in Latin or English but in some fancy language for the niggers, he said it was an African language, Yoruba or something, of course nobody here understands "head nor tail," and wait for it, the message was that despair was the great sin. What a laugh, it's like those Harlem movies about interracial sex they're feeding the people on now to keep them quiet. These people live in a world of dreams, I don't know how they believe people can stomach that kind of talk still.

In my father's house there are many mansions, I remember this from my schooldays, they'd "bust your tail" with licks if you didn't go to church. But the house is full up now, Roy, there are no more mansions. I suppose like everybody else I fooled myself that there was a mansion waiting somewhere for me, but I didn't really fool myself, you mustn't believe that, even when I was a child going to school from the back room of my father's grocery shop, knowing that back room as the only place I come from in this great wide world, it wasn't mine, I always knew I was fooling myself, I didn't believe there was or would ever be any mansion for me.

Other people had the mansions and they were full up, like the people in our so-called "exclusive" hotel the Prince Albert, they used to take us there some afternoons from school, to the park outside, to play, for the people to see us, to show us where we couldn't go. And even in England when there was some talk of me in the world, everybody was jumping on the bandwagon then, I knew there was no mansion, it was all going to end in smoke.

Things are desperate, Roy, when the leader himself begins to yield to despair, things are bad. The whole place is going to blow up, I cannot see how I can control the revolution now. When everybody wants to fight there's nothing to fight for. Everybody wants to fight his own little war, everybody is a guerrilla.

He turned, hearing light footsteps in the front porch, and saw Bryant standing in the doorway, in a dark blue short-sleeved jersey and jeans, his pigtails erect, fearsome, his twisted face sweated and shiny, his eyes inflamed. He stood beyond the blue carpet, in the shadows, waiting to be noticed.

"Bryant-boy."

"Field duties," Bryant said, and came into the room, something in his walk and the way he held his head indicating irritation, an unwillingness to talk.

He sat down in one of the chairs and took up the paper, rustling it loudly. The light from the desk lamp fell yellow on the twisted side of his face and showed up the boniness of his forehead. White spittle had gathered in the corners of his mouth, and his red eyes seemed about to water.

Jimmy knew Bryant's moods, and let him be. And, with Bryant sitting there, Jimmy became calmer. He looked at what he had been writing; it seemed far away. His despair had purged itself. He had momentarily lost control, but now he was better; now again he could see clearly.

"Yes, Clarissa," this cool and amazing man said, "I owe you a dollar and I remember you." And when he said this I got nervous, looking at his eyes I saw the game was up, I felt he could see right through me. I can't hide anything from this man, I don't know how I'll explain myself to him.

I said, "Jimmy, I seek you out to warn you. They're full of hate, Jimmy, they seek to destroy you because they're frightened of the hate the oppressed of the world feel for them and they're frightened that the oppressed might find a leader. They make it their business to seek out and destroy the leaders, Jimmy."

He said, "Clarissa, go back and tell your employers I'm not running anymore." I said, "My employers, Jimmy?" He said, "No one is getting me to come out of my unfortified castle and be shot down, Clarissa. You see, Clarissa, I've been caught by people like you once before and I'll not be caught again, you talk of revolution but you belong to the establishment, Clarissa, you think you will come and flash your milk-white thighs before the poor blacks and they will believe your story. You think you will play with the little black boys and then you will go home, but I've news for you, Clarissa, the little black boys are not playing anymore. I know your game, Clarissa, now tell me, wasn't your father in Intelligence?"

I said, "Jimmy, I've told you, I beg you to understand, that I've to do my duties but I'm amazed by the man you are." He said, "The black boys aren't playing anymore, every man in this hotel lobby understands your game, Clarissa, look around, look at the waiters, do you think they don't know that you're rotten meat, do you think the taxi drivers don't know, everybody has seen you accosting me in public and they will know that you're rotten meat, and so I must warn you that in future you must walk only in daylight and in open places, Clarissa."

As he said this the fear gripped my heart and I looked at his unblinking eyes but could find no pity there, I don't know how I can tell him that he possesses my mind, it's true I'm of the establishment and of a certain class and only bad-talk England to put people off the scent, I understand his hate which I can see in his eyes, I understood everything when I saw that hate there.

"Here is your dollar," he said, throwing a note down on the table, "I've already settled the bill with the waiters." And so saying he turned on his heels and stalked out of the lobby and leaves everybody standing in amazement not least of all myself.

I don't know where to look, I feel I'm exposed, it's true what he said, the waiters look at me in a funny way and the taxi drivers look at me in a funny way, and so it continues day and night it's as though Jimmy has blighted this place for me, I see his powerful mocking face in every face I see, and I begin to see that this obsession will drive me mad. And I'm scared like anything, I don't know what to do, I can't tell my husband now, I've to live with this, I feel I somehow have to throw myself on Jimmy's mercy and beg him to give me another chance, because I know that he's the man who controls this hate I see around me and he's the only man who can turn this hate into love.

In public places I walk with circumspection and so too in quiet places, because I don't know what will spring out at me, who are these men I ask myself whenever I see people approaching, what do they want of me. Of course I'm full of hate for these shiftless people, no wonder they can't get on, and now I'm frightened of this hate and scorn I bear for them because I feel it is bringing retribution and retribution is what I'm afraid of everywhere, in the street, on the Ridge, on the beaches with the tourists, because every taxi driver and every waiter knows what I am, and one day at midday I'm on the beach and walking in the grove when I see these boys with pigtails like the boy at Thrushcross Grange, and they begin to close in on me and when I walk faster they walk faster and they begin to mock and chase me and I know that my hour has come and that no one can save me only Jimmy and I begin to run through the grove to the open sea because at least there would be people there tourists and lifeguards and all the other things that you see but it seems I will never get to that place and I'm thirsty, dying for water on this blue and cloudless day and then I see a car in the distance and I begin to run to it and as I run the boys run and I see it is an old Ford with those curving front fenders—

"The rat!" Bryant screamed, throwing down the paper on the carpet. "Jimmy, I see the white rat today!"

Jimmy started. Light changed around him; he turned from the desk and saw Bryant, not far away, on a beach, in the middle of the day, but sitting on a furry chair, his face half-lit, close to tears. Jimmy pushed back his chair and stood up.

"Don't touch me, Jimmy!" Bryant screamed. "I will kill you if you touch me, Jimmy."

He was going to speak comfortingly to Bryant, in the language and accent of the streets. But he spoke formally. He said, "She came to see you, Bryant. She wanted to get her dollar back."

"Jimmy, Jimmy." And Bryant, throwing back his head, began to cry.

He went and put his hands on Bryant's shoulders. His fingers pressed against the gritty jersey and the damp skin below. He took his face close to Bryant's and said, "I'll give her to you."

8

IN THE mornings Roche thought: I've built my whole life on sand. He had thought of himself as a doer; it surprised him now to be so far from that self, to be a man who waited on events; and the very placidity with which he waited on events gave him, as he awakened in the mornings, a sense of alarm, which, before dying away in daylight and the day's routine, became muted in those words: I've built my whole life on sand.

He was waiting for Jane to leave him; he was waiting for his public relations job with Sablich's to be shown up as the non-sense job it was, and with that exposure for all his action to be revealed as futility. In his mind the two failures were linked and ran together. He thought: I have trapped myself. One failure by itself he could have managed; but the two, running together here, in this lost corner of the world, would overwhelm him. And he could neither act nor withdraw; he could only wait.

Yet he knew that to many people around him he appeared as a man given over to a cause. It was understandable, but it was strange; because he had no political dogma and no longer had a vision of a world made good, and perhaps had never had such a vision. If he had had a system, a set of political beliefs, it might have been easier for him to have set it aside, to have admitted error, as some of his associates had done, to have blamed the system or to have blamed the world for not living up to the system, and without any sense of reneging to have made a fresh start. But he had had no system; he distrusted systems; he had a feeling of responsibility for what he had done. Responsibility didn't end with failure, or with the abandoning of beliefs that had prompted certain actions.

There were perhaps half a dozen occasions on which he might have withdrawn and returned to the life that had been marked out for him. He needn't have been tortured in South Africa; he needn't have written his book; he needn't have taken the job with Sablich's; having taken the job, he needn't have become associated with Thrushcross Grange and Jimmy Ahmed. Responsibility; inertia, perhaps; perhaps, too, some little optimistic spasm, some feeling that out of this particular decision some good would come, some good that would finally release him and enable him to return to his old life. Yet each decision had taken him further away from what he saw as his real life, and had left him, here, at forty-five, quite adrift. And he was a clear-sighted man, even cynical. His responses to people and situations were immediate; but to act he had often to ignore what he had perceived. He said, "You have to work with what is there." Every decision he had made had been made after he had disregarded some element of the truth.

Everything that was to be known about Jane was clear at their first meeting. He had picked up all the clues; but their relationship was based on his ignoring these clues.

She was at the time doing the publicity for the firm that was publishing his book. He was still new to England, still amazed, after Africa, at the quickness of shop assistants, taxi drivers, telephone operators, secretaries. Jane, on the telephone, inviting him to lunch to discuss what might be done for his book, had been charming and persuasive; and he, abashed by what he thought to be the ritual of publication, had agreed. He had expected someone professional; but when he arrived at the publisher's office the woman at the desk could get no reply from Jane's extension; and he had sat for fifteen minutes or so in the waiting room, looking through the publisher's catalogue, and considering a bronze-colored statuette of a slender, lightly draped woman raising an empty basket or bowl above her head, before Jane had appeared, coming in, to his surprise, from the street. She had been out shopping; she had forgotten the lunch.

It turned out that she was new to the job, which she said was "awful"; and, in half apology, she invited him to share her amusement at the awfulness of the job and her inexpertness at it. She didn't quite know what she had to do, she said; but then she suggested that it didn't matter, because it was such a "ghastly" firm anyway.

Roche was modest about his book; but he couldn't dismiss these words about the firm simply as the turns of speech of an idle woman doing a job unseriously. The words were spoken with too much conviction, the irritation seemed too deep. So he had pressed her; he had asked her why the firm was ghastly. She couldn't say; she had nothing to say. And she put an end to the subject of the firm, and to that particular mood of petulance, by smiling, going big-eyed, flushed and coy. He had been taken: that smile of complicity, after the display of the passionate nature.

He was not less taken when, switching from charm and girlish incompetence, she had attempted, big eyes going moist, to talk about his book. It was immediately clear that she did not know his book; it was also clear that she had her own idea of the kind of book he had written. And she was anxious to put herself on the side of this imaginary author. She said: "The colonial police are terrible." He was struck by this sentence. It was at once glib and spoken with conviction, as though it issued out of a great store of knowledge on the subject. The anachronism—"the colonial police"—was not deliberate. To Roche the words suggested less a reading of history than a secondhand intimacy with old events: old conversations overheard, someone else's experience—these things just remembered, a reaction suddenly summoned up.

The innocence was startling—the newspapers had campaigned in vain, he had written his book in vain—but the passion stood out the more against this innocence, against this impression she created, already, of busyness and private harassment (that shopping before lunch, forgetting the lunch she had been so eager to arrange, her swift changes of mood, the busyness that apparently left her no time for the newspapers), the harassment that was no doubt responsible for those impatient gestures: flinging down her gloves on the restaurant table with a flick of the wrist, as though she were swatting a fly, or like an exhibitionist cardplayer playing a trump card.

He didn't set her right about the colonial police or about the book he had written. What he had written about was too close to him; and she knew so little. Besides, his political attitudes were complicated; the writing of the book had shown him that they were more complicated than he had realized. The book slightly embarrassed him; he knew it to be diffuse and ambiguous, even after the publisher's editing; he hadn't been able, in spite of re-writings, to overcome his instinct to muffle the personal drama of arrest, torture, imprisonment, and release.

Unwilling to explain himself, he allowed her to attribute to him comprehensive revolutionary views about Africa and race, a vision of one particular order about to be swept away. He didn't object; but when he didn't give the confirmation she was expecting she abandoned that large view and spoke instead, as to one who would be sympathetic, of the West Indian bus conductors in London, who were efficient and good-humored and yet were subjected to much racial abuse.

Jane said she had recently walked out of the house of a friend who had begun to say harsh things about "immigrants." Roche could see her walking out of the house. He could see her making some abrupt gesture, sitting forward perhaps, and then, with this physical movement, finding herself committed to the whole action: picking up lighter, bag, gloves, getting into coat—swift, large gestures, which he played with in his mind's eye and found attractive. But he doubted whether she had left the friend's house solely on account of the bus conductors; he doubted whether she had left the house at all. And though Jane said, "Nothing would ever induce me to talk to her again," he doubted whether there had been any serious breach.

Everything about Jane was simple, exaggerated and, oddly for a woman of twenty-nine, schoolgirlish. Of the simplicity of her views and her girlishness she seemed unaware; this absence of doubt, which was like an absence of self-knowledge, made her forceful and gave a certain solidity to her presence. She was not someone he wished to argue with or put right; he noted only, at this lunch, that she was flinging out what she clearly thought of as violent views for his approval and admiration. And this was unexpected and touching.

So the lunch, which she had arranged to talk about his book, turned into a display of her attitudes. She became the doer, the seeker; he became her audience. From time to time she threw some tribute at him for his book, the life he had led, the dangers she imagined he had been through; but she always returned to England, herself, and the attitudes of her class, about which she seemed anxious to instruct Roche. The words "colonial police" had suggested someone for whom the organization of the world was still simple, who still lived in a vanished age or within the assumptions of a vanished age; her critical obsession with England and her class showed her still to think that England was of paramount importance in the world.

They walked back to the office after their lunch; and there in her little room he saw her in her role as executive. Whereas, at the beginning, she had invited him to share her amusement at her incompetence, now she invited him to share the irritations of her job. She was sharp on the telephone with some man; when she put the telephone down she said to Roche, her face flushed, her eyes bright with temper, "What on earth do you expect from a man who has to bow and scrape all day long to make a living?" So carried away was he by her that he accepted her behavior on the telephone and her explanation afterward as logical; only later did he see the contradiction.

At the beginning she had made some effort to put herself on his side or what she thought to be his side. Now, already, he was half on hers. He saw her as someone at odds with more than her job, her class, or England. She was at odds with something much larger; and toward that mystery, that private harassment which he had sensed in her in the restaurant, he began to be drawn.

She had married young, at seventeen or eighteen; she spoke of it as of an abduction. For a reason Roche couldn't follow she blamed her mother and an uncle for this early marriage (her father had died when she was very young); and she blamed her school for sending her out uneducated and ready to throw herself at the first man she met.

She had married a man twice her age, a politician, thought then to be rising. He had since fallen, become a businessman; and though Jane now spoke with contempt of his politics and with sarcasm of his "beauty," it was clear that she had been attracted by both his beauty and his eminence; and though she spoke of this marriage always as something forced upon her, it was clear from other things she said that she had been the pursuer, thinking to have found in the politician a unique combination of beauty, eminence, and wealth that no one before her had recognized. It appeared that the politician, not knowing that he was being chased by this schoolgirl, had had to be told by a friend, "Don't you see that girl's in love with you?" Jane spoke of this with sad pleasure, as of her only moment of romance, before the long disaster.

The beautiful politician had, during his extended bachelorhood, become fixed in the habits of his schooldays. He had masturbated even on their honeymoon, the young girl awake beside him; for stretches of the day, during this honeymoon, Jane had been left alone. "Of course," she told Roche, giving him the first twinge of sexual alarm, "I wanted to be in bed all the time." She spoke the limericks he had taught her, the passion-killing erotic rhymes. He was excited only by prostitutes, swiftly bought and had; with Jane he was finished in a second, preferring more usually to be "tossed off," and Jane still spoke the words like a schoolgirl who had just acquired them, part of the mystery of men.

The man Jane described in this way had a modest public reputation and sometimes his picture appeared in the financial pages. He was about Roche's own age, as Roche worked it out. Once admired, he was now altogether betrayed; and this gave Roche a further alarm. Perhaps she exaggerated; no doubt there had been other aspects of their life together. But her pitilessness about the man was also a pitilessness about her own life, shaped by that early shock and violation.

After two years there had been a divorce. But that had not brought real release. She hinted at a procession of lovers, a continuing violation; she spoke, with brutal detail, of the affront of her abortions. She spoke as though she had never exercised choice. Events, society, the nature of men, her own needs as a woman, had sent her out into the sexual jungle, to play perilously with the unknown.

Roche thought he understood. And so, within a fortnight, they had fallen into a relationship: Jane the violated, he, with a life in ruins, the comforter. He had penetrated swiftly to that core of passion he had divined in her. He was the one who understood: Jane behaved as if he was. And in her big, ugly kiss, so abrupt, so oddly childlike, whose aggressiveness yet took him aback, he thought he could read all her past.

That was less than nine months ago. And that understanding, at which they had arrived so soon, had turned out to be the limit of their relationship. It was only to that they could return after jars, strains, and irritations; she the violated, he the comforter; an understanding that for her seemed to be enough, but for him was increasingly sterile.

If they had stayed in London they might have separated as easily as they had come together; and that relationship, never going beyond promise, would have left only a faint impression on him. She would have dwindled away into the London background and he would have caught glimpses of her in other people, picked up echoes of her attitudes. He would have been able to place her; he would have been content to be another of her failures. But here on the Ridge, where she was as alien as he, and there was nothing to camouflage her, where the empty company house with the too-solid wooden furniture and the view of the exploding city at the foot of the brown hills reminded him of his own failure, here on the Ridge where his own vision of his future had begun to contract and then to blur, and he had become aware of his age, here he had become obsessed with her.

All that was to be known about her was clear at that first meeting: it was her total display. But what London had masked the Ridge now, too late, made plain. How often, in London, he had seen her casual irritations and hostility mistaken, as they had been mistaken by him, for a point of view. How easy it had been in that city for her simple impressionistic comments, borrowed from here and there, and some already borrowed from himself and distorted, to suggest a complete and coherent personality. In London, Roche now saw, Jane was an exotic; and perhaps she was aware that she was an exotic. Perhaps she was aware that her simple views, which would have been unremarkable in a woman of another background, were more than simple when she claimed them.

But here on the Ridge, where the modes of English speech were not known, and where, moreover, she was associated with Roche, what she said was taken literally. Here, where everyone lived in a state of suppressed hysteria, and where ambitions and jealousies no longer had to do with motorcars or houses or fine things, but with security—money shipped abroad, residence visas for Canada and Australia and the United States—and where even Harry de Tunja, a perfect Ridge man, had quietly established his status as a Canadian landed immigrant, here where people regarded their way of life as almost over, Jane, offering her casual nihilism, her casual outbursts about the coming crash and the disintegration of systems, was saying things people preferred not to listen to. And no one believed in her passion. She was from London; she had London to return to; she was not taken seriously.

At Mrs. Grandlieu's one evening Roche had seen the young wife of a lawyer grow silent as Jane had talked on; and then the young woman, a pretty brown-skinned woman, neat in a tight-waisted blue dress, a touch of rouge on her cheeks, carefully made up for the evening in the great house, had frozen, had refused to acknowledge Jane's presence. This was done quietly; not many people would have noticed; but Roche, contrasting the woman's neatness and gravity with Jane's gobbling talk and nervous manner, which now began to appear strident and hysterical—and Jane that evening was in a sack dress made of a kind of striped North African sacking—Roche for the first time, and to his great surprise, began to detect in Jane a physical gracelessness. Jane talked on; she seemed not to be aware of the effect she had been having. But she did know, and she had been wounded. She returned gloomy from the dinner, saying nothing: it was the beginning of her detachment, soon to turn to revulsion, from their life on the Ridge.

They were dull people, she decided, sheep being led to the slaughter; they deserved their future. She continued to find proofs of their dullness, and he watched her revulsion grow. More than once he heard her say, holding out the French lighter to someone who had asked to see the unusual model, "Sahara gas, I suppose." It was the kind of comment she was used to throwing out, and this comment had doubtless been borrowed from the journalist of whom she sometimes spoke, one of those failed lover-violators. In London it would have been an interesting comment; to someone meeting her for the first time it would have suggested knowledge, alertness, a degree of political concern; it would have opened up so many conversational possibilties: France, Algeria, the Arabs, exploitation, the using up of the world's natural resources. But here it was allowed to pass as just a geographical fact; no one knew how to take the matter further.

She was among people who didn't have a world view—and a world view was what she had expected, once she had left England. She was among colonials who were interested only in their own situation and their own politicians, whose names she had given up attempting to learn. She was among people who didn't understand her language; and she was adrift. And perhaps it was this feeling of being adrift among people who were narrow and literal that made her more forthright and passionate; perhaps it was this that had led to that famous, unforgotten incident at Mrs. Grandlieu's when she had spoken of the horrors of the island and of "those black little animals ferreting about in the rubbish dump" and had, literally, stopped the conversation. It was her London manner, her wish to impose herself; she wasn't sure what point she was making; it was her manner that had swept her on too far. She understood this; and, in response to Roche's silence when they went back to their house, she gave the coy, flushed smile she had given when, at their first meeting, she had been unable to tell him why the publishing firm was ghastly.

Without an audience, then, to give her a familiar idea of herself, she had—in the house, with Roche, the only person who could half understand them—begun to relapse into her class certainties. And thus what London had masked the Ridge had layer by layer exposed. That obsession with England and her class, that vision of decay, of a world going up in flames: he had thought, in London, that it came out of her conviction that the world was not what it ought to be. The truth was simpler: the world was to go up in flames because it wasn't what it had been, or what she thought it had been. At the back of that vision lay the certainties—of class and money—of which, in London, she had seemed so innocent.

And something of innocence remained. She was without memory: he had decided that long ago. She was under no obligation to make a whole of her attitudes or actions. It was useless, as he had found, to point out her contradictions. She was not abashed because she was not interested; she owed no one any explanations. She was only what she did or said at any given moment; she was then what she was. He had been drawn by what he had seen as her mystery. But where he had once looked for passion born of violation and distress, he now found inviolability.

She had invested little in this relationship. She had from the start, as it now seemed, held herself back, for this moment of withdrawal. The gesture, of leaving London and coming out to live with him, so soon after meeting him, had appeared to him grand, part of her passionate nature; yet it was contained within this sense of inviolability, her belief that everything could be undone. And he saw that he had moved from the role of comforter to that of violator. He was another of her failures, someone else who wasn't what she had thought he was.

And from being the woman who had attempted to transmit her hysterical vision of the world to the inhabitants of the Ridge —those impressionistic, passionate comments which formed no pattern, which seemed about to lead her to some conclusion but never did, many things jumbled together: the contempt with which West Indian bus conductors were regarded in London, the shallowness of her women friends, the horror of the shantytowns on the island, the guerrillas in the hills—from this she had become calm, detached, the visitor.

She detached herself from his failure and from his job. She pretended, at first with irony, and then with indifference, not to know what he did. "Is that what Peter is up to these days?" "Did Peter say that?" So that the breakdown of their relationship was known on the Ridge; and it was thought that the inadequacy was his. On the Ridge, as he knew, this inadequacy could only be interpreted sexually; and he knew that it was interpreted as something connected with his imprisonment in South Africa.

She had come, again, to the end of a cycle. And now, from the angle of the rejected, he saw how she might get started on another. She had no audience here and was quiescent; but he saw how, in her own setting, with a familiar audience, and after another failed adventure, she might send out the same signals of passion, distress, violation: another total display, as instinctive and as without calculation as the one for which he had fallen. The sea anemone, rooted and secure, waving its strands at the bottom of the ocean.

This instinct, this innocence, this inviolability: he was obsessed with her. He longed to make some dent on that inviolability; he longed to reveal her to herself. But every day he went down from the Ridge to the decaying city, to his meaningless public relations job in the old offices of Sablich's; every day he was undermined. He was without a function; he saw himself as she had begun to see him; and there was this that depressed him now, and it was like a confirmation of his present futility, that though his attitudes and Jane's seemed to coincide, though they seldom argued because they were seldom opposed in what they said about the island and its possibilities, he had begun to long for some sign of admiration from her, some generosity, some comprehension of the life he had lived, the wasted endeavors, the spent optimism. He had never looked for this kind of approval before; he recognized it as a danger signal. Every morning he thought: I've built my whole life on sand.

9

IN THIS part of the city the streets were narrow, sometimes little more than lanes, and twisting. The houses, overhung by big breadfruit trees and mango trees, could be very small, sometimes like miniatures, each house standing in its own little plot and almost filling it. In the paintings done by local artists for the tourist trade it was still a picturesque area: red tin roofs edged with white fretwork against the tall green trees, pink oleander and red poinsettia leaning over narrow pavements, the winding lanes, the hills. But even in the paintings now the black asphalt streets could be seen to end in dirt tracks, thinning as they wavered up the hills and splitting into paths; and above the staggered red roofs could be seen the wooden shacks on thin stilts scattered about the stripped hillsides. The shacks, in this season of drought, were the color of dust; the eroded hills reflected light and heat; and the area was like a crater, enclosed and airless.

Once it had been a respectable lower-class area. And here and there respectability still showed, in some neatly fenced little house with a front gate still with a bell, or with ferns in hanging baskets shading a toy front veranda. But the community once contained in this area of greenery and red roofs and narrow lanes had exploded. Families still lived in certain houses; but many of the houses had become camping places, where young men looked for occasional shelter and an occasional meal, young men who at an early age had found themselves in the streets, without families, knowing only the older women of some houses as "aunts."

It was a community now without rules; and the area was now apparently without municipal regulation. Empty house lots had been tuned into steel-band yards or open-air motor repair shops; cars and trucks without wheels choked the narrow lanes. Where garbage dammed the open gutters, wrinkled white films of scum formed on the black water. The walls were scrawled, and sometimes carefully marked, with old election slogans, racial slogans, and made-up African names: *Kwame Mandingo (Slave Name—Butler)*. There was something competitive and whimsical about the slogans and the names. Humor, of a sort, was intended; and it seemed at variance with the words of threat and anger.

This was Stephens' area. This was where he had had his gang. It was from this, three months ago, that Stephens had allowed himself to be led to Thrushcross Grange, and the land: Stephens allowing himself to fall, as Roche had intended he should fall, for his own semipolitical slogans: the land, the dignity of labor on the land, the revolution based on land. Now Stephens was missing; and Roche was worried. Jane, returning from her visit to Thrushcross Grange, had said that the Grange was a cover for the guerrillas. It was something she had thrown out and perhaps had already forgotten. But Roche had remembered. Roche didn't ⁻lieve in the guerrillas the newspapers, the radio, and the television spoke about. But he believed in the city gangs.

Stephens' mother's house was in a dirt road that branched off one of the older, asphalted streets. Roche parked on the asphalt, away from the corner. It was two o'clock, the hottest and stillest time of day. The streets were empty and exposed; the telegraph poles hardly cast a shadow; the shadows on houses had withdrawn right up to the eaves. As he was locking the car door he heard a hiss. He began to turn, but then didn't. A boy crossed the asphalt street and came directly toward him. Roche put on his dark glasses.

The boy said, "You. Gimme a dollar."

Roche didn't turn away. He looked at the boy. He saw the dull, close-set eyes, a pimple on the right eyelid: the mind half eaten away, human debris already, his cause already lost.

The boy said, "Wash your car for a dollar."

Roche tested the handle of the car door. "You will watch my car for a dollar?" He began to walk to the corner.

The boy walked beside him, gesticulating with both hands, keeping his elbows low, flinging out his arms, making stiff, scattering gestures with his open palms, and appearing to work himself into a rage. He chanted, shouted, "A dollar, man, a dollar, eh-eh!"

Roche concentrated less on the boy than on the yard from which the boy had come: perhaps the boy's friends were there, watching.

A man was crossing the dirt road and coming toward them. Roche, turning to his left to go up the dirt road, heard the man say, "Eh-eh, why you don't leave the man?"

It was the voice that alerted Roche. A deep, relaxed voice. A calm face: a face that knew its own worth. Someone who could spend money on soft leather shoes, plain and unpolished and covered with dust, but elegant in the instep. A man with a job, a man with a purpose. After surprise, instinct: the man was a plainclothesman. And as soon as the suspicion came to Roche he knew, from a swift second glance at the man, already on his way, brisk even in this heat, his unsweated short-sleeved Yucatan-style shirt dancing above his worn jeans, that he was right. He thought: The house is being watched.

He thought, walking slowly up the hills, exaggeratedly avoiding stones, holes, and dusty litter: Should I become involved in this? But he knew that it was already too late to turn back.

The house had once been the last on the left. But the unpaved road had since continued up the hillside in an irregular dirt track, with houses on either side; the track had been worn smooth, and looked as hard and slippery as if it had been plastered; and little timber houses and huts were scattered about the hillside at the end of little branch tracks.

Mrs. Stephens' house was one of the miniature houses of the area. It had concrete walls and a corrugated-iron roof, and it stood on concrete pillars about four feet high. Chickens, open-beaked and clucking in the heat, roosted in hollows in the thick, dry, dungy dust about the pillars. The house had some pretensions; it wasn't a shack; it belonged more to the asphalt streets than to the hillside. It was built according to the standard pattern of the area: divided lengthwise down the middle, with bedrooms on the right —the frosted casement window of the front bedroom open, with a half-curtain in lace hanging from a slack curtain wire—and on the left a toy veranda, living room, and kitchen.

Roche went up the shallow flight of red-colored concrete steps to the veranda. Two morris chairs with blistered arms and faded cushions almost filled it. The white paint on the frame of the living room door was cracked and dingy. He knocked: and then, sucking on the temple of his dark glasses, he turned and looked up at the sky, the yellow, built-up hillside, and then down the unpaved road to where he had seen the man in the Yucatan-style shirt. Two blocks away he saw a parlor-bar level to the pavement, its open doorway black below a rusty corrugated-iron awning.

He hadn't intended to stay long at the house. He wanted only to ask about Stephens and to gauge whether Mrs. Stephens knew anything about her son. But when Mrs. Stephens wrenched open the rickety frosted-glass door Roche found he had decided to say nothing about her son.

Mrs. Stephens was a big, well-proportioned mulatto woman. Her dress, which went down to her knees, was tight about her breasts and her belly. Her short hair was done up in little plaits. Her eyes were sunken, and about her cheeks there was an unhealthy, shiny puffiness.

Roche was glad he wasn't going to ask about Stephens, because when Mrs. Stephens said, "Eh! Mr. Roche. But you give me a shock. I see this person through the glass and I ask myself who this white fellow is," he knew from her tone and her distant manner—she appeared to be talking to someone over his right shoulder —that she was less than friendly.

And there was a calculated casualness in the way, having let him in, her eyes seeming to search the street and the hillside the while, she turned and walked back into the room, dragging her slippers on the varnished floor, picking her way through the clutter of furniture: the remainder of the morris suite, a center table, a sideboard, a large dining table with six chairs—standard old-fashioned furniture of the island, miniatures of the furniture in Roche's own house on the Ridge.

Mrs. Stephens was not alone. In the far corner of the room, just at the side of the window, an older woman was sitting on one of the dining chairs. She was smaller than Mrs. Stephens, with slacker flesh; her squashed face was set in a smile.

Roche said, "I was just passing, Mrs. Stephens."

Mrs. Stephens said, "Yes, yes. All my friends pass in. You would like some cold juice? Neighbor, you would like some juice?" As she went through the door at the back, she said, "Is only my children who don't come to look for me."

Roche smiled at the old woman. She smiled back and said nothing.

Mrs. Stephens had made her declaration about her son. The rebuke and suspicion of her words lingered in the choked room, which was airless, even with the open casement window. There was nothing more to say; but Roche had committed himself now to the social call. The room depressed him and made him uneasy; he felt alien. On the pale-pink concrete wall there were framed photographs of some of Mrs. Stephens' children. One young man was in an academic gown: it was like a photograph in a photographer's window in London, with the photographer's satire hidden from the sitter, who saw only the flattery. And those other faces: faces of the street, unremarkable in the street, and here, oddly, where they were honored, looking more vulnerable. So fragile this world, where the furniture, heavy and excessive, filled the room and yet seemed not to belong: it was easy to imagine the morris set absent, and the dining set; it was easy to have a sense of the house as a hollow, flimsy structure in a small patch of yellow dirt.

The concrete walls were scratched, dusty plaster showing below pink distemper, with a shine of dirt at hip level; old putty had fallen out of the wooden partition that divided the tiny living room from the two bedrooms: dark caverns beyond half-open doors. On this partition was the Thrushcross Grange poster: *I'm Nobody's Slave or Stallion, I'm a Warrior and Torch Bearer —Haji James Ahmed.* Roche's nervousness grew. Fragile, fragile, this world, requiring endless tolerance, endless forbearance: the furniture, the poster, the photograph of the young man in the academic gown.

The old woman, following Roche's eye, said of the photograph of the young man in the academic gown, "That one is Lloyd. Madeleine's first." Her voice was pleasant and educated; she seemed better educated than Mrs. Stephens; and yet she spoke of Madeleine with respect and of Lloyd as a success. "He's in England." And having spoken, she smiled again, and nodded.

Roche knew about this brother of Stephens': the one who had got away to England before the barriers came down. England, Roche thought: it was so hard to get away from England here. And there were so many Englands: his, Jane's, Jimmy's, Lloyd's, and the England—hard to imagine—in that old woman's head.

"Yes," Mrs. Stephens said, coming back into the room with tumblers of grapefruit juice on a tin tray enameled with bright red apples. "Yes, Lloyd's in London." She worked through the furniture to Roche. "But Lloyd forget his mother." She worked her way back to the dining table, dragging her feet and seeming to swing her hips. She held the tray to the old woman and said, "Neighbor?" She sat down and said, as if only to the room, "Yes, Lloyd forget everybody. I don't know what the sweetness is up there that does make him behave like that." But she soon made it clear that she knew: the trouble was Lloyd's wife, the wife who had made him get out. "Yes, neighbor. I don't grudge anybody. I used to have a man too and I know what it is to want to keep a man. But Hilda gone too far. Anybody would think I do Hilda something. Hilda don't write me, you know. Hilda's only writing is to her family. Still, I hear they have everything of the best, and Hilda doing two jobs and everything. Well, let them enjoy it. All that coming to an end soon. They will want to come back here. They will learn that the only people who have anything good for you is your own. The juice sweet enough for you, Mr. Roche? Or you would like some sugar?"

"No, it's all right, Mrs. Stephens."

"Yes, neighbor. I used to have a man too. Now I have to fend for myself. When Knolly was here I used to get a few cents, but since he get taken up with that Chinee man I don't see one red cent from him. Mr. Roche, you must tell Knolly to come and look for his mother some time."

"I don't go up there very often, Mrs. Stephens. I go up once or twice a month."

"Yes, neighbor. I know what it is to want to keep a man."

"Hilda is like that," the old woman said. "That is Hilda's background. Very common. Never-see-come-see. That is Hilda through and through."

"Yes, my dear. Two jobs, and everything of the best. But they will realize. The only people who have anything good for you is your own. What is the sweetness with that Chinee man, Mr. Roche? Who give him all that big fame in England? What he doing with those boys? Knolly was a good, good boy, don't mind what people say." She began, quite suddenly, to cry.

The old woman said, "Neighbor."

Roche said, "Mrs. Stephens."

"That Chinee man," Mrs. Stephens said. "I never like that Chinee man. But I am a supporter of this government, Mr. Roche. This government will never fall."

"Not while Israel lasts," the old woman said, and shook her head up and down, smiling, at Roche.

"Yes," Mrs. Stephens said. "Israel is in her glory."

"Who ever thought the day would come, Madeleine?"

Mrs. Stephens sighed. "Who ever thought the day would come?" She stood up and made a move, between the dining chair she had been sitting on and the back of the morris settee, toward Roche. "But you not drinking the juice, Mr. Roche. It is not to your liking? You would like some more ice?"

He had been barely sipping, allowing the diluted grapefruit juice to trickle between his almost closed lips and rest without taste below his lower teeth. The tumbler in his hand felt cold and clammy; the hens below the floorboards clucked contentedly in the heat; and through the open window came the smell of dust and chicken dung. The leaves of the breadfruit tree in the next lot were a hard green. The dining table was stained and lackluster; yet Roche had known all the furniture in this room polished and shining.

Mrs. Stephens said: "You would like some more ice?"

He put the tumbler to his mouth and took two long gulps. The thin acrid taste of the grapefruit lingered in his mouth; and he swallowed and sucked, working the taste out.

"Knolly was a good boy," Mrs. Stephens said, sitting down. "When he was here I always used to see a few cents. I don't know what kind of sweetness he find up by that Chinee man. I don't know how he could believe that other people could look after him when they can't even look after their own."

She was not concealing her hostility now. Her jaw jutted; her eyes were cold and small; she was speaking more quickly, putting an edge to her voice, and occasionally tripping over a word.

The old woman said, "Madeleine."

Mrs. Stephens became calmer. "Yes. I too had a man. I too."

"Hilda is Hilda," the old woman said. "But you mustn't forget what Lloyd is."

"Everything of the best, my dear. That is the message Hilda send to me. You know what Knolly did with the first money he get? The first-first money? He went to town and he buy two bamboo vase stands and he put them up on the wall."

One was still there, in the corner: a little trapezoid shelf, edged with bamboo strips on which a pattern of diagonal lines had been burnt, braced into a diamond-shaped frame of bamboo strips decorated in the same way. The shelf was empty; little broken cobwebs hung from the dusty bamboo strips. To a child the vase stand must have seemed pretty: it was something about Stephens Roche had never known, though he knew this room well. It was something about himself that Stephens had suppressed.

"Lloyd was born in the days of bondage," Mrs. Stephens said. "When Knolly born black people was ruling here. Nobody bringing back plantation days, you hear me. Not you or Sablich's or that Chinee man."

So far, in her bare, intermittent courtesies to himself and the contrasting gravity of her gossipy manner with the old woman, in her deliberateness, Roche had seen only hostility. Now he saw that Mrs. Stephens was distracted with grief; and this unsettled him more. In her speech, which now seemed to him disordered, he thought he was getting glimpses of a personality and a world that were as alien and shut-in as that choked little room.

He looked at her with something like a smile, to show that he understood, that he was willing to draw her hostility. But as he smiled her rage grew; and he began to be alarmed.

"People have to look after their own," Mrs. Stephens said.

It was one of the ideas she was playing with, one strand of her anguish that seemed constantly to knot and unknot itself. Roche continued to smile. But the old woman, as though knowing better than Roche what was to follow, said, "Madeleine, Madeleine."

"Rotten meat," Mrs. Stephens said.

He could guess the sexual significance of the words. But he wasn't prepared for the contempt, the contempt of women for women, the contempt which, in that room, from Mrs. Stephens, was like a contempt for her own body and the body of her neighbor, slack, swollen, worn out. The grapefruit taste in Roche's mouth went bitter; he associated it with the smell of the chicken dung and dust that came through the window; and the saliva thickened nauseously on his tongue.

"That is what they feed up that Chinee man on in England. That is the only sweetness he know. That is what they feed him up on and then they send him down here. Parading through the town with their tight pants sticking up in their crutch. They *stink*, Mr. Roche. They stink like rotten meat self."

He laughed, and his lips rode up above his long molars. He laughed at the violence of her language, he thought it was expected of him. But she became enraged, and she held his eyes until he acknowledged her rage. His lips fell back over his teeth; his smile became fixed again.

"I will tell you this, Mr. Roche," Mrs. Stephens said, leaning forward. "White women marry their own. But they like the Negro men."

The old woman nodded, smiling at Roche. She smoothed her dress over her legs, worked her lips over her teeth and said softly, as though stating a well-known fact, "But they marry their own."

"I will take the glass from you, Mr. Roche," Mrs. Stephens

said, getting up and moving again between her chair and the morris settee.

He surrendered the wet tumbler, noting as he did so the small flowered pattern on Mrs. Stephens' dress, the dirtiness on the stomach and the breasts. His right hand was wet and sticky; the smell of chicken dung was strong in his nostrils. When Mrs. Stephens took the tumbler and put it on the enameled tray on the dining table he began to study the gown Lloyd was wearing in the photograph.

"But is black people fault if they allow themselves to be fooled," Mrs. Stephens said. "But those days finishing fast now. Lloyd was born in the days of bondage. When Knolly was born, Israel was in her glory. Knolly born knowing that. He born knowing that after Israel it was the turn of Africa. No matter what anybody say or do."

"Israel first," the old woman said, again as though confirming a well-known fact.

Roche stood up.

Mrs. Stephens said, "You going, Mr. Roche?" She was looking older than when he had come; the rings below her eyes had grown darker; she looked more suffering, exhausted.

"Yes," he said. "I have to be getting back to the office."

He began to move toward the frosted-glass door. Heavily, she got up from the chair and followed him. He opened the rickety door himself: the light outside was an assault.

"When you see Knolly, Mr. Roche," Mrs. Stephens said, "you must tell him to come and look for his mother some time."

She held the door open while he went down the red concrete steps. She didn't look at him; her eyes searched the sky and the hillside in an unseeing way. When, from the dirt road, he turned to wave at her he found that she had closed the door again.

The sun beat on his temples; his shirt burned. The dust was thick; he fancied it was penetrating through his socks to his ankles. The bitter saliva thickened nauseously at the back of his mouth. He worked his tongue and cheeks and spat, stickily, into the dust and watched the spit roll into a dust-coated ball. His stomach heaved; the smell of the chicken dung and the tainted dust caught in his nostrils, and he clenched his teeth; but he spat again. He walked briskly downhill, careless of dust and rubble and litter. Two blocks away he saw the black doorway of the bar: he knew that, from there, he was being observed. The boy who had asked him for money was sitting on the steps of the house opposite the car. The boy stayed where he was and stared.

The handle of the car door was hot; and the car, when he sat inside, was suffocating. The seat burned; his mouth again filled with sticky saliva; he felt dust had settled on his face and hands and even below his shirt. He drove carefully, around the obstructions of parked cars and trucks, past the blocked gutters with wrinkled films of white scum. The car cooled down; he began to sweat less.

At last he turned into a broader street, shaded by old *samaan* trees that grew out of the wide pavement. This was the boundary of the area of small houses and twisting lanes. The houses were bigger here, and many had been turned into offices or commercial colleges. The air was lighter: this street led to the main park. And it was here, some way from the park, in the thin shade of a *samaan* tree, and against a long white concrete wall hung with a vine known as the bleeding heart—heart-shaped leaves, browned by the drought, heart-shaped flowers the color of blood—it was here that Roche saw two men squatting on the pavement. Not far away, on the left-hand side of the street, an old black car was parked close to the pavement, with its two left-hand doors open over the pavement. Two men were in this car, one in the back, one in the front, both facing the pavement. The man in the back, with one foot in the car and one on the pavement, had a thick, well-trimmed mustache.

Roche thought: Stephens is in real trouble.

ABOUT FIFTEEN minutes later he was in the parking lot of Sablich's in the center of the city. The elderly mulatto watchman, seated as always in his Windsor chair, smiled at him and, little pipe in his mouth, heavy baton over his thighs, half rose to greet him. The watchman was tall and heavy, with a round face that was too small for his body; his pale brown skin was extraordinarily smooth. He was near retirement, and looked more like a ticket-collector than a watchman. Roche saw the watchman smile, saw him make the effort to rise. But he ignored the watchman; he walked past without looking at him; and he saw the smile turn to a look of surprise.

Upstairs, in the corridor outside his office, he washed his hands in the antique wash basin; the water ran black. It was cool in the office. The jalousies were sealed; the hum of the air conditioners masked the street noises; the afternoon light, coming through strips of glass painted green and falling on the dark oiled floor and pale-green wooden partitions, gave the room a soft green glow.

His sweated shirt dried; he could feel salt and dust adhering to his neck and face. He thought of telephoning Jimmy Ahmed; but he changed his mind. He had telephoned Jimmy before, to find out about Stephens, and Jimmy had been offhand. It was never good, with Jimmy, to be the one who had to get in touch; it was always better to let him make the first move; Jimmy played that little power game.

It was Friday. The day's work was almost over, and the week's; and people were beginning to stand around desks in relaxed groups, some of the men with their office towels over their shoulders. He went to the washroom and stripped for a wash: there would be no water on the Ridge until the evening. The washroom was in a renovated part of the building and was not air-conditioned. The concrete walls were white, the windows open; the light dazzled. His face burned again, and he could hear the din of the street. He could hear especially, above the cars, trucks and bicycle bells, the chant of the blind beggar, a youngish man whose legs had been cut off below the hips, who every Friday came to this part of the city. "*Help de poor! Help de blind! I am very grateful. Help de blind! Help de poor! I am very t'ankful.*" A lusty voice, and the chant never stopped: it was a performance, it had a theatrical, even comic, quality. The beggar knew he was famous.

Roche knew the beggar. But listening now to the persistent cry, not seeing the man, he felt only its strangeness and his own solitude. And out of this there came to him a feeling of apprehension, at first vague and perhaps a little willed, not focused on anything, but which then, as he stood half naked in the sunlit concrete washroom, with its heated sour smell, all at once became overpowering. He was becoming detached from his normal self; his perceptions were being distorted; and he continued to feel that he was willing it. His mood was wrong; and he was sufficiently alert to know that to go outside into that city, in that mood, was to invite physical attack. Drying his face and chest, he thought: I must drive carefully when I leave here. When he went back to the green office he thought again of telephoning Jimmy. But then he thought: I must be careful; I mustn't become involved.

At four the office closed. Doors banged in various parts of the building, footsteps resounded on wooden floors. Going down to the parking lot, he passed a door that opened into the gallery of the darkened emporium below the main offices. Clerks were doing up bolts of cloth and straightening counters: young men in neat trousers and shirts with nicely knotted ties, men who during working hours gave an impression of great civility, but who came from houses like the one he had visited that afternoon, and whose manners now, after closing time, were already changing. In the parking lot he could hear the roar of the released city: an extra volume of sound around the beggar's cry, more people, more cars and trucks, shouts, innumerable bicycle bells.

The watchman sat in his Windsor chair. He looked without expression at Roche. Roche greeted the watchman, and was relieved when a smile appeared on the man's smooth round baby face.

He had rehearsed, as far as he was able, the dangers of the afternoon drive home. In the business area of the city he watched out for the abrupt stops and starts of the route taxis, the bare arms of the drivers making dancer's gestures outside their windows. Later, around the park, he watched out for the cyclists, and especially for the exhibitionists among them: the riders without hands, celebrating the end of the working week by riding with shirts open all the way down, shirttails flapping above their saddles, riding fast and swinging out to overtake more sedate cyclists. He watched out for the mule carts and the hand carts, the queues at bus stops.

The afternoon light, already touched with amber, shot through the dust kicked up by vehicles that ran over the broken edges of the asphalt road; the scorched verges were tawny. The road began to climb; the air became lighter, the streets wider. He passed the botanical gardens; bamboo clumps that had ignited and burned down created the effect of ruins. A little later, the road still climbing, he saw the black police cars, blocking half the road.

It was routine after some incident down in the city, this blocking of one of the escape routes to the hills. After seven months he had got to know the police officers who were posted in the area. As he slowed down he recognized the sergeant. He was expecting to be waved on. But the sergeant signaled to him to stop and pull over to the side. He smiled at the sergeant; the sergeant looked embarrassed. The men with the rifles didn't smile. Other cars slowed down and were waved on. His car was searched: the trunk, the engine, under the seats. The padding on the doors was felt. And Roche stood exposed at the side of the road in the amber light.

A man pushing a bicycle up the hill, a laborer, shouted at the policemen: "Search him!"

And it didn't help when, a little later, a young brown man, whose own car had been waved on, put his head out of the window and shouted to Roche: "Sue them! Sue them!"

The sergeant, from being embarrassed, had become official. They didn't talk; and when the search was over Roche didn't smile at the sergeant. They parted as strangers. Roche drove away slowly. The light was soft; the shadows of trees fell right across the road. As he drove up into the clearer air, into the region of gardens, children, uniformed servants, and well-fed watchdogs, he thought: Something is being prepared for me. Driving as carefully in these quiet roads as he had driven in the city, he thought: Perhaps I should get out.

A golden light touched the bare front lawn. He went into the house through the kitchen. Adela was not yet available; Jane was out. The house felt shut up and hot. He opened the door of the back room and went out on the porch. The cooler air refreshed him. From here he could see the airport and the white and silver glints of the planes. The evening haze was already building up above the rubbish dump and the swamp. He watched the light turn, saw color come to the tops of clouds: rose and gold and then lilac.

Pipes hissed in the house. Adela came out to him, in her ironed white uniform.

She said softly, "Water, Mr. Roche."

He was taken aback by her gentleness.

She said, "You would like some tea?" And she spoke without aggression. She stood for a while on the porch: she had something to say. She said, "Your lady gone out with Mistress de Tunja." But that wasn't her news. She said, "You know Dr. Handy Byam, Mr. Roche?"

He had seen the posters for this latest American evangelist, but now he was confused by Adela's aspirates and wasn't sure whether the evangelist's name was Andy or Handy.

"I feel so good, Mr. Roche, after last night. So good. Handy Byam say he wasn't going to heal anybody with his own hands. Last night he say the people have to do their own healing now and he is just there to guide them. He say that Israel is in her glory and the power is now on the Nig-ro people. He ask us to turn to whoever was next to us and to hold their hands and to pray and pray hard, so that every man would heal his neighbor."

She demonstrated, standing with her firm legs apart, rocking back on her heels, and making separate clasping gestures with her hands. The clasping hands became clenched fists; she closed her eyes and quivered.

"And I hold my neighbor like that, and he hold me like that, and we pray and pray until Handy Byam call on us to stop and shout if we was cured. And you shoulda hear the shout then, Mr. Roche. You know Handy Byam, Mr. Roche? One-among-you should get to know him, you know. He is like you too, a little bit. Your size and your color."

It was like a tribute. It was the first time she had shown him such regard.

10

THE COAST here was intermittently rocky. At high tide, below what Harry de Tunja called his beach house, there was no beach; the sea came right up to the foot of the low cliff. Low tide exposed a narrow, steeply curving rim of coarse sand littered with seaweed and sea grapes, the debris of the sea. Two hundred yards away there was a breach in the cliff wall. A forest river had once emptied itself into the sea at this point. Great trees now grew in the old river channel. The river had laid its silt far out into the sea in a wide convex bed, so that the sea here had receded and was calmer, with little waves breaking at odd angles. At low tide there was a beach: an expanse of waterlogged muddy sand, declining gradually to sea, with gray islets of shingle, crushed shells, tiny brown crabs, and small stranded fish. Of the forest river there remained now the merest stream, ending in a woodland pool, dark and green from the trees it reflected; and the pool spilled over onto the beach in a miniature estuary of ever-changing channels, inches deep, that left rippled or plaited patterns on the gray sand.

It was an ancient site. Aboriginal Indians had beached their canoes here; around this shady river bed, a meeting place, there had been Indian villages and food gardens. The gardens had lasted longer than the people: even after forest, the plantations, and now the beach houses, cassava grew in unexpected places. Seafarers from Europe knew the site for its fresh-water stream. Now it was a local pleasure spot, not a place for tourists, not a place for bathing, but a place for Sunday excursions, for drinking parties, and for the celebration of certain religious rites that required the sea or a river.

At eleven o'clock it was crowded. Old buses with locally built bodies of wood and tacked-on tin were parked in the side road above, their windows hung with clothes. Clothes hung on bushes; and bundles and baskets were everywhere. Radios played the reggae. Out of the shade of the trees, on a little bluff of dry sand, men and women gowned in black or red rang bells and chanted, facing the sea. The sky, blue inland, was silver here in the heat.

Jane, Roche, and Harry de Tunja had walked far beyond the little estuary and the crowds, and were now walking back. They walked in the narrow strip of sand between the cliff and the ebbing sea; and soon they began again to see the long white candles on the sand, amid the tangle of weed, the dead coconut branches, the unfamiliar tins dropped somewhere in mid-ocean. Long white candles, still whole, still fresh, with only the tips of the wicks burned. And, here and there, the little nailed-up rafts, hatcheted strips of hairy yellow box boards, on which the candles had been sent out on the water, to be doused at the first wave or to collapse at the first turbulence: a drama taking place again, in the distance, in the shallows outside the estuary: a black-gowned man, standing up to his waist in the sea, ringing a bell with one hand, holding a little raft steady with the other hand, a blindfolded woman in a pink chemise beside him, with a lighted candle in her hand. Yellow box-board rafts, pushed far from their launching places by the wavelets that broke at odd angles, bobbed about at the edge of the sea, struck muddy sand, floated again, were stranded. Candles, splashed with gritty black mud, littered the estuary beach.

Harry de Tunja, interrupting his deep-breathing exercises, said asthmatically, "I don't know why, but I don't like seeing this thing at all." And he choked in the hot moist air.

Jane and Roche waited for him to catch his breath. After a series of gasps he fell again into the rhythm of his deep breathing.

Jane said, "Wax and water. Fire and water."

A fat barefooted woman, with three elderly women attendants in white, was preaching, shouting, chanting. *And Mary lay dong, and de chile lay dong*: they were the only words that were clear, and she spoke them again and again between passages of gibberish. She looked down at the beach; she seemed to be addressing someone stretched out there, for whom, from her gestures, she continually spread an imaginary rug or sheet. It was a private frenzy. No one was listening to her; no one stopped to watch; her three attendants in white stood quiet and relaxed, holding Bibles, not looking at her, looking vacantly at the sea and the people passing up and down.

Bells rang on the dry sandy bluff. A blindfolded group was being prepared for the walk out to the sea. They marched without moving, holding unlighted candles; and about them black-gowned and red-gowned men and women chanted. On the wet beach below the bluff people watched: half naked these watchers, black and brown bodies on which sand had stuck in patches and dried gray, and they stood and swayed as though infected by the rhythm of the bells and the stamp of the six blindfolded marchers above them, who were fully dressed, and stamping holes in the dry sand.

The marchers were in two columns of three. The woman in front was middle-aged; she held her candle upright and worked her hands and hips in an easy grinding way. The man was youngish; whenever he stamped his left foot he seemed about to collapse, but it was his own variation of the march: it was what he was allowing his body to do, this quivering descent, this mock half-fall. They stamped and stamped, digging their feet deeper into the sand. The woman sweated prodigiously; great circles of sweat had spread from under the arms of her white bodice. She held herself erect; her pumping elbows and her stamping feet created their own rhythm. She marched like a leader. The man beside her marched like a clown. The white blindfold emphasized his broad forehead, his heavy, ill-formed lips and his sagging jaw. The bells rang and rang. And though about the chief bell ringer, stylish in a black gown with a yellow sash, there was something of the showman, pleased to draw a crowd, and though among the watchers there were those who had begun, half humorously, to mimic the marchers, all eyes were on the marchers, on those repetitive steps, on the upright woman, her blindfolded face held up, her hands and elbows moving in steady rhythmic circles, and on the semicollapsing man in khaki trousers and white shirt, both man and woman seemingly locked, behind the blindfold, in a private world.

Harry de Tunja said after a while, "I think we should be moving on."

Jane, chalky white from her period, and with little red spots at the side of her mouth, said, "Do they object?"

Harry said, "For them, man, the more the merrier." As they walked off he added, "But sometimes when I watch these things I can feel the ground moving below me."

They walked past a plump woman in a yellow bathing suit and a red hat sitting with her dimpled brown legs flat on the muddy sand, past family parties and other groups detached from the ceremonies, past the wreckage of box-board rafts and the scatter of whole candles, to where the river channel ended, the cliff wall rose up, and the beach narrowed again, washed clean by the receding tide, with only the fresh sea litter of weeds and berries and entangled vines like broken garlands. Bells and radios, the reggae as repetitive as the bells, were muffled by the wind and the sea, less placid here, with shingle grating down the curved beach with every wave.

A zigzag of massive concrete steps—high tides, searching out the weaknesses of cliff and concrete, had left the lower steps exposed and isolated, like some rock formation—led up to Harry's house. Harry paused after every few steps to catch his breath. When he got to the top he put his hands on his hips, threw out his chest and breathed deeply five or six times. And then he seemed to be all right.

He said, "You see, it's under control now. I know I've got it beaten. The trouble is, I don't know whether it's the honey diet, the yoga, or the deep breathing. And the damn doctors here don't know either. I ask old Phillips about it, and he say, 'Well, Harry-boy, I don't know what to say. I feel it must be psychological.' "

Harry's speech, now that it was unobstructed, was extraordinarily musical, rising, falling, with unexpected passages of em-

phasis and unexpected changes of pace. *Psychological,* as Harry
spoke it, was like a line of song.

The air was fresher, even at this low height; it was without the
hot salty moistness of the air at the estuary. The house was set
back from the cliff end; the parched, pebbly lawn was shaded by
Honduras pines and almond trees, flat round leaves of green and
red and brown on horizontal black branches; and in the porch,
where there was only a view of the sky and the distant sea, and no
reflected glare, it was cool. Chairs had been put out, two Guate-
malan hammocks strung up. Rum punch, tumblers, and a bowl
of ice cubes were on a table.

Harry said, "When you're up here, you wouldn't believe that
that nonsense is going on down there."

This was the routine of Sunday at Harry de Tunja's beach
house: the early morning drive down from the Ridge through the
silent city, the quiet suburbs and factory area, the uncrowded
roads; the drive through the bush of what had once been coffee and
cocoa plantations, past the weatherbeaten little tin-and-timber huts
that dated from that time; along the rocky coast, little bays of
untrodden sand, sharp rocks, and white, crashing waves, turbulent
rock-bound coves; through the forest then, thinning out on the
cliff above the sea: arrival, the early morning breeze, the early
morning light, the walk along the beach, and then rum punch until
midday.

Jane had been to the beach house about half a dozen times.
This was the routine she knew. But today something was missing;
the house was missing some presence. It was missing Marie-
Thérèse, Harry's wife. She had, without warning, left him. One
afternoon she had driven their two children to the airport—they
were going back to their school in Canada after the holidays—and
she hadn't returned home. It was a drama. The de Tunja house
was one of the best known on the Ridge. To people who didn't
know them well, like Jane when she had just arrived, the gaiety of
the de Tunjas could seem excessive, even forced; they seemed to
like too many people; they offered friendship too easily. But the
naturalness of the de Tunjas had overcome all doubts; they were
like people without secrets; and they had become Jane and Roche's

only friends. It had seemed such a settled house; they had taken such pride in its fixtures and its garden and the frivolities of the dark and very cold air-conditioned room known as Harry's Bar. The breakup had unsettled many people. But there was little sympathy for Harry, because with the breakup the even more unsettling news had come out that the de Tunjas had been establishing their status as Canadian "landed immigrants." Harry had been the complete Ridge man. Now, to many people on the Ridge, his news was like a double confirmation of the instability in which they all knew they lived.

Something of this instability, of an order suddenly undermined, extended to the beach house, so that, independently, both Jane and Roche understood they had come to the end of the last pleasure they shared on the island: Sunday at Harry's beach house. The furniture in the porch was the same; the striped hammocks were the same; Joseph was busy in the kitchen; yet the day had been reduced to its routine and the house was already like something vacated.

Marie-Thérèse had left, but she hadn't gone far. The civil servant whose mistress she had become lived on the Ridge as well. She still acknowledged certain duties toward Harry and visited their house two or three times a week to see that everything worked. There was even some question that she might be coming to the beach house on this Sunday. But now, near midday, it was clear that she was spending the day elsewhere.

Harry said, "You met her on Friday, Jane. Did she tell you she was coming?"

"She didn't say."

Harry rocked in the hammock that was slung from the two front pillars of the porch. To Jane, in a chair at the back of the porch, he seemed to be swinging between the sea and the sky in his fringed Bermuda shorts and white canvas shoes and red-striped jersey. His arms were folded tight over his chest; there were dark rings below his sunken, distressed eyes.

Harry said, "I asked Meredith and Pamela. But it look as if something keeping them back too. That's the trouble. When you lose your wife it's like a wedding in reverse. Some people on the boy's side, some people on the girl's side."

Harry's turns of phrase, and his musical speech, could suggest humor where he intended none. Roche laughed. Jane watched for his tall, blackened molars. And she continued to study Roche's face as he said, in his calm, reflective way, as though no human experience was outside his comprehension, "It's the standard crisis. She'll come back. When we are forty-one we all think it would be nice to make a fresh start. It's the kind of thing we laugh at when we're forty-two."

Harry said, "Yes, Peter. That's what you told me. And that's the little philosophical bit I've been holding. But I don't know, man. This damn thing going on too long now. I begin to feel they're playing for keeps. I don't know what come over Marie-Thérèse. She is a completely different person. I don't know how anybody could change so much. I told her the other day, 'Marie-Thérèse, that guy is just having a damn good time in bed with you.' And you know what she said? Jane? Peter? She said, 'What do you think I am having?' You would believe that?"

Jane said, "I can believe it." Her face had lost a little of its chalkiness. The rum punch was having an effect: she spoke quickly, gobbling up the words, and she laughed after she had spoken.

Harry said, "Then you see more than me. I never know Marie-Thérèse talk like that. She even moving differently. She come in the house these days and she start moving about like some kind of ghost. Quiet, but *fast*. When I tell you, boy. Those hands of hers just going like that, whish-whish-bam-bam, and that's it. She straighten everything and she ready to go. She is like some kind of nun when she come home these days. You know those working nuns? Really, it's as though she's under some kind of spell. What's this guy's technique? That's what I ask her only Friday gone. 'Marie-Thérèse, what's this guy's technique? Has he read some book or something? Tell me, Marie-Thérèse. I can read too.' "

From seriousness he had moved to self-satire. He laughed, swung out of his hammock and said, "Let me go and see what Joseph is getting up to, eh." As he went inside they heard him say, as though unwilling to let go of his joke, "Marie-Thérèse shouldn't have done this to me."

Roche swayed in his hammock. Jane sipped at her rum punch and then took a gulp. She was drinking too quickly. She had no palate, Roche thought. She ate and drank as she sometimes spoke, in the same gobbling way. It was something about her he had begun to define, an aspect of the physical gracelessness he had begun to notice since they had moved apart and she no longer required his comfort. She lay back in her aluminum-framed easy chair and held her hand over her eyes. Her face was irregularly flushed now and looked blotched; her eyes were moist. She lit a cigarette; but then almost immediately, with a flick of her middle finger, shot it into the dry lawn. She lay back in the chair looking abstracted, distressed, but as though preparing to relax. She was still for a minute; then, abruptly, she swung her legs to one side of the chair and stood up and went inside.

Roche let his hammock sway. The light now had a settled incandescence. The sounds, of wind and sea, seemed to have altered, were no longer the fresh sounds of early morning. Steady, repetitive, they emphasized the midday stillness. The cigarette Jane had thrown on the lawn smoked fiercely. As if from far away there came the sound of bells; and having heard this sound, Roche continued to hear it on the wind. His eyes felt strained. It was the light; he could feel a headache building up. He got out of the hammock and went inside to get his dark glasses.

It was dark in the living room, and cool; and in the bedroom, up two or three steps from the living room, it was darker, the window facing the sea wire-netted, the external storm shutters half closed, the wooden louvers inside tilted up, with just stripes of white light showing through the slats. Jane was standing on the other side of the bed, next to the window. She was naked below her cotton blouse; her blue trousers, with the pants inside them, were thrown on the bed. Half naked like this, she looked big and tall. She glanced at Roche as he came in; then, turning her back to him, and facing the window, she seemed about to sit on the bed. She came down hard on the very edge of the bed, which dipped below her weight; but she didn't sit; she threw herself backward in an apparently abandoned attitude, opened her legs, raising her feet up against the wall, and inserted what Roche now realized was the tampon she held in her hand; and then almost immediately she was sitting, had seized the blue plastic tampon case from the bed and sent it spinning with a low, level flick of the wrist to the corner of the room where their basket was, with their beach things. The tampon case struck the concrete wall and clattered on the floor.

It had all been done swiftly, in as it were one action; and she had appeared quite athletic. Her shoulders had barely touched the bed before she had jerked herself up into a sitting position; and even while, fumbling at the bedside table with his dark glasses, which lay there with his car keys, Roche was recovering from what he had seen, Jane had pulled on her pants and trousers and, without a word to him, had gone out.

He remained behind in the room, looking at the window and the stripes of light, putting on his dark glasses, raising them above his eyes, playing with the contrast of glare and cool. Apart from the first glance as he had entered the room, she had not looked at him. That throwing back of herself on the bed, the swift gesture of insertion, and, above all, the shooting of the plastic container to the corner, that gesture with her large hands: it was as though she didn't belong to her body, as though there was some spirit within her that was at odds with the body which she yet cherished and whose needs she sought to satisfy.

He stayed in the bedroom a while longer. When he went out to the porch, Jane was again lying in her chair, smoking; and Harry was swinging in his hammock, his arms tightly crossed, as though he was cold.

"Lovely, eh?" Harry said, looking out toward the sea. And after a pause: "It could be so damn lovely here, man."

His words lingered between them. Then he said, "Well, I suppose Marie-Thérèse isn't coming. And Meredith and Pamela had better hurry up. Otherwise I am man enough to start eating without them. I feel Meredith is coming late for spite, you know. Merry's getting a little funny these days. I don't know whether you notice. I hear he's getting a little closer to the powers that be. I tell you, boy, whatever people say, I'm damn happy I've acquired this Canadian landed-immigrant status, you hear?" He laughed; it turned into a choked, asthmatic gasp. "It's a damn funny way to live. When you were inside I was sitting here and looking up at that rusty hammock hook and thinking, 'I better get the place repainted soon, before that rust take hold.' And I don't even know who will be here to enjoy the house next year. It's a funny way to live, living in a place and not knowing whether you staying."

Again there was the sound of bells from the beach. It rose and fell with the wind; and then it disappeared.

Harry said, "I hate music."

Roche said, "This is a lovely rum punch, Harry. I love the nutmeggy flavor."

Jane recognized his dry, precise, rebuking tone. It puzzled her; she dismissed it.

Harry said, "It's well cured. Most of the stuff you get in bars is raw like hell."

Jane said, "I didn't mind those people down on the beach. I was fascinated. I thought I could watch that man and that woman all day."

"And they could keep it up all day," Harry said. "Those people would dance their way to hell, man. Do you know, Jane, I have never tapped my feet to music. Never."

Roche said, "When I was in jail I would play whole symphonies in my head."

Jane said, "But, Harry, I thought you would be a marvelous dancer."

"In Toronto, you know what they call me? Calypso Harry. Up there as soon as you tell people where you come from they think you're crazy about music."

Roche said, "Harry, you were born in the wrong place."

"No, man, Peter. You can't say that. But I mean. How the hell can you respect a guy who starts tapping his feet to music and jigging up in his chair? Apart from everything else, I find it looks so damn common. Especially if the guy is a little old. You feel the feller has no control at all, and that at any moment he is going to tear his clothes off and start prancing about the room. You were saying something about jail, Peter?"

"I used to play whole scores in my head. From beginning to end. No cheating. And I would time myself."

"That's the only place where it should be permitted. In jail, and in your head. But, Peter, you are serious?"

"Other people did physical exercises. Other people kept diaries. I arranged concerts for myself."

"Better you than me. But that is a hell of a thing you are telling me, man, Peter. Jane, is this true?"

"I don't know. But I suppose I can believe it."

"If I had my way I would ban music. And dancing. Make it a crime. Six months for every record you play. And hard labor for the reggae. Jane, I am serious. This is a country that has been destroyed by music. You just have to think of what is going on right now on that beach. And think how lovely and quiet it would be, eh. None of that reggae-reggae the whole blasted day."

Jane, sitting forward, said quickly, "I know what Marie-Thérèse is doing now. She's tapping her feet to music."

Harry said, "What's that guy's technique?" He sat up in his hammock. His legs, slender, brown, and sharp-shinned below the fringed Bermuda shorts, hung free; his white canvas shoes looked very big. "Ever since that girl cut loose, the language, Jane. The language that girl now uses to me. I'm ashamed to tell you. What do you suppose they're doing now? At it, eh?" He lay back in the hammock and looked at the ceiling of the porch. "At it all the time."

Jane said, "They're probably having a terrific quarrel at this minute. Sunday's a bad day for rebels. They're probably not even talking this morning."

"Calypso Harry." Harry swayed in his hammock, considering the hammock hook. "I give up explaining now. People always call you what they want. They always call you by the last place you've been. Do you know, Jane, Peter, that the surname I carry is really the name of a town in South America? Tunja. When we were in

Tunja we were called de Cordoba. And I suppose in Cordoba it was Ben-something-or-the-other. Always the last place you run from."

Roche said, "Tunja?"

"It's in Colombia. I don't know. I never went looking for the place. Nobody has heard of Tunja. And I suppose that's why it was a good place to leave. Those wars, too, you know—1830, 1840. It was the time the Siegerts were taking their Angostura business from Venezuela to Trinidad. We came here. The British Empire, the English language: I suppose it made a lot of sense. And now at least I can go anywhere. And I suppose the time has come to move on."

Jane said, with an old brightness, "The airport. Every day I look at the airport and wonder when it will close down."

"Mrs. Grandlieu," Roche said. "I don't think it will come to that."

"But you've had a good run for your money," Jane said to Harry.

Roche said, "Not better than you."

Jane leaned back in her chair. Her lips closed slowly over her teeth.

After a pause Harry said, "I don't want to go. I love this country. But when you feel the ground move below you it is damn foolishness to pretend you feel nothing. The other day I was standing outside the office with old man Sebastien. I don't know whether you know him. He is one of those manic-depressives—all their madness come out in property. He was in one of his manic moods. And when he is like that the family can't control him. Everybody selling or trying to sell, but Sebastien just want to buy now. The man come to your house at midnight. He suddenly want to buy this or he suddenly decide to buy that. I was standing up with him on the pavement, trying to cool him down and prevent him coming inside the office. And this old black feller come down the street, pushing a little box cart. Old black feller, old rummy face—thousands like him. When he reach us he stop in the road, he raise his hand and point at me and he say, 'You! You is a Jew.' Just like that, and then he move on, pushing his little cart. He didn't make any big scene. It was as though he just stop to ask me the time. Now why the hell should an old black man stop and accost me like that? He make me feel I get off the ship in 1938 with a pack on my back."

Roche said, "He was probably drunk."

"Well, yes. Drunk. But what the hell does it mean to him? What kind of funny ideas are going around this place? I don't know whether you notice how suspicious everybody is these days. Everybody nervous and a little tense. You don't feel it? Everybody feel that the other guy have some important kind of secret. Look, like the way I know people feel about me since this landed-immigrant status. Like the way I too feel about Meredith these past two–three weeks. I don't know what it is. All I know is that Merry is up to something, and I have to be a little careful. Sometimes in this place, you know, you can wonder what century you living in. Mrs. Grandlieu ever tell you how her father-in-law died? He was going round one of the estates one morning. In the middle of the morning he went back to the estate house for breakfast. He drank some water from his own icy-hot—a thermos flask, nuh—and straightaway he feel he want to vomit. You know the first thing he ask for? A basin, to vomit in. It took him six hours to die. Six hours."

"Poison," Roche said. "That's very African."

"The man vomiting up his guts. He is a dying man, and you know all he could think of? He want people to save his vomit—all his vomit—and take it to the police. That is the only thing he is talking about. And that is how he spent his last hours on earth: thinking about Negroes and the police and punishment. As though on the last day of his life he went back a hundred and fifty years and was a slave owner again. I don't want to die with thoughts like that in my head, man. And that was just in 1938, you know. You know how they catch the poisoner? A month later, Christmas week, a crazy old black woman start parading through the town, shouting and crying, 'I see Jesus! I see Mary!' She was the poisoner. And she nearly cause a riot, eh, before they put her away in the madhouse. She had nothing to do with the estate. She'd just seen old Grandlieu in the morning, that's all. When

I hear people shouting about Jesus and Mary, and I see candles on the beach, I feel funny."

Jane said, "Mrs. Grandlieu never told me that story."

"People prefer to forget certain things. But if that happened to Mrs. Grandlieu today, she would behave in exactly the same way. These people are different from you and me, Jane. This is their place. When that black feller with the box cart point at me and say 'You is a Jew,' he didn't point to Sebastien and say 'You is a white man.' He knew it was Mr. Sebastien."

The sun was edging toward that side of the porch where Roche's hammock was hung. The black shadow of the porch roof was moving at an angle to the south. The cigarette that Jane had thrown on the lawn had burnt itself out; the wind was eroding the ashy little cylinder. Sky and sea were white; the sea, splashing out of its basin, grated on the coarse sand below the cliff. Ice floated in water in the bowl on the table. The Honduras pines bent in the light breeze; the almond trees, with their big flat leaves and solid lateral branches, hardly swayed at all. The morning was over; it would soon be time for lunch: the quick climax of these Sundays at the beach house. After lunch there would be drowsiness, no talk, relaxation, rest; and then the drive back through the forest and the coconut estates and the bush to the late-afternoon dust and heat of the city.

Faintly at first, and then with growing distinctness against the breeze and the waves, there was the sound of chatter below the cliff. It was hard to ignore; they all three listened. It was not easy to tell from which direction the chatter came. To Jane it was like the sound of chatter in the gully at the foot of their garden on the Ridge. It was a group, clearly, walking fast. Soon the voices were immediately below the house; and then the unseen walkers passed on and their voices were lost.

Jane said, "I wouldn't call Mrs. Grandlieu white."

Roche said, "Not as white as you."

Harry, coming out of his abstraction, the rings below his eyes very dark, said, "That's another question. Here she is Mrs. Grandlieu. And she is not a stranger." He began again to swing in the hammock. "And still, you know, as I look up at that hook and the rust running down, I know I will get the place repainted. You can't do anything else. But it's a damn funny way to live. Listen, I think that's Meredith." He jumped out of the hammock, and left it swinging slackly.

They heard the car come into the yard. Harry went through the living room to the kitchen; and, as the engine cut out, just behind the kitchen, it seemed, and as a door banged, they heard him say, in a tone which was at first like a continuation of the tone he had been using with them, but which then became more emphatic, brisker, a performance: "Eh-eh, Merry-boy! I was just saying that you weren't coming for spite. Where is Pamela? She couldn't make it. But this is beginning to look to me like a boycott, man. Well, come in, nuh. Peter and Jane here since morning. They nearly drink out all the damn rum punch."

MEREDITH HERBERT was the first man Roche had got to know on the island, outside his work; and for some time they had remained close. They had met at dinner at Mrs. Grandlieu's; and even if they hadn't spoken at length then Meredith would have stood out. Meredith didn't pretend, as one or two of the older, and more jauntily dressed, black men did, that he was at home with Mrs. Grandlieu. His comprehension of the situation was complete. He didn't laugh at Mrs. Grandlieu's racialist jokes; he didn't respond to her provocations. Mrs. Grandlieu was reserved with him; and in Meredith's courtesy toward this middle-aged woman with the pale brown skin, who spoke deliberately badly and with an exaggerated local accent, Roche detected something like compassion for a woman whose position in the island was no longer what she thought it was.

Meredith was about forty. He had been in politics and had briefly even been a minister; but then he had fallen out with the party and resigned. He spoke of himself, and was spoken of, not as a rejected politician but as a political dropout; and this made him unusual, because politics here was often a man's only livelihood, and political failure was a kind of extinction. More than once a new minister, rising too high too fast, had come to live on the Ridge, chauffeured and guarded, embarrassing everyone, his children isolated and subdued in a large garden, carrying the slum on their faces and in their manner, until, as suddenly as they had been called up, the family had been returned to the darkness below, broken by their taste of luxury. But Meredith had other resources. He was a solicitor; and he enjoyed some celebrity for his weekly radio interview program called *Encounter*, in which he exploited his position as a political dropout and showed himself tough and cynical and no respecter of persons.

He was happily married, with a baby daughter; and he seemed able to separate his political anxieties from his private life, where he gave the impression of being at peace. In the hysteria of the Ridge—and against what Roche had first seen as the loudness and gush of Harry de Tunja—Meredith had been a restful man to be with. It was odd: Meredith, in his lucid analysis of most situations, striking off damning points on his stubby fingers, could be gloomier than anyone. But whereas other people were enervated or made restless by their anxieties, Meredith seemed untouched by his own vision of imminent chaos. Roche had once heard him say, speaking of the breakdown of institutions on the island, "We are living in a house without walls." Yet Meredith lived as though the opposite were true. In his delight in the practice of the law, which he said exercised him totally, extended all his gifts, in his delight in his radio work, in his pleasure in his family (his wife came from an established mulatto family), in his housebuilding and homemaking, there seemed to be a certainty that the world would continue, and the place he had made for himself in it. And to Roche, new to the island, this combination of political concern and private calm had been restful.

But the relationship had not survived Jane's coming. To Jane, not looking in those early days for what was restful, and even then having no taste for the political or economic complexities that Meredith liked to analyze, Meredith was "suburban." And Meredith, holding a doll in one hand, and leading his infant daughter to the garden gate to wave good-by to Jane after her first visit, did appear too domesticated and settled: Roche could see that. Jane also decided that Meredith was boring; and then she decided that he was ugly. Roche said she was being trivial. She knew it; but, noticing the effect she had made, she insisted. "I can't get over his looks." And what had only been one of her offhand, unconsidered judgments—that Meredith was suburban—she had, perversely, cherished into a settled attitude. Between Jane and Meredith there had quickly grown up a muted mutual antagonism; and Roche, although he knew the antagonism to be artificial, issuing from Jane's casual, instinctive cruelty toward people with whom she was not concerned, this cruelty part of her laziness, her refusal to be bothered, Roche was affected.

As the two men drifted apart, as they ceased to be easy with one another, Roche began to see Meredith's personality—the personality that had attracted him and seemed so restful—as a creation. In Meredith's domesticity he began to see an element of exaggeration and defiance. He began to detect the strains behind the personality. In Meredith's capacity to enervate others without appearing to be touched himself Roche began to have intimations of Meredith's own hysteria, of the rages, deprivations, and unappeased ambition that perhaps lay behind that domesticity he flaunted. Meredith's character, once dissected in this way, could no longer appear whole again, could no longer be taken for what it appeared to be. Roche began to be wary of Meredith. And he moved then toward Harry de Tunja, who continued to be as he always had been and, surprisingly, turned out to be just as he appeared: a man without secrets, who made his private anxieties public, a man whose manner never varied, whose business life flowed into his social life.

"SO PAMELA couldn't make it, eh," Harry said, leading Meredith out of the dark living room to the porch. Harry's thick-soled canvas shoes flashed white at the end of his slender brown legs and appeared comically large. "Everybody behaving as though what happen between Marie-Thérèse and me is like a wedding in reverse. Some people on the groom side, some people on the bride side."

Meredith, coming onto the porch, and acting out his entrance, said with a heavy local accent, "I hear she giving the feller hell, man, Harry. She after him to acquire landed-immigrant status."

"Oh God, Merry, man. You too?"

Meredith was short and walked with a spring. He was slender but his body looked hard: he was heavier than he looked. He wore a white shirt with a button-down collar; it was unbuttoned at the neck but not too open, and it didn't suggest holiday dress. The shirt was too tight over his solid shoulders, the collar was too close to the neck: a tie seemed to be missing.

Still making his entrance, he stood on the porch, swinging his hands together, rapping a box of matches against a pack of cigarettes. He said, "Jane."

"Hello, Meredith." She had rearranged her legs on the chair.

Meredith said, "Peter, I want to see you."

"Is it good or bad?"

"That depends on you. Don't look so frightened. We'll talk later. What have you been doing this morning?" He sat down on the aluminum-framed stool beside Roche's hammock.

Harry said, "The usual thing, nuh. We went for a walk on the beach. And we watched those people doing their business." He made it sound a morning of pure pleasure. "Have you seen them?"

Meredith took a glass of rum punch. He said, "There's a lot of mad people in this place."

Jane said, "Are they mad?"

Harry said, "They're not sane."

"Jane doesn't believe they're sane either," Roche said.

"The visitor's courtesy," Meredith said. "Cheers. 'We're just like you. You're just like us.' What's new with Sablich's these days, Peter?"

"I'm not sure I'm the person to ask," Roche said. "I've decided to leave."

Harry looked alarmed. "But you never told me, Peter."

Meredith, sipping rum punch, smiled at Jane. "So you're leaving us, Jane."

She said, "It's the first I've heard of it."

Roche said, "I've only just decided." He laughed and showed his molars. "It's all these mad people I've been hearing about."

Harry, sitting in his hammock, and moving back and forth, the tips of his canvas shoes touching the terrazzo floor, said, "But this place is full of mad people, for truth. I was just thinking about it the other day. I was at the races, and I was buying some nuts from 'Nuts and Bolts'—you know the guy? And it suddenly hit me that all those people selling peanuts and cashew nuts are mad like hell. I say it suddenly hit me, but I've known it since I was a child. I always knew those fellers were mad like hell. The funny thing is I never found it funny. And, you know, once you realize you have madmen running about the place, you start seeing them everywhere. It's a damn frightening thing."

Meredith said, "You sound worried, Harry."

"In any other country those guys would be put away. I don't know how we start the fashion here that the moment a guy get mad he must hook up two big baskets on his arms, put on tennis shoes and start walking about the place, shouting, 'Nuts, nuts.'"

Meredith said, "I will keep an eye on you."

Jane said, "It sounds the most marvelous therapy."

Roche said, "It will give a new dimension to swinging London."

"An overgrown idiot boy lived near my elementary school," Meredith said. "He was white. A big boy. He couldn't close his mouth. He used to point at us and say, 'Bam! Bam!' That was all he wanted to do, to play cowboys-and-Indians with you. You could make him very happy if you bammed back. But that was committing yourself to a term-long relationship. We called him Bam. That was all. Nobody troubled him. He was just part of the scenery."

Jane said, "How very humane."

"Humane?" Harry said. "That is our downfall. We encourage too much slackness."

Meredith said, "I think we should ask Peter about that."

"I used to think we had to work with what was there. I don't know what I think now."

"We don't make enough allowance for the madness," Meredith said. "Read the papers, listen to the radio, read any government report: you will feel that we're all very logical, rational people and we know where we want to go. I suppose that was my mistake. I knew about the madness. I knew about it in my bones. I grew up with the damn thing, after all. Like you, Harry. But I pretended it didn't exist. I don't know how it happens, but the moment you start thinking or writing or worrying about resources and your five-year plan, you forget the madness. You forget about those people down there on the beach. A good politician should never do that."

Harry said, "But that's a hell of a thing you're telling us, Merry. This place could be a paradise, man, if people really planned. We could have real industries. We don't have to let the Americans just take away our bauxite."

"I traveled out with two of the bauxite Americans," Jane said. "They spent all their time on the plane reading pornography. The hard stuff. *Easy Lay* and *Sucked Dry*."

"We could have real industries," Harry said, lying down in his hammock, his chest singing asthmatically, creating an effect of accompanying bird song. "Not this nonsense we have. One factory, one rich white businessman, one rich black politician."

"All this is true," Meredith said. "But they may not want what you want for them. They want other things. The people down there by the river have other needs."

"Oh God, man, Merry, you know a lot of those fellers are just damn corrupt. You say so yourself. It make me so damn sad, seeing boys I go to school with going in for this thing. You always try to tell yourself, 'Oh, this guy is still right. That guy is still okay.' And then one day you see the feller with his belly hanging over his waistband, and you know he gone the way of all flesh. Jane, you know that? The moment you see one of these fellers getting to the belly-hanging-over-waistband stage you know how his mind working. You know what happen to him. It is the only thing you have to look for. The belly and the waistband. It make me so damn ashamed, man, to see those fellers at parties. Jane, they will take two drinks at the same time. And they will eat as though they've never seen food."

Meredith said, "They're very hungry."

He had been looking at Harry with a fixed wounded smile.

This smile, and the way he held his head, drew attention to the wide space between his nose and his mouth. This part of his face looked especially vulnerable: here could still be seen the bullied schoolboy he had perhaps been. And there was about his reply to Harry something of the pertness of the schoolboy.

Harry crossed his legs in the hammock and looked out at the dazzling sea. "Twenty, thirty years ago, everybody was lifting weights. You would see people exercising in every back yard. You remember the body-beautiful craze, Merry? It was a lovely thing, man. It used to make you feel so good. You remember how those boys used to walk?"

" 'Wings,' " Meredith said, and laughed. He put down his glass and acted out the posture: squaring his shoulders, raising his elbows, and letting his hands hang loose. "The gorilla walk. But those were the needs of those days."

Harry said, "We're not talking the same language."

"You are pretending you don't understand me," Meredith said. His smile had vanished, and he spoke precisely, with an edge in his voice. "If those people down on the beach were a little saner, don't you think they would burn the place down twice a year? Madness keeps the place going."

Jane said, "It's very convenient for Mrs. Grandlieu."

"Convenient for everybody. Convenient for you and me and Harry and Peter and Sablich's." But the edge had gone out of Meredith's voice. And when he spoke again it was with a rallying tone, in a local accent: "But still, eh, Harry? After Israel, Africa."

"Well, Merry-boy," Harry said, floundering. "I don't know. But if it say so in the Bible . . ."

Roche said, "Does the Bible say anything like that?"

Meredith said, laughing, and in the same rallying tone, "I suppose you have to look hard. But tell me, Jane, how did you get on with Mr. Leung's son?"

She said, "You mean Jimmy Ahmed?"

He smiled at her. "At school I knew him as Jimmy Leung. Did you look into his eyes and understand the meaning of hate?"

She was puzzled.

"I was just quoting from an interview in one of the English papers. An interview by some woman. When she wrote about Jimmy she became all cunt."

Harry said, "Merry, man."

Meredith fixed a smile on Harry and, spacing out the words, said, as if in explanation, "She was all cunt."

Harry said, "I don't know what kind of language I'm hearing these days."

"I was in London when this great Negro leader burst upon the scene. And I must say it was news to me. I had always thought of him as Mr. Leung's son, trying to get into the Chinese scene over here and talking about going to China to advise Mao Tse-tung."

Roche laughed. "Is this true?"

"You know people over here. They believe that everybody in China is either like Charlie Chan or Fu-Manchu. I was with the BBC at the time, and they asked me to go and do a little three-minuter with this black rebel. I went to an address in Wimbledon. It turned out to be a bloody big house. I can't tell you about the architecture or the period—I didn't have those eyes at the time. You grow up in a place like this, you don't know anything about architecture. To me a house was just a house. It was old or new, big or small, poor or rich. This was a rich, big house. And this was where the leader was living. With the woman who was managing him. I can see now that she was middle class or upper class or something like that. But all I saw then was a white woman in a big house. She was arranging all the publicity, and I sat down in that big drawing room and watched that man behaving like one of those toys you wind up. And that tall woman with the flat hips was looking on, very, very happy with her little Pekingese black. And he walked up and down yapping away. She was disconcerted by me. A real Negro. But you see how bogus the whole news thing is. That woman was the story. I really should have been interviewing her. But I just recorded the yapping and edited it down to three minutes for the evening program. That was my little contribution to the Jimmy Ahmed story."

Jane said, "Was she the woman he married?"

Harry said, "You see what I mean about encouragement? Jane, why did people in England give that man so much encouragement? I can't tell you the amount of nonsense we used to read in the papers."

Meredith said, "I regard him as one of the more dangerous men in this place."

Roche said, "He would be very pleased to hear you say that."

"He's dangerous because he's famous, because he has a lot of that English glamour still, and because he's nothing at all. 'Daddy, am I Chinese?' 'No, my boy. You're just my child.' The Chinese don't have any hangups about that kind of thing at all. No encouragement there at all. And ever since then you can do anything you like with Jimmy Ahmed. Anybody can use that man and create chaos in this place. He can be programed. He's the most suggestible man I know."

Roche said, "I've never found him so."

Meredith said, "You offered him the wrong things."

Harry, laughing before he spoke, said, "You offered him work."

"I didn't offer him anything," Roche said. "I only tried to help him do what he said he wanted to do."

"I know," Meredith said quickly, nodding. "Land, the revolution based on land. That was the London programing. But if you think Jimmy was going to come here and bury himself in the bush, you don't know Jimmy. Jimmy has to go on and on. There's a kind of—what's the word? Not dynamism."

Jane said, "Dynamic."

"There's a kind of dynamic about his condition that has to work itself out. In England it ended with rape and indecent assault. The same dynamic will take him to the end here."

Roche said, "How do you think it will end here?"

"He might be a millionaire. He might be the next prime minister. It all depends on how he's programed. In the kind of situation we have here anything is possible. One thing I'll tell you: Jimmy isn't going to end quietly in the bush buggering a couple of slum boys."

"That's what Jimmy feels too," Roche said. "I think you're both exaggerating."

Harry said, "I don't think so."

"Tomorrow," Meredith said, "that man might say something or make some gesture or stumble into some kind of incident, and overnight he could be a hero. The white-woman rape, running away from England, the hater of the Chinese: he can touch many chords. I know. I just have to study myself. I don't have to try too hard to remember how I used to feel when I was a child about the Chinese shops. Jimmy always talks about being born in the back room of a Chinese shop. And in England that sounded nice and deprived. But I used to envy Jimmy. And most boys were like me, eh. A shop—how could a thing like that ever go bust? A shop had everything. It was a place where your mother sometimes sent you to get things on trust. I used to pass the Leung shop four times a day. It was on the way to school. Jimmy's mother was a very pretty woman. Brown skin, lovely features, Spanish type, with a mass of black hair under her arms. I can't tell you how that hair excited me. Long before I could do anything about it. I never went through that queer phase you read about. I was always straight. I used to envy old Leung, and I used to think: You can get a woman like that only if you have money, if you have a shop. To me that was just a fact of life, that our women went to live with Chinese shopkeepers. There was nothing you could do about it. Nobody had to tell me anything: I knew that that side of life was closed to me."

Childhood, Roche thought: it was odd here how people spoke about their childhoods, as of a period only just discovered and understood. But Meredith had never spoken like this before, and Roche wondered whether Meredith knew how much he was revealing of himself.

Harry said, "I can't believe that, Meredith."

"And it wasn't even what we call a grocery," Meredith said. "A grocery was something else. Nice concrete blocks, solid, properly built, with a proper sign."

Harry said, "You can sell liquor in a grocery."

"The Leung shop was just a little shack, with a rusty galvanized roof and a broken-up floor and crooked walls coming down to the pavement. But it took me a long time to see it for what it was. I don't believe I saw that place as it was until I came back from England. We're all born as blind as kittens in this place. All of us. We can see nothing, and we remain like that even when we are educated, even when we go abroad. Look at me, working for the BBC and going to that house in Wimbledon with the tape recorder on my shoulder, and not understanding anything about the house or the woman. Just seeing a white woman and a half-Chinese man in a big house. It can take a long time to start seeing. And then you can see and see and see. You can go on seeing, but you must stop. You can start forgetting what you felt when you were a child. You can start forgetting who you are. If you see too much, you can end up living by yourself in a house on a hill. That was beginning to happen to me."

"I never thought that was true about you, Merry," Harry said. "Everything you said made a lot of sense to me. But if a man like you start talking like this, then this place has no future."

"You were never blind, Harry," Meredith said. "The one man in the country."

"If you think we should all start jigging up to the reggae, not me, eh. If I had my way I would ban music here."

"What do you mean by the future? What do you want? Different people want different things. Jane doesn't want what you want. If you had one wish, Jane, what would you ask for? Shall we play that game?"

From the beach there came the sound of chatter again, and they all listened: the group returning, walking as briskly, their voices more animated now, and one voice—hard to tell whether it belonged to a man or woman—breaking into a shriek of laughter just below the house.

Harry said, "Joseph will be wanting to go and have his dip. You are staying for lunch, Merry?"

"No, man. Pamela."

Jane said, "Let's play the game. Ask me my one wish."

Meredith said, "Tell us."

Jane said, "I want lots and lots of money."

Meredith said, "I thought you would say that."

"You took the words out of my mouth," Roche said. "You never miss an occasion, my dear."

Meredith said, "Harry?"

"Occasion?" Jane said.

"To tell us how privileged you think you are," Roche said.

Harry said, "My one wish? Well, Merry-boy, I think a lot about this one. And I suppose the truthful answer is that I want nothing. At the moment all I want is to get Marie-Thérèse back."

Meredith said, "You mean you want to be in a position where you want nothing?"

"Merry, you putting words in my mouth. I know what you driving at. No, man, I mean nothing. I don't want to want anything."

Roche said, "You want to be a vegetable."

"You can put it like that."

Jane said, "How horrible."

"What a restless man you are, Harry," Meredith said. "You've given yourself away completely. Peter?"

Roche said, lingering over each word, "I would like to have the most enormous sexual powers."

Jane, blowing out cigarette smoke in her ugly way, through wet lips, said, "That would solve nothing."

Meredith smiled. "But it would be a lot of fun."

"We can't get away from the subject today," Harry said.

Roche said, "And you, Meredith?"

Meredith continued to smile at Jane. Then his expression became serious. He raised his head slightly, so that again the great gap between his everted nostrils and his mouth was noticeable. He paused; he was creating a silence, as though to frame a prepared statement. He said, "I would like to express myself fully." And for a while he held his head in the same raised position, and the expression on his face, of the bullied schoolboy, remained unchanged. So that, black, and the only one among them sitting upright, he seemed central and solitary on the porch, distinct in

the light, sitting on the thin striped cushion of the low stool. At
last he relaxed and began to smile again.

Harry said, "But you're cheating, man, Merry. You ask us
to say one thing. And you say four or five things. It's as though
you ask a guy to tell you in one word what he want, and he say
'Everything.' "

"I don't think I'm cheating. I would say I'm asking for less
than you. When I am about to die I want to feel that I have lived.
I can even put it negatively. I don't want to feel that I've been
denied life." He spoke with seriousness, making no attempt to
match Harry's jovial tone. And again he seemed to be sitting
on the porch as on a stage, against the white sky and dazzling
sea.

Jane said, "This is getting creepy."

"You think so?" Meredith said. "The really creepy thing about
people is how little they expect of themselves. Or for themselves.
That is the creepy thing."

Roche said, "Human ambition is limitless."

"But capacity is restricted," Meredith said. "We can prove
that right now, the four of us. Do we have time?"

Jane said, "Is it another game?"

Harry sat up in his hammock. He was wheezing; the flesh
around his sunken eyes looked bruised. He said, and his chest
sang through his words, "Joseph is getting a little cantankerous."

Jane said, "Let's play the game."

Harry got out of the hammock and moved toward the living
room. "You people just hearing pots and pans in the background.
And you think Joseph is just doing his stuff. But with Joseph I am
like a mother with a baby. I know the meaning of every noise he
make. And I'm telling you: Joseph is getting damn mad."

Meredith said, "When you come out, Harry, bring a pencil
and paper."

Harry sucked his teeth and went inside. A wheezy whisper was
followed by muffled bass noises. Pots and pans banged. And when
Harry came out again, with a pencil and a "Don't Forget" pad,
he was wheezing hard.

Meredith took the pad and began to write. He said, "I am

writing down the answer you will all give to a question I'm going to put to you."

Jane said, "That doesn't sound much of a game, if we're all going to give the same answer."

"You mustn't anticipate, Jane." Meredith stopped writing and put the pad face down on the terrazzo floor. "I am not asking for one word or one sentence. In fact, I want you to be as imaginative as possible."

"If this one has a catch," Harry said, "I don't want to play."

"There is no catch," Meredith said. "You have everything you want. Right? Everything, anything. It's all been granted. All I want to know is how you spend a full day. A working day, if you're still working. I want it in detail. You can create any personality for yourself. But you mustn't duck the question. I don't want a catalogue of the things you own or your talents or your achievements. I want to see you living with all your blessings through twenty-four hours. Just remember this, though: If you're the world's greatest painter, you will be spending a lot of time painting."

Jane said, "But I can't answer just like that. I will have to think about it." `

"That's a good answer," Meredith said. "I think it proves my point."

"And then I don't know whether I want to tell you about my perfect day.'

"Who was talking about a perfect day? That's a woman's reaction. But all right, Jane. You've dropped out."

Roche said, "That doesn't mean that her expectations aren't great."

"It means they are very vague. And the whole point of the exercise is that you've got not to be vague. I didn't want to say this before, but this isn't a game that women can play. Their expectations have to do with somebody else. Like that perfect day we aren't going to hear about. A woman can't visualize too well because she has too many possibilities. She can be anything. Anything can happen to her. But it's out of her hands. It all depends on this man who's going to find her. That's a terrible thing, if you think about it. I often think that if I were a woman I would be very frightened."

Roche said, with a faint smile at Jane, "Jane doesn't look very frightened."

She said brusquely, "I've dropped out."

"Harry doesn't want time to think," Meredith said. "Start, Harry. Let's see you getting up in the morning. Lovely bedroom, fabulous view, fabulous house."

"Well, yes. I will take a little honey, and then I suppose I will do my yoga."

Meredith said, "You don't have asthma. You've got rid of that."

"I will still take the honey. And I will still do the yoga."

"Excellent."

"Then a little walk around the garden, I suppose. And I'm not looking at sand and sticks. No drought."

"Fantastic garden," Meredith said. "But where's this house? In what country?"

"I love this country. But you know the situation."

"There is total stability wherever you are. You have absolute security."

"I have to think of the children. They're more ambitious than me. I think it will have to be in Toronto. Well, after breakfast, nuh, with a little honey, I go to the office."

"Fabulous business," Meredith said.

"No, nothing too big. No fun in running something that get too big and you can't feel it. I get to the office before anybody else. I find it cool and quiet and clean. I love being in a clean office first thing in the morning. Nobody around you, nobody talking, your desk empty. That's when I do my thinking, in that first half hour. All kinds of fantastic ideas come to me. I see how I have to play this and play that, and I feel in control. Then the guys start coming in, the letters come up, and work starts. In the middle of the morning the guys come in with some problem that is driving them frantic. Well, I listen to them and I go through the papers and I straightaway see how you have to play the thing. I say so-so-so-so. And the guys fall back in amazement. And they know why I am the boss. Well, lunchtime, nuh. Nothing too elaborate. You know me. As soon as I eat or drink too much I start choking."

"This is excellent, Harry," Meredith said. He got up and passed the pad on which he had written to Jane.

"I'm forgetting," Harry said. "There is no music anywhere. I am not hearing music anywhere. In the afternoon I dictate half a dozen magnificent letters. I've been turning them over in my head all day, and at three o'clock I call the girl in and I'm ready to go. And that's it. Eight or nine problems. All settled, and I feel I can look forward to developments. I'm planning years ahead, you know. At four o'clock I'm feeling damn good. And everything I do now is like a reward."

Jane read what Meredith had written and began to laugh.

Harry said, "Am I saying something funny?"

She said, "No, no. Go on, Harry. Do go on."

"In the evening I go back home and walk around the garden and do a little yoga and splash about in the pool. Then I shower and put on clean clothes. I love clean cotton. And then some lovely friends come for dinner. And then we end up in the bar."

"And that's it?" Meredith said.

"I suppose so."

Jane said, "Meredith is right."

She took the pad back to Meredith, and he passed it to Roche.

Roche read: *The life being described is the life the speaker lives or a life he has already lived. The setting may change, but no one will make a fresh start or do anything new.*

Harry got out of the hammock and said, "Let me see, Peter."

They all stood up. The sun was slicing across one corner of the porch. The light was hard; the parched lawn was beginning to reflect heat.

Roche said, "I suppose that's true of me too. I was changing the setting. So I wouldn't feel I had to do anything about anything."

"Release," Meredith said, and at that moment was like a friend again. "That would be lovely. Just to be oneself. That's how I see it too."

Roche said, "I was trying to see myself in this new setting as a successful lawyer. I feel like you. The law engages the whole personality. Scholarship, memory, judgment, knowledge of men—"

Jane said, "But you didn't mention Marie-Thérèse, Harry."

"I thought about it, but somehow I didn't want to."

Meredith said, "Don't believe him. He wasn't sure. But that's standard. Men who play this game seldom mention sex. The man who has everything takes that for granted. Cruel but true." He was standing beside Jane. She was as tall as he. He began to rise and fall on his toes, began again to swing his arms, slapping the matchbox against the cigarette pack. He said, "But we might talk more about this, Peter. On the radio. I've had you on my *Encounter* list for a long time. As a matter of fact, it's what I wanted to see you about. You should have been on the program a long time ago. But I wanted to let you settle down. I don't think there's any point in asking a man who's just arrived what he thinks about the place."

Roche said, "Now that I know, I'm relieved. But I suppose I'll have to ask Sablich's."

Meredith said, "They'll give you a bonus. It'll be very nice for them. The format's quite simple. We'll record for an hour and cut it down to twenty-five minutes. Roughly what we've been talking about. Something offbeat. Nothing about our beaches and our wonderful hospitality or the way we look after our old people. I'll telephone you next week."

He rose on his toes, small, solid, bowed to Jane, said, "Jane," and then, arms swinging, matchbox striking cigarette pack, he walked with his springy step through the dark living room, acting his exit as he had acted his entrance, saying loudly, in a local accent, "But, Harry, where Joseph? Joseph gone? Take care he don't leave you too, eh, Harry."

The car door slammed. The engine started.

Harry said, "Well, all right, man, Merry. Nice of you to come over. Love to Pamela, eh. And tell her the boycott over. Well, right, man."

The car moved away, and Harry came back into the living room, wheezing, looking very tired.

Joseph had gone down to the beach. But he had laid the table in the alcove at the far end of the living room and had put out the food on the ledge of the wide kitchen hatch.

Harry said, "Well, sit down, nuh."

His tone was the jocular tone he had used seeing Meredith off. But his voice had grown hoarse. All at once he closed his eyes, held up quivering hands, and said, "I feel like screaming. I feel I should go out somewhere and cut my throat."

Roche said, "Count ten, Harry."

And while Jane squeezed in between the bench and the table in the alcove, Harry put his hands on his hips, lifted his head and began to take short, noisy breaths. When, eventually, the spasm was controlled, and they were all seated, he said, "That man draws something from me these days. It isn't so much what he says. It's a kind of feeling he gives off. When you look at his face and that little smile you feel: Oh my God, what's the use, why do anything. And you want to push your hand through a glass window. And he always ends up looking so damn happy. That gets me so mad, man."

Jane said, "I can't get over his looks. He mesmerizes me. When he was sitting down on that low chair I thought he looked like a wistful little frog."

Roche said, "That probably explains a lot."

"He was aggressive today, man," Harry said. "I'm sorry, Jane. I'm very sorry. But I've never heard Meredith use language like that before in company."

Jane said, "I scarcely hear what he's saying. I just sit and admire."

Harry said, "Somebody's given him a sniff of power. You notice he didn't say too much about his perfect day? I was waiting to hear whether he was prime minister. But he didn't mention politics at all."

Roche said, "I can understand that."

"No, man," Harry said. "He wants power. Or what he thinks is power. I've been hearing stories. And he is a damn fool. They will chew him up again. And this time he will really mash up his life. I don't know how he thinks he can go down to the beach and talk to those people. They don't want to hear anyone like Meredith."

Roche said, "That's why he's so worried. He knows he will be chewed up."

"I don't know how a man can change so much," Harry said. "Jane, you wouldn't believe what fun it used to be with Meredith. Terrible things would happen in this place, and then you would hear Meredith talk and he would put everything in place for you and your mind would be settled. You would feel that with people like that things couldn't be so bad. But look today. You know, I've never heard Meredith talk so much about Jimmy Ahmed. To Meredith the man was a joke. Today he talk as though he want to kill the guy."

"He's jealous of that woman in Wimbledon," Jane said. "I suppose he wants us to look in his eyes too and understand the meaning of hate."

Roche said, with his laugh, "He doesn't have to try. I was trying to work out that last game he made us play. It works, doesn't it? I suppose the proposition is really very simple. I suppose it's just a demonstration of the fact that we are what we are, and can't imagine ourselves being anybody else. I don't suppose it's more than that."

Harry said, " 'The life you will lead is the life you have led.' That's a damn depressing thing to tell people on a Sunday morning."

Roche said, "It depends on how you look at it. It can be comforting as well."

" 'Nobody will make a new life,' " Harry said. "No, man. He's got me wrong."

It was nearly the end of this Sunday at the beach house. They were heavy with rum punch and food, fatigued by the light. They fell silent. It was the time when Marie-Thérèse, in her long dress, would go round and whisper to her guests, proposing rest, or a game of draughts or chess, or a walk to the estuary, or a drive into the bush. Her soft presence then would keep the holiday alive.

Without her the house went dead. Outside was white light, the repetitive beat of the sea on the steep and narrow shore rim, the faint ring of a bell, faint chatter borne on the wind. Open to wind and light, the house on the cliff felt empty and abandoned.

11

FOR A WHILE the road stayed close to the coast: the dazzle of the afternoon sea; rocky coves now half in shadow; little bays where no one bathed, where jagged rocks pushed out of smooth gray sand; white, sunlit spray on black-brown reefs. Then the sea noise was left behind, and they were in the high woods, where three or four kinds of a wild, spiny palm grew among tall white-trunked trees hung with creepers with giant shining heart-shaped leaves. The road was like a green tunnel. But the woods which looked so thick and old had been destroyed in many places. Patches of scorched openness, where secondary bush looked collapsed and brown, showed the drought; and the light there was hard and still. Sometimes, for stretches, the woods were only a screen beside the road, and the hard light and the openness behind showed through.

Jane was tired and strained. She was pale, and her eyes, as always at times of stress, were moist.

She said, "Do you think Marie-Thérèse will go back?"

Roche said, "I used to think so until today. Now I'm not so sure. Seeing Harry today makes you understand what she's had to put up with."

"Harry's cosy little world is breaking up." She spoke absently. " 'Man, you come to de beach house dis Sunday, man.' "

Roche said, "It looked cosy to us. I wonder whether it was ever cosy."

Jane said, "Well." And a little later she added, "Everything has its season."

He recognized the sentence as one of his own. He said, "I suppose we must seem pretty cosy to them too. We're just visitors."

"I'm damn glad I'm a visitor."

The high woods gradually gave way to secondary bush: overgrown old cocoa estates and coffee estates, with tall shade trees that here and there gave an impression of forest. They passed derelict old cocoa drying houses, with once movable roofs that ran on rails, some roofs now forever open. Occasionally, in dirt yards beside the road, there were little rotting shacks, hollow and flimsy-looking with doors and windows open, tin roofs eaten up with rust, old unpainted wood the color of ashes; and sometimes there were little shack villages, with a collapsing shop on stilts, tin advertisements bright on its open doors, a glass case of soft bread and cakes on the counter, and on the shelves, as gray and mottled as the outer walls, jars of cheap sweets and upright bottles of sweet carbonated drinks. Sometimes there was a small timber church or church hall. Sometimes a signboard, as bright as a shop sign, on what looked like a private house, announced a hall of a private sect. And on the road were groups walking to worship, dressed up in the heat of the afternoon, the men in dark suits and brown shoes, the women in flimsy pink or yellow dresses showing the satin chemise below, the shadows of the walkers falling black on the black asphalt road that wound through the hilly land.

Children played in some yards. Sometimes, on a veranda, a bare-backed man, face and hands blacker than his chest, as though scorched by a fire, sat in a hammock made of an old sugar sack and held a naked baby. Father and child: the tedium of Sunday in the bush. This was a busy road. The crowded city was just over two hours away. Yet these villages seemed insulated from the weekend holiday traffic: charmed villages, stranded in time, belonging to another era, an era that contained no possibility of a future.

Jane said, "It's depressing, isn't it? It's so hard for me to remember that when I first came I was dazzled. That morning you drove me from the airport. I was very tired. I couldn't take anything in. But I thought I was going to get to know it well, and I thought it was very beautiful. That was the best day. Now that I know I'm not going to stay I don't see it any longer. I wouldn't care if I never drove along this road again. Meredith was awful, wasn't he? You see, I was right about him. You told me he was so very urbane."

"He's certainly been holding back on a few things."

"I never thought the word could be applied to someone who looked like that. He was so crestfallen when you said you were leaving."

Roche smiled.

Jane said, "His little frog's face absolutely collapsed. He doesn't like you being here, and he's hurt when you say you're going. He just wants you to stay so that he can play his little games with you."

"He was very hostile. He didn't make any secret of that."

"His hostility doesn't matter."

Roche smiled: his satyr's smile. "I don't suppose it does. Not to you at any rate."

"He's the kind of man you have to slap down right from the start. If you don't want to play there's nothing he can do about it."

"It isn't a game, Jane. You just don't make a hit and run back to base."

"All that talk of fuck and cunt. I suppose he expected me to scream and jump on a chair. And I know it's just that rich woman in Wimbledon he's riled about."

"I'd never heard of her before, I must say. I'd only heard about the interview. And I suppose that from a place like this she must look more and more goddesslike. To both of them."

"Both of them? You mean Jimmy Ahmed?"

Roche didn't reply.

Jane said, "Do you know who she is?"

He said with sudden irritation, "I don't know *everything*. I've just told you. I've only just heard of her."

"I was thinking of the photograph in his sitting room. The children without the mother." Then, after a pause, in a delayed response to his irritation, she said, "I thought you knew something about this place. Something special. Why did you come here? How did you hear about it? What did you think you could do here?"

"I knew as little as you. I knew only what I read in the papers. I thought there would be something for me to do here. Real work, not what I'd been doing before. A regular nine-to-fiver. That was the point I thought Harry was making, and I feel like him. Work is very restful. But if I'd played Meredith's game beforehand I suppose I would have known differently."

" 'No one makes a new life.' "

"It's a little more complicated than that for me. It isn't that I just can't see the future. I've got to the stage where I can't even see what a good future for me would be. If I were being really honest, I suppose I would have told Meredith what you said. That I needed time to think. Harry can dream of Toronto and his sky-scraper—I believe that's how Harry sees it, don't you? But I no longer have an idea of what I want to do. I'm afraid I've stopped thinking of myself as a politician. It's odd, but I realize that's what I've spent my whole adult life thinking of myself as. And now there's nothing to replace it. A man just has so many years of optimism. I'd never thought of that, and it isn't the kind of thing people tell you about."

"Do you think Harry will manage in Toronto? He's all right here. But he doesn't really know what business is. They will chew him up up there."

"A man like Harry will get on anywhere. You'll be all right too. You'll just make a fresh start, in spite of what Meredith says."

"You think so?" she said irritably, and looked out of the window.

He could see it so clearly. That irritation, that looking out of the window, enabled him to see it so clearly: her instinctive display, an extension of her display now, in the car, against this alien background of bush. He could see how the past few months could be reduced to another episode of betrayal and violation. He could see the irritability, the brightness, the hysteria, the reaching out toward the new person that would seem so wholehearted, so final, so full of flattery for that new person: the reaching out that would yet conceal her own certainties, would be without risk, and would commit her to nothing.

He said, "London awaits. You've huffed and puffed, but you've always known you'd never blow it down. If you knew you were really going to blow it down you'd be very frightened. Don't you think a man like Meredith understands that? Are you really so surprised by his attitude?"

"I'm not interested in what Meredith thinks."

The road was turning toward the sea again, and the cocoa-and-coffee woods had given place to bush, the yellowing bush of a treeless swampland. The shallow ponds had dried down to hard, cracked mud.

Roche said, "I suppose Meredith's being brave. This place can be blown down, and this place is all he's got. He sees what you and I see. Every day he's got to reconcile himself to it."

An iron bridge, painted silver, spanned a slow river that flowed between mangrove. The river, reflecting the mangrove, was yellow-green. The level of the water had fallen; the exposed thickets of mangrove roots were hung with shreds of old slime that had dried to the color of dust. Between massively bolted girders the car rattled over the planks on the bridge. The sunlight fell yellow on the yellow-green water, crisscrossed by the shadows of the girders. And momentarily, driving down the embankment from the bridge, seeing the shallow creeks the color of rust that flowed into the river they had just crossed, getting some idea of a primeval land-scape, sun and slime, heat and vegetable decay, momentarily Roche had a sense of desolation.

He said, "It's funny how they talk about their childhoods here. Jimmy, Meredith. As though it's so far away. As though it belongs to another century. And as though they've just found out about it."

The land flattened, the road entered a coconut plantation. And all at once it seemed to be late afternoon. The road was narrow, a crust of asphalt and gravel on the sand. The gray trunks of the coconut trees were very tall and curved. There were so many of them and they were set so regularly that from the car they seemed to be moving, crisscrossing the band of bright sky and the long, low, muddy breakers, white in the afternoon light, to which the eye was led beyond the debris of the coconut plantation: dead palm fronds, brown and shining, coconut husks in heaps, yellow-green nuts awaiting collection. It would photograph well. The camera would get everything, even the muddy olive color of the stripe of sea beyond the breakers, even the yellow froth on the beach. It wouldn't get the desolation: the desolation they had driven through to arrive at this spot, the desolation of the late afternoon, the idea of darkness and the end of the day, the desolation of the dim lights soon to come on in the white-washed hutments of the plantation workers.

Every coconut tree was numbered in black; many were ringed with an orange-colored blight-deterrent. And the plantation continued.

Roche said, "No wonder they talk about their childhoods. It is here, waiting for them. When you look at this you feel you've gone back fifty years."

It was not a beach for bathing. But here and there in the sand, in safe places away from coconut trees and falling nuts, there were old cars, with open doors, and small groups of people. Poor people: ugly girls from poor houses with all their girlish instincts: other people's pleasures, hopes, gaieties. Other people's Sundays: Jane thought of Harry's beach house, empty on the cliff; she thought of darkness falling on the estuary. She thought of darkness coming to their house on the Ridge. The coconut trees crisscrossed in the gloom; the far-away sea glinted in the afternoon light. Her fatigue and irritability began to be replaced by fear. It was not defined; it was fixed on nothing in particular; but it had been maturing all day. She decided that the time had come to leave: escape was urgent.

Roche took off his dark glasses, unnecessary in the coconut gloom. She glanced at him. She saw distress in his eyes.

She said, "It must be hard for you."

He said simply, "Yes, it is hard. On a day like this."

They passed a rough little wooden stall beside the road. A whole family sat or stood around the stall, obviously their own, which offered a few vegetables and bright, speckled fruit. And not long after they passed a group of strolling women who wore pink and blue plastic curlers, and some men who wore short khaki trousers and nothing else.

Roche said with sudden passion, "I loathe all these people. I hate this place."

Her own irritability and melancholy vanished. She had known him calm, ironic, sarcastic: saint and satyr, hard to pin down. Now, extending sympathy to him, she had drawn out of him something like a child's rage. She saw the veins on his temples, the set of his mouth; and, driving through that coconut gloom, with the line of sky and sea far to their right, for the first time she was nervous of him.

He said, "But, as you say, Sunday's a bad day. It will be all right in the morning."

This was more the manner she was used to: his saint's manner, as she thought of it, in which everything had an explanation as satisfying as an excuse, and everything, every new experience, every new fact or perception, was absorbed into a private system that kept him calm and aloof. His face relaxed, became again the ascetic mask she knew. Her nervousness abated; but she remained disturbed by him.

There was a break in the coconut trees. Sunlight spattered the road, lit up a small settlement of weathered wooden houses set in sand that had turned gray from the rotted shreds of coconut fiber with which, over the years, it had become mixed. After that the coconut planting was irregular, and the trees were not numbered. A white wooden bridge, a shallow reddish creek; and then they were out of the plantation, and again in the bright light of the afternoon.

Jane said, "You must get that man off my back."

"Who?" Roche put on his dark glasses.

"Jimmy. Endless telephone calls."

He didn't react.

"I don't know what Adela must think. And when you answer he always wants you to telephone back in five minutes at some new number."

Roche smiled. "That's Jimmy. He likes to make it appear that somebody is telephoning *him*. He always gets a telephone call when he comes to see me in the office."

"I went to see him one lunchtime at the Prince Albert. That seemed safe enough. He said he was talking to the Lions."

"The Lions don't meet at the Prince Albert. He took a chance there. But with Jimmy there's always some stupid little giveaway like that."

"He turned up in a great big American car with a driver." She saw that Roche smiled, and her tone went lighter. "A fat black driver wearing a see-through blue nylon shirt and one of those knotted vests."

He almost interrupted her. "What did Jimmy have to say?"

"Jimmy talked about this woman he'd met in London who'd been out here during the war as a child and whose father was in Intelligence."

"I've never heard of her before."

"They stayed at the Prince Albert and this little girl would look out at the park and see the schoolchildren playing. He said he was one of the children."

"I wonder where he got that story from."

"I saw that I was being softened up and that the time had come to leave. He said he would give me a lift. The doorman whistled up this awful car. It was all I could do to keep a straight face. As soon as we drove off Jimmy kissed me. On the lips. The driver must have thought I was some kind of hotel pickup. It wasn't funny. It was awful."

"I knew that something like that must have happened."

"You knew?"

"Meeting Jimmy at the Prince Albert was as good as making an announcement on the radio. Jimmy would know that."

"It was awful. That mustache, those wet blubber lips. Liver-colored lips, pink on the inside. And the driver and the car."

"Jimmy was very odd on the telephone the last time I spoke to him. And all kinds of people have been making signals to me the last few days."

He paused for Jane to speak. She said nothing.

He said, "They haven't always been kind. Look at Meredith this morning."

She was very pale. She lit a cigarette and the wind whipped her smoke through the open car window.

She said, "I don't think I want to see Meredith again."

"We can put an end to this quite easily," Roche said. "I think we should call in on the way and talk to him. It's only a small detour."

They were getting out of the area of bush and estates and coming out into the plain, with the mountains and the valleys to their right. From here the road ran straight through settlements and little towns and open fields to the factory area and the city. The brown-red mountains smoked. Here and there fires had blackened the fields.

Jane said, "I don't think I want to see that horrible house again."

"You can't be too subtle with a man like Jimmy. Otherwise he might miss the point. And it will do him no harm to be taken by surprise."

He was relaxed at the wheel, with no sign now of his earlier passion. He spoke with a satisfaction that was almost like relish; and about his determination there was something as childlike as there had been about his recent rage.

She made no further objection, surrendering to events as she surrendered to the sense of motion. The car would stop; events would reach their climax; the crisis would recede; she would be herself again. And as the landscape changed, as the car turned off the highway into the secondary bush of the abandoned industrial park, as she saw again what she thought she had said good-by to, she found she had slipped into her own state of excitement, her own little delirium, in which, each time with a kick of wonder and apprehension, in a process which she thought she could control, she intermittently came to herself and had a sense of her presence in a car, beside Roche, on a particular stretch of road, past and future blurred, with just a knowledge of the crisis to come.

The brown, tattered lawn, the hot glitter of the many-angled corrugated-iron roof, the sun on the ocher-washed concrete walls, the sloping shadows, the bright soft petals of bougainvillaea, the pink of oleander and the congealed-blood color of hibiscus blooms that had quailed and folded, the derelict bush stretching to the white-trunked wall of forest: it was all as she had remembered it. It all continued to exist.

When the car stopped in the road and Roche got out and slammed his door and she got out, the delirium was over; and she was in control of herself again, marveling at, and regretting, the now dead excitement. And it was only as they walked into the yard, through the gate that had been left open, that she thought that her second visit here might be made known to Roche, and her version of her meeting with Jimmy be shown as false.

No one was in the yard. No one appeared on the porch, white in the sun. The car port at the side of the house was empty; there was a dusty old stain of oil on the concrete. The door from the porch to the living room was open.

Roche called: "Jimmy!"

There was no reply. He walked into the living room, and Jane followed him. She saw again the electric blue carpet with the black and yellow splashes; the bookshelves, the books, the photographs in stand-up frames; the desk, untidier than it had been; the chunky three-piece suite upholstered in that tiger-striped furry material. Various sections of a newspaper, roughly folded, lay on the couch; the inky-looking comics supplement was on the glass-topped table. There was a light coating of new dust on surfaces; dust, disturbed by their passage through the room, could be seen to rise in the glare reflected from the white porch. With the room untenanted and exposed, it was possible to see it stripped of its furnishings, to see it bare, with only the mahogany-stained shelving on the wall. She considered the sulking, vacant, curly-haired children in the mutilated photograph.

Calling "Jimmy! Jimmy!" Roche began to walk through the house, and Jane walked behind him. She entered a passage she remembered. She began to know alarm and disgust again; she began to feel the need to get out quickly, to be herself again. They walked noisily, creating noise in the echoing concrete house. Roche opened the door into the kitchen; and the sight and smell of dirty plates, stale food going bad in the heat, strange food, further unsettled her. She thought: I feel like screaming. The thought came to her as words alone; but then within herself she began to simulate an imaginary scream.

Walking now like a man who knew that the house was empty, no longer cautious, and suddenly simply curious, Roche opened more doors. Jane followed him. She saw the bedroom. She saw the unmade bed, the two sunken pillows, the stiff off-white stains on the sheet, a spring or two of hair, specks of dirt or tobacco, the yellow candlewick bedspread half on the maroon-carpeted floor. The door to the bathroom was ajar and she had a glimpse of the low tiled wall which marked off the shower area. She saw the view through the high, barred window: the afternoon sky, the distant line of bush, the crests of the spiky forest palms. The room was close; it smelled of distemper and old clothes; not even the wind cleared that. On the bedside table there were two paperback books. Cheap paper curling in the heat. A pornographic cover. A shallow round jar of some cream.

She stood in the doorway with Roche, who was sucking on the end of one temple of his dark glasses. Something of his excitement had gone.

He said, "He isn't here. Shall we go across to the Grange?"

"Let's go home."

She followed him back to the living room. He stood for a while beside the tiger-striped couch, sucking on the glasses, looking. Jane studied the photographs. The room felt hotter now. The glare from the porch was fierce.

Jane said, "I hope the water's on when we get back."

He moved to the desk. He began to read a blue aerogramme letter.

Jane said, "I think we should go. This place is creepy."

He said, throwing the letter down on the desk, "Another brush-off."

She went to the desk and, not taking the letter up, leaving it on the desk, she began to read.

Dear Jimmy, We were vastly amused by your letter. That

place certainly sounds ripe for something, from your description of it. You are certainly the right man in the right place. But Lord Thomson and the Sunday Times might be a better market for the series of thirteen you propose writing. We are not in that league, as you know, and the feeling here is that something more in the nature of hard news, offbeat but illuminating, might be of more use to us rather than the psychological analysis you propose, which I know is your forte and which I personally would find fascinating, as I need hardly remind you. To tell you the truth, I don't know how much longer we can go on. I am beginning to feel that we are an incurably frivolous people and as a nation we seem resigned to giggling our way to oblivion. The scene as we knew it is no longer what it was, and I personally feel that the time has come to batten down the hatches and ride out the storm. But perhaps out of all your experiences might come some powerful and hard-hitting novel—how good, by the by, to hear that that progresses smoothly. It will certainly give a much needed fillip to the form which, like everything in this nook-shotten island, seems to be dying on its feet. You have no doubt heard of the staggering increase in property prices over here. We have managed, at enormous sacrifice, to become enfeoffed of a ruin in Dorset, which much occupies us these days, so at least we will be sheltered during the coming storm. The natives are so far friendly. At least no one has painted swastikas on our doors or dropped excreta through the letter slot. But that may come, when they get to know us better. Marcia sends her love. We will continue to scan the newspapers for news of you and your doings, which from this distance seem vastly exciting. Yours ever, Roy.

Roche stood beside her while she read.

She said, "Is he really writing a novel? Is that the novel, do you think?" She took out a writing pad from below some papers.

Somebody said, "Yes?"

And Jane turned to see the boy with the Medusa head, the boy with the pigtails of aggression, the boy with the twisted face, the tormented red eyes. He was standing in the doorway in his jeans, jersey, and canvas shoes. He moved aggressively toward them.

She was grateful for Roche's coolness.

Roche said, "It's Bryant, isn't it? Where's Jimmy, Bryant?"

The boy didn't answer. He came to the desk; he gathered the writing pad and letter and other papers together and put the blue-tinted glass ash tray on them. He went to the couch and began to refold the newspaper.

Roche said, "Where's Jimmy, Bryant?"

And when Bryant spoke, over his shoulder, it was almost with a shout. "Why you ask me?"

Roche said, "We've come to see Jimmy, Bryant."

"He's in town." And then Bryant sat down on the couch and began to sob. "He's in town, he's in town." His eyes were red: the red of aggression turned out to be the red of weeping.

Roche sat on the arm of the couch. "What's happened?"

Bryant said, "They kill Stephens."

Jane said, "*Killed?*"

"When?" Roche said. "I haven't seen the papers today. Is it in the papers?"

Bryant leaned back on the couch, turned his head to one side, and looked up at the ceiling. He was sobbing; he was waiting to be comforted.

Roche said, "Is it in the papers?" Then he said to Jane, "Meredith didn't say anything about it. He should have told me."

"Not in the papers," Bryant said, wiping his eyes with a long finger, a thin, crooked finger. "It happen early this morning. They was waiting for him. On the radio they say he draw first. They was waiting for him. Watching the mother house."

"Meredith knew!" Roche said, standing up. "Meredith knew!" The fact seemed important to him; it was like the main shock, overriding all the rest of Bryant's news. He said, "Is that where Jimmy has gone?"

"The police was giving up the body this afternoon. They taking it from the mortu'ry to the mother house. I didn't want to go."

Roche said to Jane, "I think I should go."

Bryant rolled his head on the back of the couch and used his long finger to wipe the rim of his eyes. "I should go too. But I don't think I can stand it."

"I'll give you a lift."

Jane wanted to cry: No!

Bryant said, "Leave me here."

Jane said, "I want to go home."

"Leave me here," Bryant said, looking up at the ceiling.

"Jane!" Roche ordered. "Let us go."

She started at his tone. He was already walking, brisk, athletic, his pale khaki trousers seeming looser around his waist; and she hurried after him. Yet when they were in the car—the sweat instantly breaking out on their faces and backs: the air heated, though the windows had been left open, the seats blazing—he went still.

He put his hands on the wheel and said, addressing himself, "I must drive carefully. In times like this one must drive carefully."

And very slowly, as though he was indifferent to Jane's reaction, as though he was alone in the car, he began to drive along the narrow empty road, sitting tense at the wheel, studying the asphalt surface, sometimes broken at the edge, sometimes overgrown, loosened into gravel here and there by tufts of browned grass. Jane was silent; it was as though she too was alone. The sunlight was yellowing; it softened the wall of bush that bounded the flattened wasteland of stunted shrubs and collapsed long grass. Slowly, though not as slowly as when they started, they approached the highway. The scorched hills appeared, dark-red and brown, smoking in many places. The slanting sun picked out every dip on the hills, every fold and wrinkle. They turned onto the highway, black and smooth from traffic.

Roche said, "I think I should go. It must be terrible in that house now."

There were not many cars on the road. The factories were closed. Far away, deep in the brown fields, there was a scattering of parked cars. The trunks of these cars were open, and the drivers could be seen, tiny, isolated, intent figures, cutting grass for the animals they kept at home. In open spaces in the little concrete-and-tin settlements children played, kicking up dust.

"Meredith knew," Roche said. "They stopped me on Friday, you know, and they searched the car."

He was half addressing Jane now, but she acknowledged nothing.

Past the junked cars in the sunken fields, past the factories, past more country settlements, the suburbs, they approached the city, the rubbish dump smoking yellow-gray, the smoke uncoiling slowly in the still afternoon, rising high and spreading far, becoming mingled with the pink pall from the bauxite loading station, the whole shot through with the rays of the declining sun. Sunlight gilded the stilted shacks that seemed to scaffold the red hillsides. The land began to feel choked. But the shantytown redevelopments were subdued; those repetitive avenues of red earth showed little of their usual human overspill. There were few trucks amid the smoke and the miniature multicolored hills and valleys of the rubbish dump, and not many scavengers. On each fence post a black carrion corbeau sat undisturbed; others on the ground hopped about awkwardly, two feet at a time.

Jane rolled up her window, to keep out the oily smoke and the deep dead smell.

Roche said, "Picking the carcass clean. They'll pick the carcass clean."

Fixed in the posture of alertness, though no longer driving slowly, still concentrating on the road as though watching for obstructions there, he did not sufficiently notice that the line of traffic he had been following had thinned out; and it was some time before he saw that he was entering a quiet city. They crossed the concrete canal that drained the ever rising swamp over which this part of the city had spread. But there had been no Sunday-afternoon "swagger" groups on the bridge, no plump young women in plastic curlers, no men with shirts out of their trousers and open all the way down.

No refrigerated trailers were unloading at the market. There were no groups of vendors and porters preparing, in an atmosphere of the caravanserai, for the long night and the early-morning market. Instead, half a dozen police vans were drawn up in the dusty market yard, and policemen stood in groups close to their vehicles.

Roche said, "I know that something is being prepared for me. They searched me on Friday. They saw me at the house."

Jane said, "I want to go home."

She rolled down her window. Fresher air blew in.

Abruptly he turned into a cross street, one of those that cut through the center of the city.

He said, "I must go. They'll believe that I knew."

He came to the main square and he saw it as he had never seen it before, empty, without people or cars, the wooden stalls in the center roughly shuttered. Between the square modern buildings, he saw tiled mansard roofs, corrugated-iron roofs in faded stripes of red and white, stylish finials, decorated wrought-iron balconies: domestic features of the upper parts of older buildings that normally didn't draw attention to themselves but were now thrown into relief by the emptiness below. No restaurant vans or coconut carts, no queues at the bus stops, no crowds waiting for route taxis at corners: a stripped, sunlit square, with a spread of litter in the open gutters and little dust eddies on the wide intersections. He saw police trucks in the shadowed streets leading out of the square. He saw groups of policemen. He saw rifles and tin helmets.

He stopped. A policeman with a helmet and a rifle broke from a group and came running out into the sunlight and across the intersection to the car, his boots pounding on the asphalt. He was shouting; his words were indistinct. Even with his rifle he looked vulnerable and a little absurd, with his short serge trousers, his exposed thighs, his truncheon, his puttees.

He shouted, "What the hell you doing here?"

And when the policeman came to the car Roche saw that he was young and nervous. He had shaved closely; every pore was distinct, and he was sweating on his scored top lip.

He said, "Where you think you going?"

He spoke with exasperation rather than authority. His gray shirt was sweated under the arms; an inch or so of white undershirt showed beyond the short sleeves.

Few of the other policemen looked at the car. Most were looking up the empty shadowed streets.

Roche said, "I'm sorry. We didn't know about this. Is it bad?"

"Trouble, I don't know. Big trouble. You live near here? Where you live?"

"The Ridge."

"Man, you drive there fast. Take the Circular Road and drive. Don't stop. Drive."

He turned and began to run back across the empty square to the group he had left.

And Roche drove as he had been ordered. He drove out of the square and took the road that skirted the center of the city, and he drove fast. It was a wide road of low shops and palings, cafes and rum shops, old timber houses squeezed into small plots, occasionally a more spacious, and now stranded, old-fashioned house with fern baskets hanging in the veranda, intermittent concrete developments. The road, usually lively, was now almost empty, and the slogans and posters on walls and palings stood out. Roche saw, again and again, *Birth Control Is a Plot Against the Negro Race*; he saw *Don't Vote*. He saw the posters for Doctor Andy Byam, "America's Gift to God." He saw *After Israel Africa*. He saw *After Israel*. He saw, and he realized he had been seeing it for weeks past, *AIA*, the letters written one below the other, reduced sometimes—a mystery simultaneously discovered and solved—to the hieroglyph of a two-headed arrow. And through the calm of the lower Ridge, where nurses still sat on brown lawns and children still played, he continued to drive fast. The shopping plaza was closed. Climbing higher, he passed the house labeled *Taylor*; he turned at *Chez Wen*; he passed *The Mortons*. And when at last, in their own yard, they got out of the car, to silence, it was as though they had both yielded to a private lunacy during that fast drive.

They separated without speaking. The house, with closed doors, was stuffy. Jane opened the folding doors at the back and went out on the porch. It was quiet and cool.

The shadow of the house reached halfway down the sloping back garden. Sunlight still caught the children's house, whose door was open. Sunlight fell on the brown vegetation of the hills. The city on the flat land below was only just beginning to grow hazy.

It was quiet. The radios all around and below had ceased to play: the reggae party was at last over. Far away, the airport, fading into haze, showed two white planes.

Jane thought: I've left it too late.

12

ADELA WAS in, but Sunday was her day off; and it had been established that on Sundays she was not to be spoken to. Jane and Roche could speak to her only if she spoke to them first. On Sundays Adela did her own chores. She hung her mattress out of her window to catch the sun, beat her mattress; did her washing. She also did a lot of cooking: on Sundays she was at home to her friends and relations. She had her own front entrance, at the side of the garage; and she had a back entrance, with a flight of concrete steps, useful as seating.

A wall of concrete blocks, about ten feet long, screened off Adela's little back yard from the rest of the back garden. The previous tenants had tried to cover this wall with a flowering vine and with the local ivy. In the drought the vine had shriveled; the ivy had lost its leaves and the brown stems had begun to come away from the wall. Where they were loose, the stems looked like dead millipedes, with hundreds of little hanging feet; where they were still fixed to the wall, the stems looked like encrustations of mud, the nest of some kind of wasp or ant. The concrete wall was a concrete wall; it couldn't pass as a decorative architectural feature. And behind it was Adela and her private life.

It was a life that on Sundays emphasized the neutrality of the rest of the house, with its solid company furniture and no pictures on the clean walls. The house needed Adela. Without her—or with her on the other side of the wall—the house felt empty and un-welcoming. And now, at dusk, it was the end even of Adela's day: her washing taken in, her visitors, if she had had any, gone.

Night fell. Lights came on in the city and isolated lights showed here and there on the hills. The great silence continued. It became chilly on the porch. Inside, table lights or wall lights made the large rooms gloomy; ceiling lights showed up the bareness. And there was no water.

Jane was unwilling to move about the house or to do anything that might make a noise. She was exhausted; she became more exhausted. She heard Roche moving lightly about: he too seemed affected by the silence. Before, she had always been re-assured by his presence, had almost needed it, needed to feel him reacting to her. But now, though she listened for his noises—she heard him trying the taps, opening and closing the refrigerator door, rustling the newspaper—she began to hide from him; and he too seemed to be staying away from her. She went at last to the unlighted front room of the house, where it was still warm; and she stayed there until, out of exhaustion, darkness, silence, she became, to her surprise, quite calm.

They met later in the kitchen, where the fluorescent light fell hard on white formica surfaces. They ate sardines, cheese, bread; and drank lager and coffee. Roche's manner was as light as his movements; he too was recovering from strain. But there was no connected conversation between them.

They heard Adela's radio. It was nearly half past seven by the kitchen clock, nearly time for the Sunday evening program of hymns sponsored by one of the Southern American churches. And soon there came the tune that, for Jane, marked the deadest hour of Sunday on the Ridge, the deadest hour of the week. Adela turned the volume down, but the words were still distinct.

> Oh come to the church in the wild wood.
> Oh come to the church in the vale.

Roche said, "Adela isn't worried. I wonder if she knows."
Jane looked at him and didn't reply. She thought: I should

have left that day when he dreamt about being tortured, the day I saw the wild man in the children's house.

Such a straight new road led to the airport. More than once, during her first few weeks on the island, they had driven in the late afternoon to the airport, for the sake of the drive, and to sit in the glass-walled lounge and drink rum punch and watch the planes, the flat expanse of asphalt and grass that seemed to stretch to the hills, the late sunlight on the hills. The hills had been green then; and the sugar cane fields through which the airport road ran had also been green, the sugar cane tall and in arrow, gray-blue plumes above the green; and sometimes on the way back they had stopped at the basketwork and raffiawork stands beside the airport road, tourist enticements. But then, almost as soon as she had got used to the sugar cane and the arrows, the fields had been fired, the canes reaped; and what had been green and enclosed had become charred and flat and open. Then the drought had set in, and those excursions had stopped. On the highway that afternoon they had passed the airport road; she hadn't given it a thought.

For so long she had held herself ready to leave. She had her return air ticket; in London she had been told she needed one to enter the island. Her passport was in order. It was a new one and—she had been born in Ottawa during the war—it was endorsed *Holder has right of abode in the United Kingdom*. A virgin passport still: it had not been stamped when she had arrived. No official had asked to see her passport, or her return ticket, when the bauxite Americans had taken her past the immigration desk. She had eluded the controls; there was no record of her arrival. She remembered it as part of the dislocation of that first morning when, exhausted by the night-long journey, unslept, the airplane noise still in her head, the airplane smell still on her, she had, coming out of the customs hall and seeing Roche, had a feeling of disappointment and wrongness. She had always been ready to leave.

Looking at Roche in the hard light in the white kitchen, Jane thought: Now it's out of my hands. I am in this house, with this man.

On Adela's radio, between passages of grave, deep, indistinct speech, the hymns continued. The hymns held more than the melancholy of Sunday evening. For Jane now they held the melancholy, the incompleteness, of all her time here; and the Ridge felt far from everywhere.

In the dead fluorescent light she considered Roche's face, which once had seemed to her so fine, so ascetic and full of depth. Now, seeing the face attempt easiness, even jollity, she saw it as worn and weak; and she wondered that she had ever been puzzled by him. She had, long ago, seen him as a man of action, a doer. Later, she had seen him as an intellectual, infinitely understanding, saint-like in the calm brought him by his knowledge. Now she saw that he was like herself, yielding and yielding, at the mercy of those events which he analyzed away into his system. His intellectualism was a sham, a misuse of the mind, a series of expedients. She understood now why, when he was at his most analytical and intelligent, he irritated her most. Ordinary: the word came to her as she watched him. It surprised her and she resisted it: it seemed vindictive and untrue. But she held onto the word. She looked at him and thought: In spite of everything he's done he's really quite ordinary.

A metallic hissing from somewhere in the house obliterated Adela's hymns. Then there was a series of snaps and sighs and a prolonged rattling. The water had come on: open taps ran, tanks were filling up.

Roche said, "I'm glad they've remembered. I'm sure that's all it was, you know. Somebody just forgot. I think I'll give myself a proper bath. It may be the last one for a long time."

The water pipes settled down. Adela's hymn program ended and she turned off her radio. There was silence.

Later, in her room, as she was adjusting the redwood louvers, Jane thought: I am alone. And she was astonished at her calm.

She heard Roche running his bath. She lay in bed, longing for drowsiness and sleep and the morning, playing with images of the day: the brown bush around Jimmy Ahmed's house, the specks of blood on the globules of sweat on the policeman's too closely shaved top lip, his curiously dainty run across the empty square, the lost gray villages in the overgrown cocoa and coffee estates, the bright sea seen though the coconut plantation, the fast drive up to the Ridge, the estuary and the candles and the blindfolded stampers. She thought: I have always been alone since I've been here. With that the panic and the wakefulness came. And then the telephone began to ring.

The telephone rang in the sitting room with the nearly empty shelves on the concrete walls, the solid three-piece company suite; and the ringing bounced into the open hall and down the concrete walls and parquet floor of the passage to the plywood of her own door. Roche didn't leave his bathroom to answer; and the telephone rang and rang. At last she put on her light and got out of bed. She left her bedroom door open, and the light from the bedroom went down the passage, reflected in the hall, and from there cast a diminished glimmer into the sitting room.

She stood beside the ringing telephone. She thought: I'll let it ring ten times. She caught sight of herself, barely reflected in the picture window that looked out on the front lawn: so solid-looking with the dark outside, that sealed pane of glass, so vulnerable. She lifted the telephone.

"Hello."

"Jane. Harry." He pronounced it Hah-ree. "You were getting me worried, girl." His musical voice was always a surprise. "You get through?"

"Yes."

"I get through too. How you liking the little excitement?"

"There isn't much up here."

"Jane, I don't know whether you and Peter have any plans for going out tonight. But they're going to declare a state of emergency in a couple of hours. And I think they must know their own business."

"Do you know what is happening?"

"Nobody knows what the hell is happening. Or what is going to happen. Is the police fault, nuh. They surrender the body of that boy they shoot, without asking anybody anything. They thought the body was going to the mother's house. But you should know that man Jimmy Ahmed start walking round the town with the body, picking up one hell of a procession. Everybody washing their foot and jumping in. Everybody carrying a piece of palm branch or coconut branch. The Arrow of Peace. You ever hear of that before? I never hear of that before. Imagine a thing like that happening to your own body: people toting it round the town. Those people crazy like hell, man."

"Is Marie-Thérèse all right? Have you heard from her?"

"Well, child, Marie-Thérèse telephone just this minute, to find out whether I get through. Is she who tell me about the state of emergency. She talk to Joseph too. He is in one hell of a state. How is Adela? I shouldn't say too much in front of her, you know."

"That's easy. She isn't talking to us today."

"Sunday. I remember. Well, Jane, we'll keep in touch. The telephone is still working, thank God. It may be nothing at all, you know. They'll probably just chase a few white people and burn down a couple of Chinese shops, that's all. It'll be a nice little excitement for you. It isn't the kind of thing you get in Chelsea or Tottenham."

She met Roche in the passage, bare-chested and in his pajama trousers.

He said, "Who was that?"

She said, "Jimmy."

"Jimmy! Why didn't you call me?"

"I don't mean Jimmy. It was Harry. He says they're rioting and there's a state of emergency."

"Who's rioting?"

"I don't know. Why don't you telephone him and find out?"

Her words came out more impatiently than she intended. As she made to pass him she saw him surprised; she saw his face harden.

He said, in his precise way, "I'll do just that."

And when she was in her room, and in bed, the light turned off, she heard the ping of the telephone bell as the speaker was taken off the hook.

She thought: It's out of my hands.

.   .   .

SHE CAME out of sleep to the dark, enclosed room, to that sense of the nightmare journey and of an unstable, dissolving world; and to the half-knowledge of a catastrophe. She was quickened into wakefulness. Her mind cleared; confusion and nightmare receded. She opened the louvers and was startled, as always every morning, by the brightness of the light. Dew was heavy on the brown front lawn. When she opened the folding doors at the back she saw that the metal chairs and table on the brick porch were wet. No smoke on the hills yet; the city lay clear below, and the thick tufted mangrove swamp and the smooth gray sea; and the early sun glinted on the white planes at the airport. The city was silent. This was always the sweetest part of the day.

She walked out to the front gate in her striped sacking dress, the one she had worn to some dinner parties and now used as a dressing gown. The newspaper was in the newspaper box on the gate: it was a second or so before she thought it was strange that life should continue, that newspapers should be printed during the night and delivered in the morning.

The front page showed no hysteria. It preserved its regular format, and the events of the previous day had been reduced to a number of separate and apparently unrelated stories. The main headline announced the state of emergency; the text, in heavy type, was the official proclamation. A single column on the left, with a grotesque old photograph, told of Meredith Herbert's recall to the government as minister without portfolio. A double-column story at the foot of the page, *Guerrilla Slain in Dawn Shoot-out*, was about the shooting of Stephens and the recovery of banknotes from his mother's house. Another item reported, more or less in the words of an official communiqué, a "police operation" in the center of the city.

Standard news, a normal day: the items were like items Jane seemed to have been reading in the newspaper ever since she had arrived.

Adela was up. From her room came a tremendous throat-clearing which was probably intended to conceal other noises. And after this there was her morning radio program, *I Hear the South Land Singing.* Half-past six.

So life was continuing. And when, in her white uniform, Adela started striding through the large rooms, thump, thump, on parquet and terrazzo, the house was like itself again. Clearing away the things from last night's supper, Adela thrust her fingers down the sides of the beer glasses. She went still for a second, and then had a little frenzy. A tremor ran through her body, she knitted her brow, bunched her lips together and made an angry noise which sounded like *stewps.* Then, the frenzy over, her protest made, she lifted the glasses and became active again.

At seven o'clock, as always on a weekday, they listened to the BBC news, which was relayed by the local radio station. There was no mention of their own crisis.

After breakfast and the newspaper, Roche said, "So Meredith was a minister when he came among us yesterday. I suppose he liked the idea of keeping it secret. I must say I feel more and more at sea here. I can't read these people. All these little secrets. I suppose I'm an easy man to fool. Mrs. Stephens certainly fooled me. I never guessed—the idea didn't even occur to me—that she was hiding all that money for her son."

Though Jane was listening to what he was saying, and though she was letting her mind play with his words, she was without the energy or will to acknowledge his words. And then it was too late. Her silence became pointed, and his face hardened as it had hardened the previous evening.

He left the kitchen and went to the back door and looked down the hills to the city.

He said, "Jimmy's big moment. It just goes to show. I never thought that anything like that was possible. The one gesture. Meredith knew what he was talking about." He paused and then said, as if speaking to himself, "I should have gone to the house. They'll believe I knew and didn't go."

Abruptly he turned and walked with determination back to the kitchen, to the dining area behind the cupboard divider. Jane was drinking coffee out of a heavy earthenware cup, company issue. She was aware of him walking toward her; she was aware of his sudden rage. She steadied the cup with her left hand and held it against her lips, her elbows on the white formica table. Her eyes were large and moist. He was infuriated by her air of expectation, her posture, her lips on the coffee cup.

He said, "I've been thinking about it. I've been thinking about it all night. I've heard you talk about your friends. Who are your friends? What do you talk about? What do you offer them? What do you *have* to offer them?"

He had never spoken to her like that before. And she was not at all dismayed by his anger. She put the cup down. More decisively, then, she took the newspaper, stood up and, lifting the long sacking dress above her ankles, walked out to the porch and sat down in the sun in one of the metal chairs Adela had wiped dry.

She sat there and was confirmed in the feeling of solitude that had come to her the evening before. And, unexpectedly, from this feeling of solitariness she found that she had begun to draw strength.

She sat out in the sun, steadily less pleasant, until she was dazed. This she did on most mornings, until the heat, increasing together with the noise of the working city, drove her inside: the individual noises of horns and motorcycles, children's cries, bicycle bells, trucks and buses in low gear, gradually multiplying and becoming a steady rhythmic throb which, mingled with the noise of a thousand radios tuned to the same station, turned into what the ear could take for a reggae beat, a creation of sun and heat. But the city remained silent this morning. Sun and heat awakened no life and seemed instead to deaden the city. The sun dried out the wet clumps of long Bermuda grass that grew against the retaining wall of the back garden; obliterated the beads of dew on hibiscus leaves and flowers; dried out the lawn around the porch. Threads of smoke began to rise here and there from the hills and, far away, from the great plain. Mangrove and sea blurred together in the heat haze.

Just after noon she saw the first fire in the city below. Not the thin white smoke of bush fires, or the brown-gray spread of the burning rubbish dump; but a small inky eruption of the densest black, erupting and erupting and not becoming less dense or less black, with little spurts and streaks of red that then fell back into the blackness. Explosions, but the sound didn't carry up to the Ridge. From the Ridge the sunlit city continued to be silent. Then two other fires could be seen: two little leaks of dense black smoke.

Harry telephoned. Jane answered.

Harry said, "They're burning a few liquor shops. They take out another procession this morning. That man Jimmy Ahmed, nuh. You know, I hear they chase Meredith. The police too damn frighten now to shoot. Look, Jane, I think we should telephone at regular intervals. Just in case, nuh. I hear the government about to resign. One or two of the guys fly out already."

Jane said, "But I haven't seen any planes leave."

"Me neither. But that's what they say. Truck after truck just taking furniture and china and things like that to the airport. China! You see those people! Anybody would think that Wedgwood and Spode close down. It would be pathetic if it wasn't so damn frightening. But, look, we must telephone, eh. Just to keep in touch, nuh. While the telephone still going. What is the food situation like by you? You have enough?"

"I don't know. But I think so."

The fires continued to burn in the silent city. Adela came out and stood on the porch and looked down at the city. But she never mentioned the fires to Jane or Roche; and neither of them spoke of the fires.

Between one and five Adela was free. But when Jane went to the kitchen in the middle of the afternoon to get a glass of water she saw Adela there, in her uniform, buttering sliced bread: two or three stacks of buttered slices on one side, unbuttered slices on the other. Around the bread stacks were dishes of mashed tuna and salmon, bowls of chopped chicken, sliced cucumber, and sliced eggs. Adela didn't acknowledge Jane's presence; she went on buttering bread.

Jane said, "Sandwiches?"

Adela bunched her lips and knitted her brow, buttering now with the air of someone too busy to waste time on idle talk.

Jane recognized Adela's explosive mood and said no more. She drank a tumbler of cold water—there were four bottles in the refrigerator to see them through the waterless afternoon—and went back to her shuttered room. There she began to think. The electricity might fail. No electricity, no water, no refrigerator, no lights, no cooking: sandwiches for the long siege. Would they eat all those sandwiches? Would the sandwiches keep? She remembered what Harry had said about food, and she became dismayed. She went out into the passage and saw Roche. He had been to the kitchen and had seen what Jane had seen; he too was dismayed.

He said, "It looks as though we're losing some of our rations."

Jane went to the kitchen and said, "You've made a lot of sandwiches, Adela."

Adela said, "I taking it down to the station."

The station: the police station. Jane could say nothing. She stood by, watching and not interfering, while Adela, still with knitted brow, and still with deft hands, lined two wickerwork shopping baskets with a damp cloth, packed the sandwiches in, covered them with another damp cloth, and then knotted the bundle within each basket.

Feeding the warriors, the protectors. Where had Adela acquired this knowledge? She behaved as though she had been through crises like this before, as though, at times like this, certain things had to be done, as certain things had to be done when a baby was born or when someone died. She hadn't asked for permission to prepare the sandwiches; she hadn't asked for help. And when she was ready she didn't ask for a lift. She hooked the baskets on her sturdy arms; and Jane watched her stride down the drive to the gate, brisk in the sun, her shadow dancing, looking like a nurse in her white uniform, which dazzled. It was oddly reassuring.

The sun was now falling on the front of the house, on the concrete wall and the louvers and the sealed glass of the picture window. It was time to open the back door, which had been closed after lunch to keep out the glare. When Jane opened the door she saw the shadow of the house was just covering the porch; and she sat in one of the metal chairs, still warm, and waited for Adela to return. The silent city burned in four or five places now. The smoke from the first fire was still black, but less dense.

Then she saw the plane. She had heard nothing. It was the faint brown smoke trail, rapidly vanishing, that led her eye to the plane climbing above the airport and away from the city.

She stayed where she was, in the metal chair, and watched the shadow of the house move down the slope of the back garden. She saw the heat waves disappear and felt the porch and the ground about the porch grow cool. She heard Adela come back. She had been waiting for Adela, for the reassurance of her presence, for the life she would give to the house, which she knew better than Jane or Roche and treated with a respect she withheld from them. She had also been waiting for Adela's news. But she didn't go to see Adela. She remained in her chair, and Adela didn't come out to her.

She heard Roche moving restlessly about the house. But he too didn't come out to the porch. She heard him talking to Adela and attempting in his polite and roundabout way to get some news from her. Adela's tone was abrupt and sour; and though later Roche succeeded in getting her to talk, her words were not easy to follow and Jane didn't listen.

The sunlight yellowed. The shadow of the house spread further down the garden slope. The light turned amber and gave a richness to the choked soft growth of Bermuda grass against the retaining wall, where the grass seed had been washed down, during the now distant time of the rains, from the clay of the front and back lawns: thin blanched stalks of grass, pale green at the tips and browning toward the roots. The amber light deepened and fleetingly the garden and the dusty brown vegetation of the hill glowed.

She heard the telephone ring. She didn't get up. Roche answered; she heard him talking to Harry; she closed her mind to his words.

The amber light died. The city remained silent. Below the splendor of the early evening sky the city and the sea went dark and the fires in the city were little patches of glow. They became dimmer when the electric lights came on. Yet occasionally, in a brightening glow, the movement of black smoke could be seen. It became cold on the porch. The fluorescent light began to jump in the kitchen and then the blue-white light fell on the back lawn and melted away into the darkness of the sloping garden. Jane heard a tap running in the kitchen. Water. She got up at last, to go inside. She was thinking: After this, I'll live alone.

Throughout the evening that resolution, which was like a new comfort, was with her. It was with her in the morning: the silence continuing, a strain now, the lawn wet again, the metal chairs on the porch wet, the fires in the city thinner, less black, seemingly almost burnt out.

Her calm did not break through all the routine of Tuesday morning: Adela's bedroom noises and radio program, the BBC news, breakfast. Her calm came to an end, and for the first time during the crisis she knew panic when, lunchtime past, with no call from Adela, she left her louvered room and looked for Adela and couldn't find her. The back door was open: the brick porch baked.

Without Adela the house was empty. Adela had been the link for the last day and a half between Roche and herself. Without Adela the house had no meaning. Jane could feel the thinness of its walls, the brittleness of the louvers, the breakability of its glass, the exposed position of the house on the Ridge. So that even in the dark of her bedroom she no longer felt protected or confined. That was where she stayed, waiting for Adela through all the heat of the afternoon, through fantasies of bigger fires starting in the city, around the squarer, taller buildings that rose above the brown tufts of trees in the main park. She waited until sunset. And when the telephone rang she hurried to the warm sitting room to answer it.

It was Harry, telephoning for the second time that day.

He said, "It's bad, girl. They say the police cracking up. Guys taking off their uniforms and running away. But I don't know. The police are still at our station. And Joseph is still taking food down there."

"Oh, is Joseph taking food too?" And Jane realized, from the difficulty she had in getting out those words, that she hadn't spoken for twenty-four hours.

"Marie-Thérèse telephone him," Harry said. "Is what everybody around here doing."

Jane said, "Adela took some sandwiches down."

"I don't see how you can blame the police. They don't know who they fighting or who they fighting for. Everybody down there is a leader now. I hear there isn't even a government. You hear about Meredith? He went out braver-danger, you know, to try to talk to them. They chase him."

"Meredith can look after himself."

"Well, I suppose you right, child."

"How is Marie-Thérèse?"

"She's all right. She's telephoning all the time. I don't know what she's saying to Joseph, but he is keeping very cool."

"Adela has left us."

"Jane."

"She left this midday."

"She's probably just gone for a little stroll. With all the excitement, nuh, she's probably deciding to put first things first. She's probably got some little thing going down the gully somewhere."

"She's taken her transistor."

"Well, child, I don't know whether you lucky or unlucky. I don't know whether I should ask you to come over here for the night. Or whether I should be coming to you. To tell you the truth, I am not too happy living alone in this house with Joseph."

When she put down the telephone, there was again the silence. Time had jumped: it was night. The lights had come on, but not everywhere. Parts of the city remained in darkness. The irregular shapes of the lit-up areas, linked sometimes by the white lights of main roads, created an odd pattern, as of something seen under a microscope. The smoldering rubbish dump glowed faintly in the darkness that surrounded it. In the dark areas of the city itself there were about half a dozen fires. Abruptly sometimes a fire glowed and lit up the smoke that rose from it; then the glow faded and the smoke was hard to see.

. . .

EARLY IN the morning Harry came. Jane had not been long on the back porch—the sea glassy, the smoke from last night's fires in the city white and thin, the newspaper Roche had left out on the metal table on the porch sodden with dew (one of the things that infuriated Adela)—when she heard the car idling at the front gate and then driving in. She walked round to the front lawn. Harry had parked in the drive and was closing the gate.

He made it seem like a Sunday. He was dressed as for his beach house, in his fringed knee-length shorts and a long-sleeved jersey with a high neck, for his asthma. His white canvas shoes made his feet look very big and busy as he walked across the wet lawn.

Jane was glad to see him, but after greeting him she found it hard to speak. They went around the house to the back porch and passed through to the kitchen. Roche was there. He ignored Jane; he looked strained, distressed. But he was as anxious as Jane to claim Harry; and Harry seemed to hesitate before the warmth, and near wordlessness, of their welcome.

The right-hand pocket of Harry's tight shorts bulged.

Roche said, "I hope that thing isn't loaded."

"No, man. I don't want to blow my balls off—excuse me, Jane. I'm just hiding it from Joseph." He took out the revolver and showed it, and they all sat down at the breakfast table. "It used to belong to my father."

Jane plugged the kettle in. "Have you ever used it?"

"Not me. And I don't know whether my father ever used it. It resemble him a little bit. He was about five foot high, with a temper to match. It looks a damn unreliable little thing, you don't find? I feel the only person you would damage with this would be yourself." He tucked the revolver back in his pocket and said, "But it's so damn peaceful up here, man. So peaceful. Adela come back?"

Jane said, "I haven't heard her."

Harry pushed the revolver deeper into his pocket. He said, "You know, we used to laugh at the old people. And they had their funny little ways. But they were damn right about certain things. My father never employed anybody he couldn't beat with his own two hands. He used to say to me, 'Harry, if you're employing anybody who is going to be close to you in the house or in the office, forget about qualifications and recommendations. Worry about that last. The first question to ask yourself is: "Should the occasion arise, would I be able to bust this man's arse?" ' Nowadays they're sending people up to the States to do diplomas in personnel management and that kind of nonsense. The only personnel management you have to study is whether you could bust the feller's arse. It's not funny, Jane. You hear me talking like this now. And you know what? I got that big, hulking, hard-back nigger man walking about my house and yard. I am telling you, Jane. I am frightened to say good morning to Joseph."

Jane brewed instant coffee in the heavy company cups. She said, "But, Harry, your asthma. It's gone."

"Well, girl, is as they say. Fire drive out fire."

Roche said, "Does anybody know what is happening?"

Harry said, "I don't think so. I don't think anybody knows what is happening with the police down there. I don't think even our local police people know. They're just sitting tight and eating our food."

"What about Jimmy?" Roche said. "Any more about him?"

"Jimmy kinda drop out of the news. At first it was all Jimmy Ahmed and the Arrow of Peace. Now you hearing about all kinds of guys popping up everywhere. Peter, tell me. Before Sunday, did you ever hear about the Arrow of Peace? How did I miss a thing like that?"

"I'm the last person to ask. I miss everything. I never thought Jimmy had it in him to start anything like that. I always thought that Jimmy was the kind of man who would disappear at the first sign of trouble."

"That's probably what he's done. Events move too fast for him. And for Meredith too. The two of them wanted to play bad-John, and the two of them get licked down."

Roche said, smiling, "Meredith was certainly planning something more long-term."

Harry said, "A child could have told Meredith that they were calling him back to the government just to throw him to the crowd. You see how a man can destroy his life in two days. They did terrible things to Meredith. Joseph was telling me. They strip him naked. Joseph say somebody even put a knife to the man's balls—excuse me, Jane. Then they give him a piece of palm branch and make him run for his life. You see the kind of thoughts that can get in those people's head? And Meredith is one of them. He will have to hide now, you know. He can't live here after this. The place is too small."

Roche said, "I wanted to telephone Jimmy. I even went to the telephone once or twice. But I changed my mind."

"Like me and Meredith. I don't know what to do. I want to show some kind of solidarity with the guy, but I don't know what the hell I can telephone him and say. And then I don't even know whether half I hear about him is even true."

Jane said, "You can telephone him and congratulate him on being a minister."

"Yes," Harry said. "You can say that Merry looked for what he got."

Jane said, "Did you see the airplane on Monday afternoon?"

"Girl, I can't tell you the stories. If everybody who they say leave was on that plane, the damn thing wouldn't have got off the ground."

Roche said, "It isn't only Mrs. Grandlieu who can't get to the airport."

Jane ignored this. She said to Harry, "But the place just can't stay like this. It can't just turn into a great ripe cheese."

Roche looked at her. He said, "Why not?" It was the first time he had spoken to her for two days, and the words held all his secreted rage.

Jane continued to look at Harry. Her eyes went moist; she took the coffee cup to her lips and held it there.

Harry, responding to Jane's eyes, and then looking away, began talking, softly at first, and slowly. He said, "Those guys down there don't know what they're doing. All this talk of independence, but they don't really believe that times have changed.

They still feel they're just taking a chance, and that when the show is over somebody is going to go down there and start dishing out licks. And they half want it to be over, you know. They would go crazy if somebody tell them that this time nobody might be going down to dish out licks and pick up the pieces."

Jane looked at Harry while he spoke. Roche saw the look in her eyes: the violated. His anger grew again.

Roche said, almost shouted, "They *know* what they're doing. They're pulling the place down."

Harry said uneasily, "All right, boss."

Jane said, still looking at Harry, "So what are we to do?"

Harry said, "What are we to do? Nothing. We can only sit tight and wait."

Roche, looking between them, addressing neither of them, said, "The world isn't what it was. So it must go up in flames."

Harry stood up. "Jane, I want to make a telephone call."

She said, "You can use the one in the sitting room."

"No, it's nothing private. I'll use the one here."

He went to the wall telephone near the door that opened into the garage, and he began to dial.

Roche leaned across the white breakfast table and brought his face close to Jane's. She saw a face of pure hatred: the face whose existence she had intuited ever since that day when, too late, already committed to him and this adventure, she had seen him grin and had seen his long, black-rooted molars.

He said violently, "Yes, it's going up in flames. But it's taking you with it."

Harry said into the telephone, "Bertie. Harry."

Jane caught Harry's pronunciation of his name: she understood now that he pronounced it *Hah-ree* when he used the name by itself, without his surname.

"But, Bertie, you're like the Scarlet Pimpernel these days. How you liking the little excitement? . . . Still, I glad I catch you. Bertie, what the hell is happening? Your paper is telling me nothing. The damn thing is more like a crossword puzzle these days. Clues down and across all over the place. You saving up the solution for next week? . . . I understand . . . I understand the position. . . . But that is damn good news, man. If it is true. . . . Well, stick in a little something for us too, nuh . . . I don't know. I hear some people talking about vigilante patrols. . . . I agree with you, Bertie. We don't want to be provocative neither. To tell you the truth, I was thinking more of something like *Ridge Residents Starve Dogs*. I think there may be one or two guys down there who ought to be informed that the dogs up here haven't fed since Sunday . . . no big fuss, but don't lose it in the paper. Page one or page two, nuh . . . I wouldn't say it is too obscure. It is a fairly straight message to whom it may concern. And is a nice little story too, I think. . . . All right, Bertie-boy. I'll be reading the paper tomorrow please God. . . . 'Please God'? Yes, man, these days we all start talking like the old people."

He came back to the breakfast table. Jane and Roche were sitting silent, not looking at one another.

Harry said, "Good news. If it's true. Bertie says he thinks the police are holding out. It was just that airplane on Monday. It demoralized a lot of people."

Jane filled the coffee cups again, and they all went out on the porch. Jane cleared away the sodden newspaper, and she and Harry wiped the wet table and chairs.

When they were all seated, Harry said, "Can you imagine this green, Jane?"

She said, "It was green when I came. But that's how it always is. I always have to imagine what I'm missing."

Roche said, "Did Bertie say anything about the government?"

"He didn't say anything. But I assume the boys are still in control. The only lucky thing is that none of the big guys have been killed yet. Because, once that kind of killing starts, it isn't going to stop. It's going to be South America for a couple of generations. Meredith frightened me on Sunday. He talked about Jimmy Ahmed as though he wanted to kill the man. I'd never heard anything like that before. But that was when they were dressing Merry up to throw him to the crowd. Now the two of them have to run."

Roche said, "So Jimmy is washed up?"

"I think so. According to what I hear. Nobody is mentioning him anymore. He gambled and lost."

Roche said, "I can't imagine Jimmy taking that kind of gamble. I wonder whether things didn't just happen around him."

Harry said, "Jimmy was always washed up here. I don't know who told him otherwise. I don't know what they told him in London. But at a time like this he is just another Chinaman."

Roche said, "I suppose I'm washed up too."

Harry said, "I wouldn't say so."

Roche smiled. "Sablich's will also want to dress up somebody to throw to the crowd."

Harry said, "Let us listen to the news, nuh. Bring out the radio, nuh, Jane. They had a little thing on it last night. I don't know whether you hear it. 'The causes of the disturbances are still not clear.' "

She went and got their plastic-cased transistor and tuned it to the local station. *Bringing Christ to the Nation* ended. The announcer hurried through a commercial, identified his station; and the news from London was relayed. Reception was good. There was nothing on the headlines, nothing during the first half of the news. Then it came, after an item about Argentina.

". . . still tense after two days of rioting. Earlier reports of police desertions and the resignation of the government have now been officially denied. Government sources now say that the police have returned in strength to most areas of the capital from which they had previously withdrawn, and that most services are working normally. There are no reports of casualties. The causes of the disturbance are still not clear. But a correspondent in the area says in a despatch to the BBC that speculation about a concerted anti-government rebellion can be discounted. It seems more likely, the correspondent adds, that the disturbances were sparked off by radical youth groups protesting against unemployment and what they see as continued foreign domination of the economy . . ."

Jane said, "I'm glad to know what it's all about."

Harry said, "You mean about the 'foreign domination.' But

in the end, you know, that is what those guys down there would believe they were doing. Because what they're doing is too crazy."

"That's how it will go down in the books," Roche said. "That's how it will be discussed. That's what you can start believing yourself. And start acting on."

Dazzle, like the dazzle of the sea, came to a part of the city: the new tin roofs of the shantytown redevelopment, catching the sun.

Harry said, "Police withdrawing from areas of the city? I am damn glad I didn't know it was so bad."

"Perhaps in a couple of days we'll know how bad it is now," Roche said.

They sat and watched the silent city. They began to feel the heat of the sun on their faces and legs. The wet Bermuda grass was drying out. In the light the old fires in the city hardly seemed to smoke.

Harry said, "We used to have a private security patrol up here. Ten dollars a month. Twenty-four hours. I bet you a lot of people now wish we still had it."

Jane said, "Why did you stop?"

Harry made a theatrical sour face and hunched his shoulders up and down. "Some people say they didn't like it, some people say it was too expensive. But mostly it was because in a situation like this people never cooperate. They always think they can buy peace for themselves when the time comes, and so they get picked off one by one. They much prefer doing what they're doing now. You know Yvette, Jane? She is baking cakes for the police. And, my dear, icing them. As though is some kind of kiddies' carnival going on in the station. And Joseph too. Making his nice little sandwiches. He even chopping off the crust."

Jane said, "Ten dollars a month? Was that all they charged?"

Roche said, "It was cheap, wasn't it, Jane?"

"Per house," Harry said. "But they weren't so hot, you know. Some smart guy came down from the States and decided to give the guards motorbikes and two-way radios, and to increase the charge to twenty dollars a month. And that was that. Those guys just went crazy about their bikes and radios. They start going so fast that if you stand outside your gate and shout 'Help!' you'd be damn lucky if they hear you."

PRECISELY AT eight o'clock the helicopters arrived. A magnified mosquito hum at first, and then, very quickly, a roar and a clacking, destroying silence, making conversation impossible on the porch. They came from the right, from a source in a part of the bay hidden by the hills. The noise of one helicopter overrode the noise of the others. The house seemed to shake, and the brick-floored porch on its platform of packed earth felt unstable. (The porch, built on sloping land, had sunken in once before; the surface bricks had been taken up then, and there had been nothing below, a depression, the packed earth having subsided.) Noise engulfed the house; dust blew about. The pale shadow of the flying craft rippled down the sloping garden and then fell on the tops of the trees beyond the gully at the foot of the garden. The American markings on the helicopter were large; the men inside weren't in uniform.

Other helicopters were flying over other areas of the hills. And, in the distance, helicopters of another type, seemingly broken-backed, were moving in staggered flights of three across the sea that was still smooth, across the gray-green mangrove and the brown plain to the airport, hovering close to the ground there, then rising and flying back the way they had come, black insects returning to their hidden nest.

Harry said, "Licks."

Noise engulfed the house again: the patrol helicopter returning. It covered them with its shadow; the porch felt fragile. And the air was full of dust.

Away on the plain the helicopters continued to move in threes, coming down to the airport and almost settling, and then whirling away as if angered.

Harry said, "Peter, you have glasses? Binoculars, nuh."

Roche shook his head. His face had gone blank.

Harry said, "I hope Joseph ain't running out into the garden with my glasses. It's just the kind of thing he would do. Foolish, nuh. But they would pick him off easy-easy from up there. I must say I feel naked like hell sitting out here. The Americans shoot everybody. They're worse than the South Americans."

Roche said, "We didn't have to wait too long to find out how bad it is."

Harry said, "And I was trying to hide a little revolver from Joseph. I was wondering when this was going to happen. The Americans are not going to let anybody here stop them lifting bauxite. You see, Jane? They don't just read pornography."

They heard their helicopter come close, and they waited. But this time it flew lower, seeming to follow the road down to the city.

Harry said, "I knew this government could never fall. It's like that advertisement for Rawlplug or whatever it is. Fix and forget."

Roche said, "I saw this once before. Or something like it. I saw a small town emptying. It was in the middle of the day. The cars were racing out in one direction. Along the same road in the other direction a column of armored vehicles was moving in. They don't move fast, but they always look as though they do. Behind them was a column of mounted policemen with guns. They were taking their time. They had all the time in the world. Even a small man looks tall on horseback. They were wearing flak jackets, so that they looked like invalids with weak chests, as though they were all feeling very cold. I believe it was the most obscene thing I had ever seen. Preparations for a killing."

Jane said, "You mean we just have to sit here and watch this happen?"

Roche said, "You won't see anything from up here."

They remained on the porch, talking little, watching. But there was little new to see. They saw only what they had already seen: the helicopters patrolling the hills above the city, the other helicopters ferrying men and vehicles to the airport.

The sun grew hotter; slowly over the hills and the plain the bush fires were rekindled. They left the porch and went inside. They were subdued. They sat in the front room, still cool, and looked out through the picture window at the brown lawn and the contracting black shadow of the house.

Harry said, "I can tell you what is happening down there now. A lot of guys are running for cover. Every man is sobering up fast. Everybody forgetting about the palm branch and the Arrow of Peace. 'Me? How you could think I had anything to do with that nonsense?' The same people who were going to pull the place down. Every man is now a government man, and they love the Americans. The whole thing can make you cry."

Then silence returned, and they listened, waiting for disturbance. The light hardened; the heat began to have a settled quality. From time to time, with relief, they heard the clacking of a helicopter. The brown lawn became bright; the picture window began to radiate heat. They were silent. The emptiness of the house became oppressive; they became dissatisfied with being together. Each of them wished to be alone.

In the cool of the early morning both Roche and Jane had been glad to see Harry. Now, with a formality they would have used with a stranger, they saw him to his car. His white canvas shoes made his feet look as big and busy as before; the antique revolver bulged in the pocket of his tight shorts. But he took desolation with him; and he left desolation behind.

At midday they closed the back door, shutting out the glare of the porch and the view of the city, where here and there, on a tin roof, sunlight glinted, where swamp and sea and land blurred in the heat haze. They waited for disturbance. But the city remained silent. There was no sound of disturbance, no sound of gunfire. All afternoon there was silence.

There was silence when they opened the back door again and sat out on the porch in the shadow of the house. The declining sun touched the rainless clouds and the high-banked smoke of bush fires and the rubbish dump with bright color. A bicycle bell rang somewhere below and the noise came up clear. Then a radio was heard, and another radio seemed to answer from another part of the hills. The city was returning to life at sunset, slowly, returning to life as it did—in times that now seemed remote—after very heavy rain. The lights came on. There were few patches of darkness; there were no fires. And all around and below the hills radios played.

But the house on the Ridge remained empty, dead. Adela, reappearing in the morning, moved without her thumping strides. Her flesh seemed to have grown softer; she moved as though not wishing to draw attention to herself. The tension seemed to have gone out of her body. Her nostrils no longer quivered, and there was a little smile in her round eyes. No one asked her about her absence, but she said, "My godmother was very sick."

13

"HELP DE poor! I am very grateful. Help de blind! I am very t'ankful." The blind and legless beggar was back, red blank eyes in an upturned face, his chant steady and loud, gliding about his stretch of pavement on his little low cart.

Friday afternoon, and the city center had filled up again: the vendors of sweets and cigarettes and Turf Club sweepstakes; the middle-aged women with "belly-full" cakes and currant rolls in glass cases; the bicycles and the route taxis, the drivers from time to time putting out an arm and making an involved gesture, like a dancer's gesture, to indicate their route; the coconut carts and vans. Water from a thousand waste pipes ran in the open gutters. But there were no school uniforms among the pavement crowds, and, though there were few policemen, no loitering groups. People looked about them as they walked, and some people walked as if on broken glass. They were rediscovering their city: the arrow daubed and scrawled everywhere, some shop windows still shuttered, some boarded up. One or two shops, smashed open and exposed, seemed to have been abandoned by their owners: the walkers moved away from those, as though part of the pavement had been roped off.

Roche stood outside Sablich's parking lot and waited for Meredith.

Meredith was on time. He was driving his little blue car. Roche had expected something more official. He wasn't sure how he should greet the friend who had become the minister. For a minute, though, greeting Meredith, opening the car door, getting in, looking with Meredith for traffic before they drove off, it seemed that nothing had changed since Sunday. But as soon as they were in the stream of traffic, and the time had come to speak, Roche felt ill at ease. The words he had been hoping would come to him didn't come. He was unwilling to say anything about the events of the week, remembering what he had heard from Harry, and from people in the Sablich's office, about Meredith's part in those events. He was silent a little too long; and then he saw that it was also too late to say anything about Meredith's appointment as a minister.

Meredith said, "I'm glad we were able to do something, Peter. I'm sorry it was such short notice."

The friend, the minister, the radio journalist.

They were driving to the radio station to record the interview for Meredith's *Encounter* program. Meredith had mentioned it on Sunday; and Roche hadn't forgotten. He had speculated about it; he had run through various kinds of interviews in his head; he had prepared. The recording had been arranged the previous day, and apparently in something of a hurry. And it had been arranged rather officially. Meredith's secretary in the ministry, and not Meredith, had telephoned.

Roche said, "It may be our last chance."

As he spoke, Roche remembered what Jane had said on Sunday. She had said that Meredith didn't like Roche being on the island; but that when Roche had said he was leaving, Meredith's face had fallen. Roche glanced now at Meredith. But Meredith's expression hadn't changed.

Meredith said, "Why?"

"I feel there's nothing for me to do here."

"Don't say any more. We'll save it for the studio. Otherwise we'll lose it. When I spoke to you at Harry's on Sunday I was thinking we might do something philosophical and offbeat. But it's all become highly topical. That happens a lot of the time. If you chase the topical too hard you can end up being stale."

Everywhere walls and windows were scrawled and daubed with the arrow. But the city showed little damage. Not many buildings had been totally destroyed by fire; and often, even in the streets of the Chinese wholesale food shops and the Syrian cloth shops, though a shop had been blackened at pavement level, its upper floors still looked whole.

Meredith said, "Miraculously, it still works."

And for a moment he was like a friend again, like the man Roche had known in the earliest days. But the alertness was new: the small hunched figure at the wheel, the small gripping hands, child's hands. The wounded, determined smile, hinting now at secrets, was new, and belonged to a new man—the man receiving looks from people in the streets, and acknowledging the looks with a slight movement of the head: a nod to someone who was looking for a nod, but, to someone who might resent a nod, nothing, just an involuntary movement of the head. He had been confirmed in his power; he was a minister in a government that had survived. But Roche thought that Meredith was still uncertain; he was still a man who thought he was presuming.

Roche had been embarrassed. Now he began to feel sickened.

Meredith said, "Jimmy sprang a surprise on us."

Roche thought, but without anxiety: He's prepared something for me.

Meredith said, "How is Jane?"

"Jane has very much withdrawn into herself."

"I imagine we've sunk even lower in her estimation."

"She's leaving us, you know."

"One day, I suppose, we'll go over the brink. It was a close thing, Peter."

"Were the helicopters necessary?"

"I don't know. The soldiers didn't leave the airport. But I don't know."

The radio building, a new building on three floors, was set far back from the road. The in-gates and out-gates, on either side of a brick wall, were open. Inside, policemen with rifles stood behind a wooden barrier; they were the first armed policemen Roche had seen that day. Between the whitewashed curbstones of the in-lane and the out-lane there was a garden: the ornamental blue-tiled pool empty; shrubs and plants dusty, growing out of dusty earth, but their flowers bright; clumps of the small *gri-gri* palm with their curving, notched trunks. The lane was black, freshly surfaced, the asphalt tacky in the heat. The parking lot, marked with new white lines, was in the shadow of the building. Meredith parked carefully, avoiding the white lines.

When they had got out of the car and were together again, walking to the entrance, which was at the side of the building, out of the sun, Roche said, "What about Jimmy?"

"He's not present."

"Not present? What do you mean? He's been arrested?"

"That would be excessive. There are other people who will settle accounts with Jimmy. He's in retirement. But you know more about Jimmy than I do."

It was cool behind the glass doors. Meredith had lost his uncertainty. Here he was the journalist and the minister; he had stopped smiling and his manner was businesslike and official. The big brown woman at the desk stood up and was introduced to Roche. The policeman with the rifle stiffened and stared.

Meredith said to the woman, "We'll use E studio." He said to Roche, with a smile, "It has a nice view."

They took the elevator and went up two floors. Meredith turned on a light in a dark corridor. They went a little way down this corridor, and Meredith pushed open double doors and turned on another dim light. The small room ahead was in darkness, the larger room to the left was bright.

Meredith said, "The studio manager's not here. But I think we can go in. As you can see, it isn't exactly BBC."

He led Roche, through double doors, into the larger room. And when they were there he said, "Peter, do you mind waiting here for a little? I'll go and see what's happening to the SM."

The double doors closed behind Meredith as he went out, and there was silence in the studio. The sealed picture window gave Roche a view of the city such as he had never had. In the city center there was nothing to be seen except other buildings. But, here, in what had once been a good residential area, no tall buildings blocked the view, and Roche looked over roofs, silver or red, dramatized by the tall pillars and the dark-green fronds of the royal palm, to the sea, and to the hills that ran down, ridge after ridge, to the sea. The hills were bare and fire-marked, smoking in patches, but the sun was going down behind them, and the sea glittered. In the deep water behind those hills, doubtless, the American warships lay. But Roche, imagining the sunset soon to come, the hills and the royal palms against the evening sky, thought: It is, after all, very beautiful. It is a pity I've never seen it like this, and have never enjoyed it. And some time later he thought: But perhaps one never enjoys these things.

He was reducing his thoughts to words, formulating whole sentences. It was almost as if, in the silent room, waiting for Meredith, who seemed a long time, he had begun to talk to himself.

A silent room, a silent view: the picture window was made up of two panes of heavy glass, separated by a gap the width of the wall. The glass was radiating heat. Discovering this, Roche soon discovered that the room had a warm, stale, furry smell, as though dust and fluff were rising from the carpet.

The double doors were pushed open, and Meredith came in.

Meredith said, "The SM's coming."

"This studio's stuffy."

"The air conditioning can take a little time."

They sat down at the round table with the microphone, the green bulb, the heavy glass ash tray.

Meredith said, "I have no notes. Let's keep it like a conversation. What always matters is what you are saying or what I am saying, and not what you think you're going to say next. Don't worry about repeating or going back. Don't worry about referring to things we've talked about in the past. Let's keep it conversational, and let's not pretend we don't know one another. I'll call you Peter and you'll call me Meredith, if you want to call me anything at all. It's going to be rough, you know, Peter."

Roche said, "I've nothing to hide." It was a line he had prepared.

A weak light came on in the adjoining cubicle and through

the glass window a very tall man wearing a white shirt and a tie could be seen. He smiled at Roche and Meredith and sat down before his instruments.

Meredith said, "The SM."

Roche was perspiring. He said, "I'm smelling dust everywhere. It's the kind of thing that would give Harry asthma in a second."

The voice of the studio manager came through the speaker: "Can we have something for voice level, please?" For such a big man, his voice was curiously soft, even effeminate.

Meredith, lifting his head slightly, smiled, for the studio manager, for Roche; and Roche noticed that Meredith was perspiring all over the wide gap between his everted nostrils and his mouth. Meredith said to the microphone, "Every day in every day I grow better and better."

The studio manager gave a thumbs-up sign, and Meredith said, "Peter?"

Roche said to the microphone, "You need to do some vacuuming here."

The green light on the table came on.

Meredith said, "We'll go into it straight away." He said to the microphone, "This is the Peter Roche interview for *Encounter*." He paused, and when he spoke again his voice was lighter and more relaxed than it had been so far. "Peter, you were saying as we were driving here to the studio that you didn't think you had anything more to do here. Would you like to go into that a little?"

"I've begun to feel like a stranger. Recent events have made me feel like a stranger."

"Do you feel more like a stranger now than when you came— seven, eight months ago?"

"I never thought about it then. I was very happy to be here."

"But didn't you think, when you were coming here, a place you'd never been, that you were going to be a stranger?"

"A stranger in that way, yes. But I thought that there was work for me to do. I thought that certain problems had been settled here, and there was work I could do."

"You mean racial problems?"

"Yes, racial problems, and all the things that go with it. I mean not carrying that burden, not wasting one's time and one's life carrying that burden. I thought there was work I could do here. Work."

"I see you gesturing with your hands. I suppose by work you mean constructive work."

"It's a human need. I suppose one realizes that late."

"Creativity. An escape into creativity."

"If you want to put it like that."

"But some people will find it odd, Peter, people who know your background—and now you tell us of your need for creative work—that you should look for this with a firm like the one you chose."

"Sablich's."

"You've mentioned the name."

"It wasn't what I chose. I would say it was what offered itself. And I liked what they offered. I didn't know much about them when I took the job."

"But you know now."

"It doesn't alter my attitude. I know they have a past here, and that people think about them in a certain way. But I also know they have done a lot to change. The fact that they should want to employ me is a sign of that change, I think."

"Some people might say public relations."

"There is that. I always knew that. But isn't that enough? I was more concerned with the work they offered, and what they offered seemed pretty fair to me. In a situation like that I believe one can only go by people's professed intentions and attitudes. If you start probing too much and you look for absolute purity, you can end up doing nothing at all."

"I can see how some of our attitudes can irritate you, Peter. And we're all guilty. We have a special attitude to people who take up our cause. It is unfair, but we tend to look up to them."

"But I didn't think I had to keep to a straiter path than anybody else. I'm not on display. I don't know why people here should think that."

Roche's temper had suddenly risen. He was sweating; his shirt was wet. He turned away from the microphone and said, "The air here is absolutely foul."

"The air conditioning doesn't seem to be working efficiently," Meredith said. He too was sweating. He looked about him, perfunctorily, and then he spoke to the microphone again.

"Peter, you say you came here for the opportunity of doing creative work, unhampered by other pressures. And you've done quite a lot. But in the public mind you have become associated with the idea of the agricultural commune. You know, back to the land, the revolution based on land. I don't believe it's a secret that it hasn't been a success. Are you very disappointed?"

"It would have been nice if it had worked."

"Did you think it would work?"

"I had my doubts. I thought it was antihistorical. All over the world people are leaving the land to go to the cities. And they know what they want. They want more excitement, more lights. They want to be richer. They also want to be brighter. They don't want to feel they're missing out. And most of them are missing out, of course."

"You didn't think the process could be reversed here?"

"Not after I'd been here. You can't just go back to the land as a gesture. You can't pretend. The land is a way of life."

"And perhaps also a way of work. Not a way of dropping out. But I believe you've used the key word, Peter: pretend."

"Only very rich people in very rich countries drop out. You can't drop out if you're poor."

"But that's our trouble here. You've probably observed it. We are too vulnerable to other people's ideas. We don't have too many of our own. But, Peter, you say the idea of the agricultural commune in a society like ours is antihistorical. And yet you helped."

"It was what they said they wanted."

"Your theory of professed intentions."

"If the choice had been mine I would have chosen some other project. Something in the city."

"And yet for this antihistorical project, which you didn't think would succeed, all kinds of people and organizations were pressured, to put it no higher."

"We wanted to involve everybody. Or as many people as possible."

"You certainly succeeded."

"That way it seemed the thing might just work. And we received a lot of government encouragement. A lot of help."

"The government too believes in professed intentions."

"We were all misled. Perhaps we were all hoping against hope."

"And perhaps, hoping against hope, we misled others. Where do you think the error started?"

"I suppose you can say it started here. In the society you have here. It isn't organized for work or for individual self-respect."

"We won't quarrel about that. But you don't think the leadership might have had something to do with it as well?"

"You mean Jimmy Ahmed."

"Tell us about him, Peter, now that you've mentioned him. It's a strange thing to say, but you know him better than most people here."

"I found him attractive, a leader. He seemed to be able to get things done. And he had a following."

"I know. I went to school with Jimmy. He was Jimmy Leung then. I've told you this before. And to me Jimmy's always been something of a problem. I was in London when he suddenly emerged as the black leader. In fact, I was one of the first people to interview him. He was living in a big house in Wimbledon, and I thought he was quite well looked after. Even then he had powerful friends. But, you know, when Jimmy talked about this country, I couldn't recognize it. Some of the things he said I found quite humiliating. I've told you about the banana-skin game he said he played at school. You would drop the banana skin and if it fell one way you were going to marry a fair-skinned person, and if it fell the other way you were going to marry a yellow person with freckles. You can imagine how the women columnists took that up."

"I think you're making too much of a small thing."

"But sometimes small things can tell us more than professed

intentions. I never played that game at school. I don't know anyone who played that game. It sounds to me more like a Chinese
game. But the people in England took it seriously."

"I wonder. But I don't know much about that. I didn't know
Jimmy in England. I met him here. I'd only vaguely heard about
him before I came here."

"We're a dependent people, Peter. We need other people's
approval. And when people come to us with reputations made
abroad we tend to look up to them. It's something you yourself
have been complaining about. But I have another problem here.
You know the position of black people in England. You know
the difficulties, the campaigns of hate. Yet some of us get taken
up by certain people and are made famous. Then we are sent back
here as leaders."

"You think there's a conspiracy? People aren't that interested."

"That's what I mean. People aren't interested. They are ig-
norant, they don't care. But certain people get taken up. It is this
element that is my problem, this element in a place like England
that takes up some of us. Is it guilt? A touch of the tarbrush, as
they say over there—black blood? Or is it something else? Some
other kind of relationship. Services rendered, mutual services."

"I think you worry too much about those people."

"You think I do?"

Since he had smiled to speak his sentence for voice level,
Meredith had been serious, unflustered, his expression neutral in
spite of the sweat and the heat that had inflamed his eyes. Now,
for the first time, he had spoken angrily. But Roche didn't believe
in the anger. He thought it forced, self-regarding, a lawyer's court-
room anger; it astonished, disappointed him, and it left him calm.

Roche said, "How much longer are we going on?"

Meredith, readjusting his expression, said, "Not much." Then
he spoke to the microphone again.

"But we'll leave it, Peter. You say you found Jimmy Ahmed
attractive."

"He seemed to get things done."

"But what he was trying to do was antihistorical. Did you think
someone with a shopkeeping background was really equipped for

the task he set out to do? Or did you think, since it was antihistorical, it didn't matter?"

"I thought he might have chosen another project. With Jimmy, you always had to bring him down to earth. Farming is a serious business. It requires a lot of boring application. It isn't for someone who's easily bored or wants quick results."

"I think you are being naïve, Peter. You were a stranger when you came. I accept that. But did you think, after you'd got here, that someone with a Chinese shopkeeping background could be in tune with aspirations of black people?"

"He seemed to have followers."

"Yes, followers. That's why our brothels are full. But let's leave that too. You said you came here because you wished to do creative work. That implies you felt you were needed."

"I was wrong."

"But it's nice to feel needed. And that also implies that you felt you would be welcome. And you are welcome. But what a nice world you inhabit, Peter. You have so much room for error. I wouldn't be welcome among white people, however much I wanted to work among them."

"That's the way the world is."

Roche looked away and said, "I'm choking. I can't think clearly in this studio." But he spoke without temper.

Sweat was running down Roche's forehead into his eyes and down his neck into his shirt. He was aware of the studio manager in the dimly lit cubicle; and he had half addressed those words to him. But there was no response from the big man behind glass, cool in his white shirt and striped tie. The man had missed the appeal; he remained neutral; his expression didn't alter.

Roche looked away, past Meredith and the microphone, to the picture window, radiating heat. Beyond the two panes of glass was the silent view: the sun going down behind the hills, the sky turning pale ocher, the sea silver, the hills red-black, the royal palms darkening against the sky.

The studio manager, responding to the silence, said, "Shall we stop?" The curiously soft voice again, singsong and slightly effeminate.

Meredith, his face wet, his shirt wet and sticking round the collarbone so that his skin and vest showed, said, "We'll go on for a little longer. It's bad for me too, Peter." He pulled out a loose white handkerchief from his hip pocket; but then he changed his mind; he didn't use the handkerchief, and he left it on the green table.

"I don't want to embarrass you, Peter. Especially now that you say you're leaving us. Have you any plans for the future? Do you know what you'll do?"

"I suppose I'll go back to England and try to get another job."

"In the same field?"

"No."

"So you're washing your hands of us. I feel we've let you down. I feel you haven't enjoyed your time with us."

"I wish my life had taken another turn."

"What do you mean? Do you wish you hadn't done what you did? Do you think it's all gone to waste?"

"We've talked about this before, Meredith. I don't think regret enters into it. I suppose I would do it again. I would have no option. I don't suppose I ever thought about it going to waste or not. I just wish it hadn't been necessary to do what I did. I wish the world were arranged differently, so that afterwards I didn't feel I had been landed with a side. I wish I hadn't walked into that particular trap."

"Trap?"

"Thinking I had somehow committed myself to one kind of action and one kind of cause. There is so much more to the world. You know what I mean. You mustn't pretend you don't know what I mean."

"As you say, you feel like a stranger here. You don't feel involved. And I can see how some of our attitudes can irritate you. I feel we've let you down. We haven't used you well—and that's true of a lot of other people besides yourself. Because you're a brave man, Peter. People who've read your book know that you're a brave man and that you've suffered for your beliefs, in a way that most of us will never suffer. Can we talk about your book? It wouldn't embarrass you?"

"We can talk about my book."

"It's an extraordinary book. Quite a document. But I'm sure you don't want me to repeat what the critics have already told you."

"They didn't say that."

"One of my problems with the book is that, although it's very political—and I know that you consider yourself a political animal —there seems to be no framework of political belief."

"I'm not sure I know what you mean."

"We've talked about this. You write as though certain things merely happened to you, were forced on you."

"Some people have said this to me. It was what the publisher said. I suppose that's what's wrong with it as a book."

"You describe the most monstrous kind of white aggression against black people. Monstrous things happened to you and to people you know. And some of those people are still there. You describe individual things very clearly. But it isn't always easy to see where you were going or where you thought you were going."

"I began to feel that when I was writing. What was clear at the time became very confused as I was writing. I felt swamped by all the people I had to write about, and all the little events which I thought important. I thought I would never be able to make things clear. But I was hoping people wouldn't notice."

"But the astonishing thing is that you risked so much for so little. Looking back now, the guerrilla activities you describe in your book, the little acts of sabotage—they really cannot be compared with the guerrilla activities of other people in other countries. Would you say that was fair?"

"We were amateurs. The situation was different in other countries."

"And perhaps the motivation was different as well. It isn't for me to pass any judgment, so far from the scene. I can only admire. But I find it hard to imagine that you expected what you were doing to have any result. Tearing up a railway, bombing a power station."

"I'm amazed myself now at the things we tried to do. I suppose we led too sheltered lives. We exaggerated the effect of a bomb."

"It was a gesture. You were making a gesture."

"It didn't seem so at the time."

"And you and your companions paid heavily for that gesture. You were tortured, Peter."

Roche, warm sweat tickling through his hair and down his forehead, stared at the microphone.

"Even that you write about as something that just happened."

Roche turned his head and looked at the picture window. The royal palms were dark warm silhouettes against the glowing sky.

"No bitterness," Meredith said. "No anger. Many people have remarked on this. But I have a problem with it. At school—many people will remember this—we were sometimes given a punishment assignment. I don't know what happens nowadays, but we wrote lines. 'The way of the transgressor is exceedingly difficult.' "

The tone of Meredith's voice, and a certain rapidity in the delivery, indicated that this was something he had prepared. Roche heard the professional laugh in the voice. Dutifully—the duty owed to someone who had prepared so well and was trying so hard— Roche turned to face Meredith again. He saw the smile, not the smile of the uplifted face, but Meredith's other smile.

"That was what we wrote," Meredith said. "We would write fifty of those, or a hundred, even two hundred. Some boys sold lines. And that to me is the message of your book. You transgressed; you were punished; the world goes on."

"That's how it's turned out. If you want to put it like that."

"It's the message of your book. You've endured terrible things —you've got to try to come to terms with it, and I can see how that attitude can give you a kind of personal peace. But it's a dead end. It doesn't do anything for the rest of us. It doesn't hold out hope for the rest of us."

"Perhaps it's a dead end for me. But I don't know why you should want me to hold out hope."

"We look up to people like you. I've told you. I'm trying to determine what you have to offer us. No bitterness, Peter. No anger. Don't you think you've allowed yourself to become the conscience of your society?"

"I don't know what people mean when they talk like that."

"But you do. It's nice to have someone in the background

wringing their hands for you, averting the evil eye—what we call over here mal-yeux. You've heard the word? People are perfectly willing for you to be their conscience and to suffer, while they get on with the business of aggressing, and the thugs and psychopaths get on with their work in the torture chambers."

"They're not thugs. They're perfectly ordinary people. They wear suits. They live in nice houses with gardens. They like going to good restaurants. They send their grown-up daughters to Europe for a year."

"And people like you make it all right for them. Your society needs people like you. You belong to your society. I can understand why you say you are a stranger and feel a little bit at sea among us."

"I came here to do a job of work."

"We've been through that before. I don't want to embarrass you, Peter. But you'll understand that we look at things from different angles. Have you really come to terms with your experience? Do you really think the effort has gone to waste?"

"I haven't come to terms with it. All my life I've been frightened of pain. Of being in a position where pain could be inflicted on me."

Meredith crumpled the white handkerchief on the table. "You talk about that as though it was something that had to happen."

"I know. I used to wonder about that. And it used to frighten me."

"This obsession with pain. It's something we all share to some degree. In your book—we've talked about this—in that chapter about your early life you talk about the German camps."

"The publisher asked me to write in that chapter."

"In that chapter you talk about the extermination camps. You say it was the most formative experience of your adolescence."

"I'm forty-five. I imagine most people of my generation were affected."

"It made you sympathetic to the Jews?"

"What I felt had nothing to do with the Jews."

"Did you want to revenge the people who had suffered?"

"I wanted to honor them. In my mind. Not to dishonor them."

"No anger?"

"What I felt wasn't anger."

"What did you feel, Peter?"

"I was ashamed." Roche touched his left arm and felt his own warm sweat. "I was ashamed for this." He let his hand rest on the wet arm. "I was ashamed that the body I had could be treated in that way."

"And the test came. You made your gesture. You cut your railway line, you blew up your power station. The gesture was important. And you were prepared for the consequences. The psychology of bravery. It's a very humbling thing. But now you're at peace with the world. No bitterness, no anger. This obsession with pain and human suffering is in the past."

"No, it's much worse now."

Meredith, crumpling the handkerchief, looking at the studio clock, appeared not to hear. "I feel we've gone a long way from the problems of white aggression in Southern Africa. Anyway, here we are, I can't say at home, but at the end of your personal odyssey. You're a stranger, you don't feel involved. You're involved with an agricultural commune which you consider antihistorical and which you don't think can succeed. But for you it's an opportunity for creative work. The human need, as you say. For you work is important. You aren't too concerned about results. Peter, our time is almost up, and I must ask you a plain question. And I must ask you to answer it, because it is important for those of us who have to live here. Didn't you think, didn't it ever occur to you, that the Thrushcross Grange commune was a cover for the guerrillas?"

"It occurred to me once or twice, but I dismissed it."

"You were wrong. But why did it occur to you, and why did you dismiss it?"

"It occurred to be because I'd read about guerrillas in the papers. But it seemed to me farfetched. I didn't believe in the guerrillas."

"What did you believe in?"

"I believed in the gangs."

Meredith raised his face and for some seconds he fixed a smile on Roche, looking at him above the microphone. Then he turned to the studio manager's cubicle, pushed back his chair carelessly, and said, "It's finished. It was marvelous. Let's get out and breathe."

Meredith stood up. Roche remained sitting. Meredith's shirt was wet all the way down: Roche could see the bump of Meredith's navel below his vest. It was like noticing a secret. Headachy, temples throbbing, not sure why he was focusing on Meredith's navel, Roche thought: Yes, that was my mistake. I should have looked for that first. That, and the waistband.

In the studio was the amber light of late afternoon. Just beyond the double doors was dim electric light that emphasized the darkness. And it was very cold. The refrigerated air struck through Roche's wet shirt, seconds before so hot, and chilled him instantly into goose flesh.

The studio manager, in his white shirt and striped tie, was as cool and calm as he had always seemed. The old-fashioned respectability of his white shirt and tie, the smoothness of his very black, hairless skin, the fullness of his pure African features, his heavy broad shoulders, the languor of his manner as he filled the duplicated form pinned to his writing board, the unhurried civility with which he turned to look at Roche and Meredith, marked him as a man from the deep country, perhaps the first of his family to be educated, the first to hold a respectable job in the city. He raised himself in his chair and smiled briefly at Roche and Meredith.

In his soft singsong voice he said to Meredith, "Twenty-two t'irty-five."

Meredith said, "With the intro we'll make it twenty-five minutes. We won't have to hack it about."

Meredith's step was springy in the dim, chill corridor.

"It was very good, Peter."

"Are you going to take out the interruptions?"

"Yes, those will go. You sound worried. I have an editing session tomorrow. The intro will be recorded then. You have nothing to worry about. It was better than you think. In these matters I'm a better judge than you." His talk was as springy as his walk.

Roche said, "The studio manager seemed pretty cool."

"Those people hear nothing. They only hear sound and level. They can read a book or write a letter while they're listening."

When they were getting into the elevator, which hissed and felt very cold, Roche said, "I'm sorry I said that about the gangs. Can that be taken out?"

"Why? I thought that was very good."

"I was thinking about that boy's mother."

"But it's true. She knows it's true. And it's what people here need to be told."

Roche didn't want to say any more. They came out into the lobby. The policeman with the rifle stiffened; and the big middle-aged brown woman half rose from her chair.

Outside the light was soft. But they stepped from the air-conditioned building into heat, rising from the black, newly laid asphalt forecourt. No view of the hills and the sea from here, only the tops of a few royal palms against the sunset sky: charcoal streaks, dark-red rainless clouds.

A great exhausted melancholy came to Roche: the sense of the end of the day, a feeling of futility, of being physically lost in an immense world. Melancholy, at the same time, for the others, more rooted than himself: for the studio manager, the man from the country, for the policeman with the rifle and the woman at the desk who were both so deferential to Meredith, melancholy for Meredith: an overwhelming exasperation, almost like contempt, confused with a sense of the fragility of their world.

Meredith said, "Am I taking you back to Sablich's? Is your car there?"

"No, Jane's using it today."

"I'll drive you home."

They didn't talk. As soon as they were out in the streets and people began to look at them, Meredith appeared to remember his earlier uncertainty; and his excitement abated. Roche's melancholy subsided into concern about what he had said. He thought he had managed well, except for that slip at the very end, when he had spoken about the gangs. But as they drove through the populous flat areas of the city, one or two lights coming on in the open stands at crossroads, as they climbed up to the cooler air of the Ridge, he remembered other things; and what had seemed to him, in the suffocating studio, a logical and controlled performance appalled him more and more. Meredith had gone far; he wondered now that he had allowed Meredith to go so far. Roche felt he was coming out of a stupor; in that stupor he had trapped himself. And by the time they came to the house he had begun to have the feeling that a calamity had befallen him.

The car was in the garage.

Meredith, already less uncertain up here on the Ridge, in the growing dark, away from the crowds, said, "Jane must be in. I'll go in and greet her."

Roche didn't take Meredith in through the garage door. He led him across the lawn, past the ivy-hung, rough-rendered concrete wall and the picture window, to the front door, which was little used; through the hall into the almost empty back room, used for nothing; and out onto the brick-floored porch.

Jane was there, in trousers and blouse. The evening paper, a glass of lager, cigarettes, and her blue lighter were on the metal table.

She said, "Hello, Meredith." She barely turned her head; her voice was casual.

The city below was in darkness. But up here the light still lasted. The hibiscus flowers glowed.

Meredith smiled, that smile at once self-satisfied and wounded.

Jane said, "How did it go?"

Meredith said, "It went very well. Peter's worried, but he doesn't have anything to worry about."

Jane said, "Peter talks very well." She spoke neutrally, stating a fact.

Meredith sat down heavily in one of the metal chairs and picked up the newspaper. Jane looked down at the dark city: lights coming on.

"We ranged far and wide," Meredith said. "We talked about mutual acquaintances." He folded the paper and dropped it on the table. "So you're leaving us, Jane."

Adela came through the back room to the porch. Jane raised her head and looked at Adela.

Meredith said, "I hope we haven't frightened you away."

Jane said, "Adela?"

Adela, not looking at Jane, stood beside Meredith's chair. She bent softly, deferentially, toward him and said, in a coaxing voice neither Jane nor Roche had heard her use, "Mr. Herbert would like to use a beer?"

Meredith stood up, rising on his toes. "No, thank you, Adela. I've got to be going."

Adela was approving. The look on her face suggested that her deference, and the polite words she had used, had been rewarded.

For some seconds Meredith rocked on his toes. "You must come back, Jane. Come back as a tourist. For a holiday."

She looked at him with moist eyes and nodded. She appeared to hesitate, but then she said, "Good-by, Meredith."

Roche didn't move to interfere.

The light had gone. The hibiscus flowers were lost in the darkness. The sky in the east was a very dark blue. The mood of sunset was on Roche, the sense of the fragility of all their worlds. The studio manager, secure in the respectability of his clothes and his radio job; the policeman with the rifle in the lobby of the radio building; the woman at the desk, so deferential to Meredith; Meredith, Jane, himself. For all of them the world was fragile. And there had been a calamity.

Meredith, acting out his exit, his leather heels rapping on terrazzo and parquet, said loudly, as Roche walked with him to the front door, "You must listen tomorrow, Peter. It's better than you think."

14

ROCHE SAID, "It was awful."

They were still sitting on the porch.

Jane said, "But why did you do it? There was nothing to make you stay there."

"Vanity. The terrible vanity that makes you behave so stupidly on these occasions. And there was a third person there. A big black man from the country. He was in the cubicle. That's always fatal: a third person. You start acting for this third person. You can't let yourself down. You slip into a kind of lunacy, and it's all of your own making. You think it's all very logical and that you're acting sensibly. But that man in the cubicle wasn't even listening. Meredith called him the studio manager. Those people only hear sound and level. I don't think he noticed anything."

"Do you think they were in it together?"

"I don't know. I thought at first that Meredith had had the air conditioning turned off deliberately. Then I thought I was wrong. Then again I thought he had done it deliberately. And then, you see, I wasn't really surprised. I was half expecting something like that."

"You didn't ask them to check to see whether the thing was working?"

"No. I didn't want to do that. I didn't want to mention it."

"You didn't even say 'This room's very hot,' or something like that?"

"I said that. I said the room needed vacuuming. But I didn't want to mention the air conditioning. It's one of those things that gets fixed in your mind. Vanity. Exasperation. Rage, contempt. I was half expecting something like that—I thought they had prepared something for me—but I was amazed that Meredith should want to try it on. And I can't tell you how quickly on these occasions you begin to feel you have nothing to defend."

Jane said with decision, "He did it deliberately. You made it very easy for him. And after that he wants to come to your house?"

"They like doing that. I could see so clearly what he was doing. That made it much worse. This nervous little man. Being anti-imperialist, antiwhite. Mopping up after the riots. The government man doing the black populist thing, laying all the enemies low. And so nervous. I could see him believing and not believing in what he was doing and saying—just like a lawyer. I found it so stupid, I can't tell you. I was exasperated. Because Harry is right, you know. They're just fattening up Meredith to throw him to the crowd at some future date."

On the porch it was already cold. The fluorescent light from the kitchen fell on the back garden.

Jane said, "The water's on. Go and have a good shower. You'll feel much better."

She spoke briskly, and she got up after she had spoken, picking up her lighter and cigarettes. But the tone of command in her voice went with a tenderness he hadn't expected. He was comforted; he rose to obey her.

She surprised him like this sometimes, when she appeared to be natural and easy, another person, obeying instincts that had suddenly risen within her. The occasions were rare and abrupt, and remained separate from the rest of their life together; he remembered them. About a month after she had arrived, Jane had said to him one evening, "Your hair's absolutely filthy. Come and I'll wash it for you." In his bathroom she stripped to her pants and brassiere; he took off his shirt and sat on a stool before the wash basin. Washing his hair seriously, speaking only about its filthiness, she had pressed against his shoulder; he felt her hairs and the bone beneath the pad of flesh. But there had been no overt sexual play; no sex had followed; they had been like children playing house.

THEY HAD dinner at the white table in the kitchen. Adela was in her room.

Roche said, "I didn't say anything bad. Nothing that wasn't true or I didn't feel. In fact, nothing I said would have been bad last week, when publicly everybody was on Jimmy's side. It would have been good publicity. Jimmy would have regarded it as good publicity: controversial figure and so on. But with Meredith today I should have acknowledged that Jimmy was washed up. That would have given the whole thing a different slant. But I didn't. And that was the trouble. When Meredith picked me up outside Sablich's I just felt I didn't want to refer to anything that had happened since Sunday. I didn't even talk to him about being a minister. And so in the studio I was still pretending that Jimmy hadn't fallen. You do get these ideas in your head on these occasions, and you never let them go."

Jane said, "Perhaps Jimmy won't hear the broadcast."

"Meredith will make sure that he does. But I didn't say anything bad. I said that Jimmy was easily bored and that you had to bring him down to earth. It's the kind of thing I've said to him on many occasions. I said I didn't think the commune was a good idea. I suppose I shouldn't have said that. And of course Meredith made it all much worse. He made us out to be frauds."

"Which is what he is. Did he talk about the woman in Wimbledon?"

"He brought her in."

"Give a dog a bad name and hang him. Do you know what I think you've done? You've left Jimmy out there for Meredith and those other people to kill."

"Yes, it will get to that. I don't think those people know how close they're getting to that situation. It's so frightening when you begin to feel the sands shifting under you and there's nothing to cling to. There's no law."

"You're getting out, though. That man's got to stay in that house and wait for them to do whatever they're going to do."

"Yes. One day there's going to be an accident. I hope it doesn't get to that. It's so odd. When you're out in the country, in the old estates, and you see the country people walking to church or rocking in their hammocks or drinking in their little bars, you don't think it's that kind of country. But every country is that kind of country. People would be frightened if they know how easily it comes. Meredith wanted to know about torture. I should have told him. You only have to start. It's the first kick in the groin that matters. It takes a lot to do that. After that you can do anything. You can find yourself kicking a man in the groin until he bleeds. Then you find you've stopped tormenting. You've destroyed a human being. You can't put him together again, and all you can do is throw the bleeding meat out of the window. At that stage it's so easy."

Jane said, "But you're getting out."

Roche said, with irony, "Yes. I suppose I will just go back to London and forget it all."

The mood in which he had left the porch, the mood in which he had sat down at the kitchen table, had vanished. For some time they said nothing.

Then he spoke again. His face was drawn and strained. He said, "I used to go to Lisbon sometimes. It was a nice place to be in. Dangerous, full of agents, full of South Africans. But it was out of Africa. I used to go to the bullfights. They told me that in the Portuguese bullfight they didn't kill the bull. I believed them. I went a lot. And then I heard that the bulls were killed afterwards, after the fight. There was nothing else you could do with them. I'd somehow believed that the spears or barbs would just be taken out and the wounds would heal. Oh my God, why is any of us allowed to live at all? That's the miracle, the sheer charity of man to man."

He was alarming her. But he didn't notice.

"When I eat food and enjoy it, I wonder why I am allowed to do so. When I lie down in my bed at night and make myself comfortable, I wonder why I am allowed to do so. It would be so easy to take it away from me. Every night I think about that. It would be so easy to torment me. Once you tie a man's hands you can do anything to him."

Jane said, "This is too morbid. I don't want to hear any more. No one's going to do anything to you here, and you know it."

It wasn't what he had been expecting. He had been half hoping for the comfort, the mood of the earlier part of the evening, the glimpse of the other side of her.

When she left the table, he remained in the kitchen; he heard Adela's radio, turned low. Then he went out to the porch. It was cold, but he sat on one of the metal chairs, listening to the roar, the reggae beat, of the city down below.

Later, after he had closed up, brushed his teeth, and changed into his pajamas, he went to Jane's room. Her door, as always when she had closed the redwood louvers for the night, had been left ajar, for the air. He went in without knocking.

She was in bed, reading a paperback of The Woodlanders, no sheet over her, and she seemed very big in a plain white cotton nightdress. Her arms were exposed; he could see her breasts. He sat at the end of the bed. A door of the fitted wardrobe was open: he could see signs that she had been packing. She hadn't brought many clothes. He looked at the wardrobe clutter, and she continued to read. It was how, in spite of everything, they still occasionally came together: sex as physical comfort and mutual service, changing nothing.

He said, in a tone that was consciously calm, as though he was listening to himself, "You know, what happened today reminded me of something that happened in London. You've probably forgotten. Perhaps you didn't even take it in at the time. You weren't the keenest of publicity managers."

She looked up from her book.

He said, smiling, "You sent a man to see me. You gave him my address and he came to see me. Oh, you telephoned me about it. You said he wanted to do a profile or an interview."

"There were so many people like that."

"Not for my book. Well, he came. I was very pleased to be interviewed. It was like being a writer, you know. Well, he came. He was an enormous man. He was wearing a black leather jacket and rimless glasses. A really enormous man. He was wearing three-quarter-length boots. Swinging London. Gear, you call it, don't you? I remember the boots—pretend-cowboy, pretend-Nazi. He was very polite. He knew a lot. He was very well informed. Then something strange happened, and it happened very quickly. So quickly I couldn't even work out in my own mind how it happened. From being someone who was asking me for my views, he became someone who was giving me his views. And those boots began to change their character. It wasn't swinging London and pretend-Nazi. It was the real thing. The accent changed too. And my room changed character too. I was pleased to have a reporter in it—it seemed the kind of thing an interviewer or reporter would find of interest. But then it became another kind of room. This man had a message for me. If I didn't shut up or, better, get out of England, I was going to be killed. He used the word. He rather enjoyed using the word."

"But that was London. You could have told the publisher. There were all kinds of things you could have done."

"Your England is different from mine. This man was very big. I keep on talking about his size. It isn't only because I'm small. You know I'm not afraid of people. I've a good idea of what the odds are in any given situation, and I can be cautious. But I'm not afraid. It's the way I am. It probably has to do with the school I went to. I suppose if you accept authority and believe in the rules, you aren't afraid of any particular individual. But I was afraid of this man. I could see that he was enjoying himself, acting out the role a little. People in that kind of situation always put on a little style. Perhaps it was a hoax. But I didn't think so. I took him seriously. I believed what he said."

"Was that why you came here?"

Roche smiled. "It was a powerful incentive."

"You didn't come to do the job you told me you wanted to do? I thought that was why you left in such a rush."

"Oh yes, the job. You had your own ideas of the job I was coming out to do. Meredith wanted to know about the job too."

"But he's right to want to know. You talked about working with what there is. So there is something in what they say about you here. You are a refugee."

"The job offered itself. And it seemed the kind of thing I could do."

"And now you'll just leave Jimmy out there for those people to kill. Who's going to give him a job? So Jimmy's right. You've all turned him into a 'playboy.' A plaything. And now you're throwing him to Meredith."

"It's what Jimmy's turned himself into."

"Well, I've news for you. I've news for both of you. He's been my lover."

The book had been resting on her breasts. She took it up again. Her face was as flushed as her arms.

Roche turned to face her. He said, "I don't believe you're lying."

"Why should I lie to you?"

He stood up. "But I don't think it would be news to Meredith."

He went out of the room, closing the door behind him, remembering too late that she left it ajar, for the air.

Some time later he went and opened the door. She was still reading. He stood in the doorway. She looked and saw the satyr's face.

He said, "Has he taken a picture of you naked? Did you pose for him with your legs open?"

A half-smile, of puzzlement and nervousness, settled on her face.

He said, "Isn't that what they do with the women they've degraded? Keep them in their wallet to show the others? Or did he do the other thing? The other act of contempt."

She didn't reply. He left the door ajar and went back to his room.

15

HELLO MARJORIE, Well this will be a surprise to you I bet, I can see you holding this between your slender well-manicured fingers, you wouldn't believe you use toilet paper and do other things (joke) and snorting, Is it Jimmy, what does he want this time, he's had all he's going to get from me. That is my Marge these days I know, different from the old days, older and wiser as you say, but I understand all that, sweetheart, and I don't want anger to come between us anymore.

Sweetheart, I sit in the peace and stillness of this tropical night to pen these words to you, because I want to clear my heart, you are the only person I can write to, and I want you to know that you were right, what you prophesied is all coming true, I am dying alone and unloved and I will die in anger, no other way is possible now. That is a bad way to die, and Marjorie I feel death is close to me tonight, I can hear it in the tropical stillness, fitfully broken by the occasional hoot of an owl, and to tell you the truth sweetheart I feel relieved, I feel I should go now. When we were children and you heard an owl at night you stuck pins in the wick of the lamp to keep death away from the house, but I don't think it stopped the coffins coming.

Will this letter get to you or will they clear it away with the rest of my possessions saying this is another piece of his junk, that is all he's left, junk. No Marge don't snort, I am not appealing for

your sympathy or crying wolf as you may think. You can't help me
now, I know that at least, at least give me that, nobody can help
me, and this letter may never get to you.

I will tell you Marjorie when I was a boy I used to think that
childhood was just a time of disguise and that it was something
I had to go through before I came into my own and that it was
going to be all right when I became a man, what a laugh Marjorie
what a laugh.

It is very black outside, in England you don't know how black
night can be here, I forgot myself when I was in London, and
when I think of London and those places I cannot work out how
I got here, so far from human habitation, and I cannot understand
why I should end here like a ghost, this is my part of the world,
I was born here, this is not London, it's like a bad dream, but I
know I'm not waking up.

I feel tonight, sitting here among my books and letters and
other dead things, like the last man on the earth. I wish I was the
last man, but in the darkness outside there is someone I love, someone who would frighten you, Bryant a young boy, I gave him so
much love, now he's gone mad with grief, a young boy mad think
of it, think of what's going on in his head and heart, I can feel it,
and he wants to take it out on me. He blames me for everything,
but I know that he is only sick of his life and of what he is, I
understand him though we are so different, and he is waiting to kill
me. I can go out and break his neck anytime, it would be easy,
a slum boy's neck. I can go out and challenge him and make him
run, but then I think of the two of us alone here, and how the
others would laugh if they could see us, two billy goats fighting
it out for nothing at all, just amusing the crowd, it is what they
would like, the last laugh. They mustn't have that, and I am
thinking now I will just walk out into the night and wait for him
and turn my back and let him do what he wants to do. That
would be the best way out, I'm tired.

I know that in life a man has always to keep on picking himself
up when the count reaches nine. That is the test of a man, not
when he's on his feet but when he's down, but I've picked myself
up too often and I've nothing to show for it. The corridor of time

is now a room of mirrors, it just shows me forever picking myself up, and this time I want them to count me out.

He's been waiting outside for three days. Thrushcross Grange is empty, he goes there and back, there and back all the time, through the bush, but I know no cooking is going on in the Grange, nothing much in that line ever went on there, they were too pampered, I made it too easy for them, and he is shiftless and feckless like the others, a slum child and starving but they don't mind, yam and breadfruit and salt fish is all they know about. I leave food for him outside the door, you would think he is a dog, and he comes like a dog and eats the food I leave out for him. The world is full of things like this that frighten you and make you ashamed, people always make you hate them, because I treat him like a dog he comes like a dog in the night and eats the food, I hear him, before he eats he rubs the cutlass on the concrete steps, like the giant in the story sharpening up his knife, just to let me know he has a cutlass, and the white plate is empty in the morning on the step.

You see how the pain comes Marjorie, you see how the glory of manhood ends. I picked him out of the gutter, you wouldn't believe the sight, the poisonous black scarecrow with pigtails like macajuel snakes on his head. He thought he was dirt, dirt, I showed him his beauty, but he's forgotten, he's gone mad with his manhood. You understand the glory and pain of manhood Marjorie, you will understand that it was too much for me to bear, and every time I look at my nakedness I feel the pain and think of you, you showed me my manhood, you made me a man for the first time, never mind what the others said, to this day Marjorie when I look down at myself I think of you. I didn't have to hide anything from you, I didn't have to pretend I was anybody else, you do not know the joy. But I suffered more as a man. When I was a child I was a child, when you made me a man I couldn't bear being that child in the back room of that shop. The things women do and can do they have no shame and thought for the children who come after them who will have to endure all that they did, women don't know how men can hate them for the things they do, make sure your children don't find out about you.

In this quiet night Marge I want to clear my heart and wipe the slate clean. You made me a man so late and I had to behave like a man. The others were jokers, you thought I didn't know, but I knew they were joking with my manhood and pain, but I was joking with them too, they didn't know and when they found out they didn't like it, they sent me back here, to make me nothing again, I knew what they were up to, don't think I don't know, I played along. You shouldn't have let me down Marjorie, you shouldn't have sided with the others, I didn't want to hate you like the others, you were my maker, you broke my heart, you made me and then you made me feel like dirt again, good only for dirt. But it's funny how people always catch me out and let me down, so I am dying in anger Marge as you prophesied and isn't that a terrible way to die.

You people sent me back here to be nothing but I picked myself up, I must have surprised you, you must have read about me in the papers, the people here knew who I was, they knew what I had done, they knew what I was offering them, the glory and pain of manhood, never mind the revolution, they knew that and that was why last week I could have burned this place down to the ground, until that dead boy's mother refused to have me in her house and those crazy black people started shouting for Israel and Africa, and I was a lost man, but I was always lost, I knew that since I was a child, I knew I was fooling myself. But I am a man Marjorie, it is what you made me, the pain you brought me, and you see how it is ending. Sweetheart, sweetheart even as I write those words my nakedness rises and it makes me sad to think it's useless, these things make sense only when there's someone else who needs it, they get life from it, you know what they say, dead men come once.

The open pad lay before him, part of the paper debris on his desk. But he no longer saw what he had written. He had stopped writing, long ago, it seemed; he had returned to himself.

The room was full of shadows; only the desk lamp was on. The house was full of noises, the scattered metallic snaps of the corrugated-iron roof, the creaks of the rafters. At last, above these

noises, he heard what he had been waiting for: a disturbance outside, no clear sound, more like a disturbance of the air.

He said, "Bryant?" and then, distinctly, through the open
barred windows he heard footsteps outside, soft, rubber-soled,
moving swiftly down the side of the house. He stood up and
shouted, "Bryant!" The sound of the cutlass blade being dragged
flat over the concrete steps outside the kitchen set his teeth on
edge. He moved quickly about the room, putting on all the lights.
He said, "Bryant, don't try anything tonight. Do you hear? Don't
do it, boy."

He went to the kitchen and stood against the door. He looked
up at the ceiling and said, "You're tired. You're not well. Why
don't you eat, then go and rest? Go and rest, Bryant. We'll talk
tomorrow. I'll come over to the Grange to see you. We'll talk. It
isn't the end of the world. We'll leave this place and go somewhere
else. There's nothing to be afraid of. You'll get better. But you
must go and rest."

16

THE OLD truck ahead, its untrue double tires hissing on the soft tar, was carrying a load of river sand. The sand was wet and dripping, but the truck left no water trail on the road. The broken trickles of brownish water, whipped about by the truck's speed, and evaporating in the afternoon heat, vanished as soon as they touched the asphalt.

Jane was in a taxi. The taxi was a large American car past its prime, its pieces no longer absolutely fitting together. In spite of its size it gave little protection against glare and heat. Hot air and exhaust fumes came through the windows, and the sun struck through on the driver's side, scorching the plastic seat cover.

The truck went past the turning that led, through young sugar cane, to the airport. The taxi continued to follow the truck: the airport was not Jane's destination. Presently, a bare and dusty black arm signaling, the truck turned off into a factory yard. Some miles later, the traffic less regular, the area of factories left behind, the taxi turned off the highway. And Jane saw the landscape she thought she would never see again: the rough narrow road, broken here and there, overgrown at the edges, the flattened scorched areas, the rows of brick pillars, still looking new, but stripped of their timber superstructures and hung with dried-out creepers, the distant wall of bush.

The taxi stopped at the house. Bougainvillaea and hibiscus were bright in the burnt garden.

Jane said to the driver, "Can you wait? I won't be long."

"How long?"

"Fifteen minutes, half an hour."

"Better you telephone the office when you ready."

She paid him and went through the open gate. He turned in the gateway, the big car dislodging a light rubble of stray pebbles, the tires crushing to ocher powder little clods of dry earth blown there by the wind; and he went back the way they had come.

No one had appeared at the sound of the car. The car port was empty, the oil stains on the concrete floor dry and dusted over. The front door was closed; Jane had remembered it open. The shallow terrazzo steps and the porch, already slanted with sunlight, were gritty, unswept.

Before she could knock, Jimmy opened the door. He held it open, and for a second or so he appeared not to see her: he was looking over her shoulder. He was as she had first seen him that day at Thrushcross Grange, when, after walking bare-chested down the aisle between the iron beds, he had put on the drab-colored Mao shirt. He was wearing that shirt now; his plump cheeks were as coarse from close shaving as they had been then, his full mouth as seemingly clamped shut below the mustache, his eyes as blank and assessing.

He said, after that little silence, "Jane. You made it, then?"

"Why do you sound so surprised?"

"I'm not surprised."

She passed into the room, and he locked the door behind her. The room felt airless, though the barred windows were open. And she saw disorder: she saw he had not prepared the house for her visit. Disorder emphasized the cheapness of the furniture, its impermanence in that room: it no longer gave delight. There were newspapers on the furry upholstered chairs, and cups and plates and tins and sticky marks on the dining table. The electric-blue carpet, loose on the terrazzo, curled at the edges: the floor could easily be imagined without it. There was dust on the glass-topped table, and a confusion of papers, writing pads and blue air-letters on the desk.

She sat down in the upholstered chair next to the glass-topped table. The synthetic furry fabric was warm. She remembered to stroke it: it was as tickling smooth as she had remembered.

Jimmy said, "Make yourself at home. Can I get you anything? No rum punch. That's your drink, isn't it?"

"It's too hot for that. I'll just have a glass of water."

He went out to the kitchen, and from that room, which she had seen once, he said, "Supplies are running low, Jane."

Hot air came through the windows. The sky was pale blue.

He came out and handed her a glass of water, without ice. The glass was wet on the outside; his hand was wet. He sat at the desk.

"Well, Jane. What can I do for you?"

She was taking the wet glass to her lips. But she saw that it was stained, with dark brown trickles, and she just held the glass a little way from her mouth. She said, "I'm leaving."

"You told me on the telephone. You're going back to London. And massa?"

"I suppose Peter's leaving too." She put the glass down on the glass-topped table. "But I don't know about him."

"So in a few days you'll be back. In a few days you will be watching television. BBC and ITV. And listening to the radio in the mornings. *Today*."

Don't remind me. I can see it all so clearly. It makes my heart sink."

"Does it?"

"Is there anything I can do for you? Is there something you want that I can get? Can I see anyone?"

"What will you tell them?"

"I will tell them that I've seen you."

"Is that all you'll tell them?"

She avoided his eyes. After a while she said, "Will you stay here?"

"Jane, do you know why you came?"

She didn't answer.

"You came because you're going away. That's why you came. If you were staying you wouldn't have come. You've caused me so much pain, Jane."

"I don't see how I've caused you pain."

"I'm not asking for sympathy, Jane. You mustn't think that. What would be the point? You know the score as well as anybody."

She was unwilling to let the question go. "How have I caused you pain?"

He said, in another tone, "You're wearing your Moroccan necklaces."

She put her hand to them and then let them fall back on the overtanned, coarsened skin in the opening of the blouse.

Jimmy said, "The ones given you by a lover."

She gave the smile with which she acknowledged her exaggerations, mischievousness, or untruths.

"He didn't want money to come between you."

"Jimmy, are you sure there's nothing I can do for you? Isn't there something you'd like me to take for your children?"

"You wouldn't be welcome there. You've caused me a lot of pain, Jane. You mustn't make it worse."

He broke off, making a sign to her with his open hand, raised his head and turned it to one side. A breath of warm air made the curtains move and disturbed the dust in the room. Jane listened with him and heard, far away, the rustle of the bush, a sound so steady it was like part of the silence.

He said, "And now you're leaving." But he was still listening. Then, abruptly, he relaxed and looked at her. "I like those necklaces."

She held the three pendants together between her thumb and forefinger, flicked them stiffly up, then down.

He said, "I remember them."

She let the pendants fall again on that part of her skin that had aged from too much sun. She said, "They're quite worthless."

"That was what you said. I suppose I like them because I see them on you. Why did you wear them today?"

"I didn't really think about it."

"You didn't think about it, Jane? But you were coming to see me. I remember them very well. I've remembered everything about you. And now you're leaving. Does massa know you're here?"

"I told Peter I was coming to see you."

"Did he tell you to tell me anything?"

"Should he have?"

"He's very worried about you, Jane. He's coming here. Did you know that? He said there was something he wanted to see me about. That's a good laugh for a hot day. Massa isn't going to let you go, Jane. It will kill him to lose you. Did you know that?"

"Peter? Are you saying that Peter cares for me? Peter cares for nobody."

"You're his last chance."

"I don't believe anybody is anybody's last chance." She opened her bag and brought out her cigarettes and her lighter.

"I remember that."

"What do you remember?"

"The way you're looking now. Your eyes. Your mouth."

She lit her cigarette and kept the lighter in her hand. He went to the shelves and took the heavy, round ash tray, bubbles in the blue-tinted glass, and put it on the glass-topped table. He stood above her and she could see up the short sleeves of his loose Mao shirt to his armpits. Her eyes went moist. He sat on the furry arm of her chair; her smoking gestures became smaller, constricted.

He said, "I was frightened of what I saw."

"Why were you frightened?" She touched the tip of her cigarette, as yet without ash, on the thick rim of the ash tray.

"It always happens like that. I knew I would be involved with you. I knew you were going to come back." He whispered, "You told massa?"

She looked at him. Her moist eyes were full of irritation, alarm.

He looked at the lighter in her cigarette hand and said, "I remember that. From the Sahara."

She held out the cigarette to the ash tray; she was about to swallow. He squeezed her hand hard over the ash tray; and her face moved to his, her mouth open, the cigarette falling from her fingers, the lighter hurting in her palm. Her mouth opened wide and pressed against his, and her lips and tongue began to work.

He took his mouth away and said, "Be calm. You're too greedy. You give yourself away when you kiss like that. A woman's whole life is in her kiss."

He released her hand; the lighter fell on the glass-topped table. Her head remained thrown back on the chair; when he went to her mouth again he found her lips barely parted, her tongue withdrawn. He said, "That's better." Very lightly, he ran the tip of his tongue between her lips, then on the inside of her lower lip. Then, still lightly, he sucked her lower lip. He took his mouth away and looked at her. Her eyes were still closed. She said, "That was lovely." He held her face between his hands, jammed the heels of his palms on the corners of her mouth, covering her almost vanished period spots, distending her lips. He covered her mouth with his; her lips widened and she made a strangled sound; and then he spat in her mouth. She swallowed and he let her face go. She opened her eyes and said, "That was lovely." He put his hands below her wet armpits and began to lift her. But she stood up of her own accord.

She said, "Your eyes are shining."

"Your eyes are screaming still."

He touched her with the tips of his fingers in the small of her back, and casually, like old lovers, they walked into the bedroom.

She saw the bare ocher-washed walls, the shiny brown fitted wardrobe, and, through the high wide window, the pale sky. The bathroom door was ajar: she saw the low tiled wall around the shower area, the dry concrete floor. Standing separate from one another, they began, without haste, to undress. The bed was unmade, the mattress showing at the top, the middle of the rumpled sheet brushed smooth and brown from use and spotted with stiff stains. The yellow candlewick bedspread hung over the end of the bed and rested on the maroon carpet.

Jane, unbuttoning her blouse, smiled and said, "Your candlewick bedspread."

"So you remember it. You didn't seem to care for it the last time."

She nodded slowly, once, and gave her mischievous smile. She took off her blouse and threw it on the brown chest of drawers. Against the rest of her the red, aged skin below her neck looked like a rash; the little folds of flesh in her shaved armpits were wet. She let the Moroccan necklaces fall, with a little ripple of metallic sound, on the chest of drawers. She didn't take off her brassiere: her breasts were small: he noted that shyness. She stepped out of her shoes and was at once small. She didn't step out of her trousers, but lifted one leg after the other, in an athletic movement, and pulled the trousers off: a rough, masculine sound. Suddenly, then, her pants a shrunken, wrinkled roll on the carpet, she was on the unmade bed, sighing, smiling at him, her head on the oily pillow; and she looked big again. She opened her legs, put her hand there, and drew her fingers upward through moist flesh and hair. The wanton's gesture: he noted it, and he seemed to say, "Hm."

She said, "I hate that shirt."

"I am taking it off." His voice was soft.

When, looking very big, he moved toward her, she closed her eyes. She said, "Kiss me, Jimmy," and waited with lips open, tongue withdrawn. Crouching beside her, he jammed his palms against the corners of her mouth. She made the strangled sound and he covered her mouth with his. He made her swallow, and she rested her hands on his back and said, "Love, love."

She felt the pressure of his hands on her shoulders, and suddenly she was turned over on her belly and he was squatting on her, her hips and legs squeezed between his knees, thighs, and feet. He said, "It's going to be different today, Jane. We're doing it the other way." She made as if to rise, but he held her down between the shoulder blades with his left hand, and opened her up with his right. She began to beat her hands on the bed. As soon as, moving down from the base of her spine he touched her where she was smaller, she cried out, "No!" And when he entered, squatting on her, driving in, his ankles pressed against her hips, she began to wail, a dry, scraping, deliberate sound. He said, as though speaking to a child, "But you're a virgin, Jane. Isn't it a good thing you came to see me today?" She shouted with real pain, "Take it out, take it out." She began to wail again. He said, "A big girl like you, and a virgin, Jane? It's hard. I know it's hard. But you didn't bring your

Vaseline, you see. A big girl like you should always take her own Vaseline when she goes visiting." She said, "Oh my God, oh my God." He said, "It's better like this, Jane. You didn't know that? You mean they never told you it was better with your legs closed? Aren't you glad you came? It's always better with your legs closed, whatever way you do it." He drove deeper and deeper, until he was almost sitting upright on her. He said, "We're breaking you in today, Jane." He began to withdraw; sweat from his face and chest dripped on her back; she sighed; but he drove in hard and she shrieked. Her hands stopped beating on the bed; her inflamed face was pressed on one side on the pillow. She stopped wailing; she took her right hand to her mouth and began to bite on her thumb; real tears came. Sobbing, biting her thumb, she began to plead, now with a suppressed scream, now with a whisper, "Take it out, take it out." Her body went soft; she was sweating all over. He withdrew and said, "There now." She said, "Have you taken it out?" He said, "Yes, Jane. You've lost your virginity."

She remained just as he had left her, her face on the pillow, the tears running down her nose; her untanned buttocks together, spreading slightly, wet with sweat where he had been sitting on her, the fine hairs there flattened in the sweat and showing more clearly. She sobbed and snuffled.

When he was off her, and beside her, not touching her, she said, like a child, "You made me cry! You made me cry!" Her face was red and wet with tears; but she was oddly calm.

He said, "I knew this about you as soon as I saw you that day. As soon as I saw your eyes and the shape of your mouth."

"My 'bedroom eyes.' "

He said, very softly, "You are rotten meat."

It was his tone, rather than the words, that alarmed her. When she turned over to look at him she saw that his eyes were very bright and appeared sightless, the pupils mere points of glitter. He was still erect and looked very big.

He put his hand lightly on her shoulder and said, "You look frightened, Jane."

"I'm thinking I have to go back."

She swung her legs over the edge of the bed, he allowed his hand to slip off her shoulder, and she stood up.

"But I haven't come, Jane."

His eyes were on her. She bent down to pick up her pants, heedless of the hairiness and open flesh, her secret once again, that she was exposing. And, bending down, straightening up, she had in one movement pulled her pants on, covering herself where she was untanned and naked.

He said, "Your mouth, Jane. You have a sweet-mouth too. As soon as I saw you I knew you had a sweet-mouth. We must christen it."

He continued to look at her. She pulled on her trousers; stepped into her shoes; buttoned her blouse, put on the Moroccan necklaces, and shook her hair into place.

She said, "I think I have to go."

He sat on the edge of the bed; his erection was subsiding. He said, "You have to go. But you know what you are now. You'll come again for more."

"I'll ring for a taxi."

"You'll be lucky if you get one to come here. But you don't have anything to worry about. Massa is coming for you. Massa isn't going to let you go." He stood up; he had shrunken. "We'll walk across to the Grange and meet massa."

The telephone was on the chest of drawers but she didn't lift it. She didn't leave the room. She stood where she was, between the chest of drawers and the door, and waited for him to dress. The pillow was as she had left it, pressed down and damp; the stained sheet had patches of damp. He dressed slowly. When, lifting his chin, he did the top button of his Mao shirt, he said, "The shirt you don't like." She responded in no way.

When they went out into the living room, the cigarette in the blue-tinted ash tray had almost burnt itself out, a disintegrating cylinder of ash. The glass of water on the glass-topped table was where she had put it down. She picked up her lighter and bag and followed him out to the porch. The sunlight on the terrazzo was dazzling. He didn't shut the front door.

They walked out into the heat and the openness. No trees grew between the house and the wall of bush. The road was lightly rubbled: stray pebbles, loosened bits of tarred gravel, clods of earth. The road ended abruptly, cracked asphalt giving way to a dirt path through a dried-up field, overgrown and then flattened by the drought. The path led to the wall of bush.

Jimmy said, "Massa will be waiting for you. A short walk. Ten minutes."

She didn't speak.

He said, "We'll also meet Bryant. You remember Bryant?"

"I don't want to see Bryant."

"But he has something for you. Bryant has something for you."

The green wall of bush, which from a distance had seemed solid, threaded with the slender white trunks and branches of soft-wood trees, became more pierced and open as they got closer to it.

Jimmy said, "Bryant and I are not friends now, Jane. You'll help to make us friends."

It was cooler in the bush. The ground was dry, covered with dead leaves, and spotted with big patches of sunlight. There seemed at first to be no path, just an intermittent disturbance in the dead leaves; and for the first time since she had followed him out of the bedroom she hesitated. He touched the top of her arm and moved the tips of his fingers down the short sleeve of her cotton blouse. Lightly, then, he held her arm and led her on. Ants' nests, of dried mud, were like black veins on the white trunks of softwood trees. The wild banana was in flower: a solid spray of spearheads of orange and yellow that never turned to fruit, emerging sticky with mauve gum and slime from the heart of the tree.

Jimmy said, "They say there's always a snake at the bottom of that tree. So be careful. See but never touch. It's the golden rule of the bush."

They were now in the middle of the bush, no light and openness behind them, trees and trees ahead of them.

"So you're leaving us, Jane. That was why you came. Because you're leaving. Do you have a nice house in London?"

"I'm used to it."

"Everything nicely put away, I bet. Is it near Wimbledon?"

"No. It isn't near Wimbledon."

"Suppose it burns down while you're away?"

"It's insured."

"You'll just build another?"

"I suppose so."

He suddenly squeezed her arm and said, "Smell it, Jane!"

She stopped and looked about her.

He said, "You can smell it?"

"What?"

"Snake."

"I can't smell anything."

"It smells of sex, Jane. Bad, stale sex. It smells of a dirty cunt."

He released her arm. The bush was becoming brighter; they were approaching openness. And soon, through the trees, the clearing on which the Grange stood could be seen: an expanse of brown in a hard white light. There was a latrine smell, which became sharper. The latrine, with corrugated-iron walls and roof and a sagging, open corrugated-iron door, stood on a rough concrete foundation just outside the bush, in direct sunlight. Brilliant green flies buzzed about it and within it, striking the corrugated iron.

They had come out into the back yard of the Grange: no shade, the bush laid waste, the land sterile. The main building blocked a view of the road and of the fields beyond the road. The corrugated-iron roof glittered; the concrete-block walls were in shadow. A roll of wire netting, old scantlings, a junked metal icebox, white enamel basins: this was part of the debris at the back. A low lean-to shelter, its palm thatch sloping down almost to the ground, was fixed to the back wall; below the thatch there was black shadow. Scattered about the ground were back yard structures and relics of back yard projects: a wire-netting pen, torn in places; chicken coops of wire netting and old board; a dry pit, the dug-out earth heaped up on one side beside a load of concrete blocks.

There was a boy in the shadow of the lean-to. He was sitting on the ground in the angle of the thatch and the ground. His knees were drawn up, and his head and arms rested on his knees. He seemed asleep. His white canvas shoes were yellow with dust; his washed-out jeans were dusty; his elbows were scratched and there was dust on his black arms.

"You remember Bryant?"

Jane said, "I don't remember him."

"He remembers you."

The boy raised his head. His face was twisted and he wore the pigtails of aggression. His eyes were red and blurred, one lid half stuck down. He stood up. He ran back into the lean-to, and when he turned to face them he had a cutlass in his hand and he was in tears.

He cried, "Jimmy! Jimmy!"

Jimmy locked his right arm about Jane's neck and almost lifted her in front of him, pulling back the corners of his mouth with the effort, and slightly puffing out his shaved cheeks, so that he seemed to smile.

He said, "Bryant, the rat! Kill the rat!"

Bryant, running, faltered.

"Your rat, Bryant! Your rat!"

Her right hand was on the arm swelling around her neck, and it was on her right arm that Bryant made the first cut.

The first cut: the rest would follow.

Sharp steel met flesh. Skin parted, flesh showed below the skin, for an instant mottled white, and then all was blinding, disfiguring blood, and Bryant could only cut at what had already been cut.

He cried out, in tears, in pain, in despair, "Help me, Jimmy!"

Jimmy, responding, tightened his grip around the neck. He scarcely felt the neck; he felt only his own strength, the smoothness of his own skin, the tension of his own muscles. He concentrated on that smoothness and tension until she began to fail. She grew heavy; his strength became useless; and as he felt her fail a desolation began to grow on him. And then there was nothing except desolation.

He was squatting on the ground, beside the dry pit of the septic tank and the heap of dug-out earth, looking at the earth and not the face, and not seeing the earth. He saw a day of sun at the

beach, sea and sky bright beyond the coconut grove, the girl bleeding on the fender of the car, accepting water from his cupped
hands, and love coming to her frightened eyes. But the eyes below
him were closed. They knew nothing; they acknowledged nothing;
they had taken away everything with them. He entered a void; he
disappeared in that void.

Then he was lost, lost since the beginning of time. But time
had no beginning. And he was disembodied. He was nothing more
than this sense of loss that grew deeper and deeper as he awakened
to it; he would have liked to scream, for the relief. The world
cleared up, time defined itself. He was himself, in a stone room,
full of incense, with stone coffins on stone shelves, where dead
women lay without being dead among white lilies. A woman sat
up in her stone coffin; the lilies tumbled off her. She was Sudanese,
like those he had seen in London: he could tell from her fine white
cotton dress, her pallid brown skin and the healed slashes on her
cheeks. She had the wanton face, the leer, the degraded mouth of a
French prostitute he had seen in a pornographic photograph at
school, sitting clothed but with her skirt pulled up, her legs open,
her great hairiness exposed. She sat up in her roughly chiseled
coffin, leering, the lilies falling off her, and she said, holding out
her hand, "Nigger, give me a dollar."

So that even here, though he had been lost since the beginning
of time, though he was lost in time itself, and didn't know who or
what he was, he was betrayed, his secret known.

The secret recalled him to himself, and his desolation was
complete. He was squatting beside the girl on the edge of the
dry pit, its crumbling walls still carrying fork marks, and Bryant,
the cutlass in his hand, was crying, like a man who at any moment
was going to scream.

"Jimmy, Jimmy."

He stood up and held Bryant by the arm. He said, "Bryant!"

"Jimmy, Jimmy."

"In here, Bryant."

"In the latrine, Jimmy."

"No. The corbeaux will come."

And Bryant looked up with Jimmy at the pale sky.

They put her in the pit, with her dead hair, still loose where it was not stained and stiff, with her necklaces, her open bag. The heaped-up earth beside the pit, dug out weeks before, had settled and seemed hard; but it broke up and crumbled at a touch, red-brown below the straw-colored, powdery crust. At first with their hands and feet alone, then with concrete blocks, then with a spade, they broke up the earth and shoveled it in, until there was nothing to be seen; and there remained only dust and labor, burning faces and arms, sweat and the stinging sun.

Far away, from the road, it seemed, there came the sound of whistling. No recognizable tune, and it stopped almost as soon as they heard it.

They looked up at the sky: it was empty.

Then the whistling came again, closer. Bryant looked at Jimmy. Jimmy said, "Bryant." Bryant ran for his cutlass. Jimmy said, "Bryant!" And this time Bryant obeyed. He began to do what he saw Jimmy doing: rubbing clods of red-brown earth on his trousers and shirt. Jimmy undid the buttons of his Mao shirt, and the two men, Bryant with his cutlass, walked to the back door of the main building, into sudden shade.

A young man was coming up to the building from the road. He was small, his blue shirt slack and bulging above his tight striped brown trousers. He was wearing white-rimmed shades; his shoes, too tight for him, gave him a dainty walk; a white airlines bag hung from his shoulder.

Bryant said, "Mannie."

Jimmy said, "Nowhere to go. They'll start coming back. All of them. But it's too late."

"Jimmy, Jimmy."

"It's too late for them now."

"Let me take him out, Jimmy. Let me take him *out!*"

Jimmy didn't reply. He went into the building and walked halfway down between the empty beds. Bryant remained in the back doorway.

Mannie came in out of the sun. He took off his white-rimmed shades: his nose was shining and there was sweat all over his face. He looked at Jimmy and said shyly, "Mr. Ahmed," and looked down. His small black shoes were extravagantly pointed; the points tilted up, the heels were worn. He went to his old bed and sat on the edge of the bare mattress, with his back to Jimmy and Bryant. He opened the airlines bag and began taking out small green tomatoes and laying them on the concrete floor.

Bryant said from the back doorway, "Let me take him out, Jimmy."

Mannie didn't turn.

Jimmy sat on one of the empty beds and said, "Mannie."

Mannie turned. "Yes, Mr. Ahmed?"

"You come back?"

"I walk down from the highway, Mr. Ahmed."

"That's a long walk for a hot day. We've been working."

"Mr. Ahmed."

"And now you come back. And you start picking my tomatoes."

Mannie's face went small and closed. Little beads of sweat began to grow on his shiny nose.

Jimmy stood up. He slapped his hand hard on his right trouser pocket and said, "Mannie!"

Mannie stood up. The corners of his eyes were red.

"I lose my pen, Mannie."

"Mr. Ahmed."

"My red biro. Yellow with a red cap. I think I drop it outside somewhere. I don't want to lose it. Go and look for it for me."

Mannie came out into the aisle. He hesitated there. He looked at the bright front door. Then he began to walk slowly toward Jimmy, Bryant, and the back door.

Jimmy said, "Go and look by the septic tank."

Mannie walked daintily in his tight shoes, his buttocks high and hard in his tight trousers, his loosened handkerchief bulging in his hip pocket, with one corner hanging out.

Jimmy said, "I don't want to lose that pen, Mannie."

Jimmy sat on another bed. Bryant remained standing in the doorway.

After some time they heard light steps. They saw Mannie. As soon as he saw them he stopped, about five or six feet away from the back door. There was dust in his hair; his blue shirt was dark with sweat around the collar and below the arms; dust discolored his trousers from the knees down.

Jimmy said, "Mannie."

"Sorry, Mr. Ahmed."

"You didn't see anything?"

"No, Mr. Ahmed."

Jimmy said, "Lie down, Bryant. Take a rest. Come in, nuh, Mannie."

Mannie came in, his sweated face tight, his eyes burning, his walk still dainty.

Jimmy said, "But you spoil all your pretty clothes, Mannie."

Mannie didn't seem to hear. He went to his bed and, not dusting his hair or trousers or hands, sat on the mattress. He looked down at the concrete floor and his eyes began to water.

Jimmy said, "We're all tired. We all have to rest. But what about you, Mannie? Where you going to go? No food here now. The Grange is closed."

Mannie, his eyes still watering, didn't turn.

Bryant got up from the bed nearest the back door. He said, "Somebody coming."

Jimmy, going to the wall and tiptoeing to look through the louvers, saw the car far away on the road, beyond the last cleared field. There was dazzle on the bonnet, but the windscreen was in shadow and the driver could not be seen.

Jimmy said, "Lie down, Bryant. Save your strength. Mannie, I'm going to clean up."

He went out through the back door. Bryant put his cutlass on the concrete floor between the wall and his bed and lay down flat on the bare mattress. The coconut-fiber filling bristled through the ticking. Bryant looked up at the corrugated-iron roof, so new still, with the cockerel emblem and the name of the manufacturers, far away in Canada, stenciled in blue.

The car came nearer. It stopped; a door banged. A disturbance of dirt clods and pebbles, and Roche appeared, with his short-sleeved white shirt, his light-colored khaki trousers narrow around his flat waist, and his dark glasses. He came into the building, took off the glasses and put the end of one temple in his mouth. His face was drawn and he looked impatient. He saw the tears in Mannie's eyes.

He said, "Mannie."

Mannie didn't look up. He said, "Mr. Ahmed gone to wash his face."

"You've been working?"

Mannie didn't reply. And Roche, waiting, considered the table with the junked office equipment, the dusty stalled standard typewriter, the rusting duplicator; the timetable on the wall, the newspaper pinups above the beds; the Jimmy Ahmed poster with the crude portrait of Jimmy, all hair and mustache: *I'm Nobody's Slave or Stallion, I'm a Warrior and Torch Bearer.* The concrete floor was dusty; the iron beds were stripped; and the bare mattresses gave off a smell of coconut fiber. Roche saw that the bed at the far end of the room was occupied.

He said, "Bryant."

Bryant didn't reply.

Jimmy appeared in the doorway. He was bare-chested, and his face was blank, the eyes assessing, his mustache masking his mouth.

He said, "Massa. We were giving you up. A tour of inspection? You're still inspecting?"

Roche said, "You all seem to be in a state."

"We've been working. Life has to go on. Bryant will take you out and show you. Mannie too."

Bryant rose and sat on the edge of his bed, facing the wall.

Jimmy came down between the beds and stood a few feet away from Roche.

Jimmy said, "Mannie has come back, massa."

Mannie half raised himself off the mattress and took out his handkerchief from his hip pocket.

Roche said, "Did Donaldson come?"

"We don't have anything to do with Donaldson. All that's gone with the wind."

Jimmy's chest, paler than his face and forearms, was moist with perspiration. Stiff little coils of hair, unexpectedly Negroid, were scattered between his purple-brown nipples, which were as large as a woman's.

Roche sucked on the end of the temple of his dark glasses. He said, "Didn't he come to see you about the tractor?"

"To take it back, you mean?"

"I don't know about that. He didn't come?"

"If he came we didn't see him. We've been busy all afternoon. Bryant will show you."

"Nobody came?"

"We didn't see anybody."

Roche looked at Mannie. Mannie's eyes were still wet and he was still looking down. His loosened handkerchief, unused, remained in his right hand. In that same hand he was holding a cylindrical blue lighter and, absently, he was polishing the bronze-colored metal at the top with his thumb. Roche hesitated. He thought: Sahara gas. In his hesitation his eyes caught Jimmy's— surprise there, and for an instant something like an appeal. And almost at the same time he saw Bryant standing at the far end of the room, looking at him.

Roche took the temple of his glasses out of his mouth and, swinging the glasses between his thumb and forefinger, took a half-step toward Mannie's bed. Then he stopped and turned and, slowly, looking at the beds, mattresses, and the posters on the wall, he walked toward the bright door. He said, "Everybody at the office knows I'm here. I'm sure they told Donaldson. A wasted journey." He was in the sunlight. He put on his glasses and said, "But never mind," and stepped from the concrete floor onto the dry red earth.

And he was walking away—the land graded down to clay, baked hard, dusty on the surface—when he heard Jimmy call, but uncertainly, "Massa."

He kept on walking.

He thought: This place has become a slaughterground. The words seemed to have been given to him, and he thought: I've just done the bravest thing in my life. He concentrated on Jimmy and addressed him mentally: You wouldn't do anything to me. You wouldn't dare.

He came to the dry ditch and the bridge of tree trunks and packed earth. He got into the car. He didn't look at the land he had just traversed or the building he had just left. He thought: If you try anything now, I'll kill you.

He turned in the road—two movements, and still no one called out to him—and then he was driving into the sun, past the field with the broken-down tractor standing against the wall of bush, past the dry flattened ridges and the furrows choked with bright green weeds, past the blocks of old bush, the spiky wild palms, the red-and-black-striped barrier pointing at the sky, the Sablich's sign, still new, announcing Thrushcross Grange, past the ruins of the abandoned industrial park, the overgrown pillars still standing in rows, the flat paved areas cracked open by grass and wild young trees, rusty reinforcing metal showing here and there through broken concrete.

And then he was on the highway, locked in the afternoon traffic, and he was being taken past all the stations of that familiar drive. The sun, already yellowing, picked out all the ridges and dips of the scorched hills, which smoked. Far away in the brown fields people were cutting grass. The junked cars beside the road; the country settlements; the burning rubbish dump, trucks and people amid the smoke and the miniature hills of confetti-like refuse, the big-breasted black corbeaux squatting on the fence posts or hopping about on the ground; the shantytown resettlements, their population spilling out of rows of identical tin-and-concrete huts, back to back and face to face down long red avenues that seemed regularly to open and close as he drove past; the bauxite pall; the hot, squalling afternoon city, melting tar, honking buses and taxis and enraged, sweating cyclists.

As he climbed to the cooler air of the Ridge, the more spacious gardens, the wider verges, Roche thought: I won't be safe at home. They'll come for me. I can't watch all night. I'll have to spend the night at the Prince Albert.

The afternoon light was mellow on the Ridge. Thin rainless clouds of pure white were building up high in the sky, for the sunset. He parked in the garage, but he didn't go through the door into the kitchen. He walked back to the front lawn and went through the front door, bleached and mottled by the sun, into the hall, and down the parquet passage to Jane's room. The flush plywood door was ajar.

He said, "Jane," and lightly pushed the door open.

The louvers were open, the room was bright and warm. The bed was made up, but there was no bedspread; the white cotton nightdress could be seen below the pillow. On the bedside table there was the paperback of *The Woodlanders*, the cover and the opening pages raised and curling in the heat. The suitcase, on the floor of the fitted wardrobe, was half packed. Only the striped North African sacking dress was on a hanger. All the shelves except one were cleared. On this shelf, with a small jewelry box, some bottles and phials and tins, and a necklace of sandalwood beads, Roche saw Jane's passport and her airline ticket folder. In the passport was the disembarkation card Jane had filled in months before but had not surrendered.

He took the ticket out of the folder and tore it up and put the pieces in his pocket. He tore up the disembarkation card. But the passport couldn't be so easily destroyed. His mind, racing, rejected all the possibilities. The passport couldn't be torn up and flushed down the toilet. It couldn't be burned: there was no open fire in the house; there was only a metal contraption beside the porch for barbecues.

He went, the passport still in his hand, to the sitting room. It was very warm there, from the sun, the heat thrown out by the brown lawn, the fixed picture window.

He telephoned Harry de Tunja. Joseph answered.

Waiting for Harry, Roche opened the passport and considered Jane's picture: a washed-out print, the cheeks too full, the hair lank and schoolgirlish.

"Harry. Peter."

"Well, well, man."

"Harry, Jane has left me. She's left her clothes behind, but she's taken her ticket and passport."

Roche, looking at the passport, read Jane's handwritten responses to the printed queries. *Occupation: Publisher. Place and Date of Birth: Ottawa 17 July 1943.*

Harry said, "That's a hell of a thing you're telling me, man, Peter." But there was no surprise in Harry's voice. "You sure, boy?"

Country of Residence: England. Height: 5'6".

Roche said, "I don't know what else to think."

"You would know better than anybody else. But you know, Peter, I feel this is just a kind of chain reaction that Marie-Thérèse set off."

"The clothes she's left behind aren't very valuable. She didn't bring out a lot."

Roche turned the page and read: *Valid for All Parts of the Commonwealth and for All Foreign Countries.* On the page opposite: *Observations: Holder Has Right of Abode in the United Kingdom.*

Harry said, "Perhaps she went on that BOAC flight. You could check in the morning. But, look, I'll telephone Mackenzie at the airport. The immigration people will be there now for the Varig flight. I'll telephone you back."

"Thank you, Harry."

There was no exit or arrival stamp in the passport. It was like a passport that had never been used.

And when Roche put the telephone down he was alarmed at what he had done.

He sat on the porch and looked down at the city.

He heard Adela call out, "Water! One-among-you, water!"

The clouds turned pink. Streaks of gray appeared in the sky. The telephone rang, and when he went to the sitting room he saw that he had left the passport beside the telephone.

"Peter. Harry. Has Jane come back?"

"She hasn't come back."

"The immigration people have no record of her departure. But they don't know anything about her arrival either. Officially she's never been here. You and I and a few other people know she's been here. But officially she hasn't been. The best thing would be for you to telephone BOAC in the morning."

"That would be the best thing."

"What do you think you'll do? You'll be going up after her?"

"I think that is what I'll have to do."

"It's the best thing, I think."

"Thank you, Harry."

Roche went to Jane's room. It was as he had left it. The wardrobe doors were open; *The Woodlanders* was on the bedside table. The louvers were open and the room was full of an amber light. He threw the passport into the half-packed suitcase on the floor of the wardrobe, and then he went and sat on the porch.

The sun set. Lights came on in the city. Adela was in the kitchen; fluorescent light came through the kitchen windows.

When the telephone rang, he was quite prepared. He went to the sitting room. It was in darkness; he didn't put on the light.

Jimmy said, "I want to see you."

"I don't want to see you."

"I'm not asking you. I'm telling you. I want you to get in your car and drive here immediately."

"Who do you think you're talking to?"

"You must come, massa. There's no one else I can ask. They've left me alone, massa."

"You'll have to stay where you are, Jimmy. And I won't be coming out to see you."

"Bryant's not well. You've all made him mad. You must come and help me with him, massa."

"And you shouldn't think of coming here. It isn't safe for you to be out these days, Jimmy. You know that. There are police road blocks everywhere. There's one on the Ridge road. I think you will find that they will be particularly interested in you. Do you understand? I'm leaving you alone. That's the way it's going to be. We are leaving you alone. I am leaving. I am going away. Jane and I are leaving tomorrow. Jane is in her room packing. We are leaving you here. Are you hearing me? Jimmy?"

"Massa."

A NOTE ON THE TYPE

This book is set in Electra, a Linotype face designed by W. A. Dwiggins (1880–1956), who was responsible for so much that is good in contemporary book design. Although much of his early work was in advertising and he was the author of the standard volume *Layout in Advertising*, Mr. Dwiggins later devoted his prolific talents to book typography and type design and worked with great distinction in both fields. In addition to his designs for Electra, he created the Metro, Caledonia, and Eldorado series of type faces, as well as a number of experimental cuttings that have never been issued commerically.

Electra cannot be classified as either modern or old-style. It is not based on any historical model, nor does it echo a particular period or style. It avoids the extreme contrast between thick and thin elements that marks most modern faces and attempts to give a feeling of fluidity, power, and speed.

COMPOSED, PRINTED, AND BOUND BY
THE HADDON CRAFTSMEN, INC., SCRANTON, PENNSYLVANIA
DESIGN BY GWEN TOWNSEND